"This weekend has meant a lot to me, Kelly," Seth said quietly. "I don't know how I would have made it without you."

Kelly smiled, looking up at Seth in the darkness. "That's okay. There are times when I can't imagine having made it without you, either."

And then something happened. Kelly would not afterward know whether the change happened within her or within him; it just happened. Their lips touched lightly as they had done many times before, an impersonal gesture of affection, and then suddenly they met fully in a kiss that was deep and lingering and took both of them by surprise.

Kelly could not believe that Seth had let them go this far. But she wanted him....

## Dear Reader,

It is our pleasure to bring you a new experience in reading that goes beyond category writing. The settings of **Harlequin American Romance** give a sense of place and culture that is uniquely American, and the characters are warm and believable. The stories are of "today" and have been chosen to give variety within the vast scope of romance fiction.

*Best of Friends* is a very current story. The subject matter represents a life-style that will probably be with us for generations to come. Land expense and population overcrowding leads to some very interesting relationships. Rebecca Flanders has again proven that she is a writer of the times with an eye on society as it evolves.

From the early days of Harlequin, our primary concern has been to bring you novels of the highest quality. **Harlequin American Romance** is no exception. Enjoy!

Vivian Stephens

Vivian Stephens
Editorial Director
Harlequin American Romance
919 Third Avenue,
New York, N.Y. 10022

# Best of Friends

## REBECCA FLANDERS

*Harlequin Books*

TORONTO • NEW YORK • LONDON
AMSTERDAM • PARIS • SYDNEY • HAMBURG
STOCKHOLM • ATHENS • TOKYO • MILAN

Published September 1983

First printing July 1983

ISBN 0-373-16024-0

Printed in Canada

# Chapter One

Kelly Mitchell lay back on the lounge chair on the deck and stared with bleary, unseeing eyes at the sunset over the canyon, trying not to think about what a fool she had been. The breeze was warm against her cheek and the square of chest and bare arms that the sundress revealed, and the tendrils of hair the wind loosened tickled her skin, but she hardly noticed. How could she have been so stupid? How was it possible that her whole life could have changed in a matter of a few minutes? But it should be no surprise to her, Kelly reflected with a weary sigh. It seemed she had traveled this ground before.... Only that did not make it any easier.

Susan came out, wearing a halter top and shorts, drying her short dark hair with a towel. She had been in the shower when Kelly came home and was surprised to see her. "I thought you had a date," Susan said, sinking into a webbed chair in one of the scattered patches of fading sunlight. "'Early dinner, late swim, and don't look for me to come home tonight'?" She quoted Kelly's words with a suggestive grin and Kelly winced.

"David's leaving," she said shortly, and that was all she could manage through the lump in her throat. Could it really be that only two hours ago she had believed in those plans, she had hugged them to her like an excited secret all day, seeing David's soft eyes across a candlelit table, tasting the salt spray on her tongue, and later ... *don't look for me to come home tonight.* ... The pain washed upward from her stomach again, sudden and sharp and aching through her arms and chest and stinging her eyes, and the quick concern in her friend's face only made it worse.

"What happened?" Susan inquired gently.

Kelly shrugged, buying time while she swallowed the lump in her throat and blinked back tears, absently picking at the embroidery on her peasant skirt. "I knew it was too good to last, I suppose."

And that was exactly what she had thought when David Hampton had singled her out at a cast party to which Seth had invited her—too good to be true. Seth had been dating a member of the cast at that time, a rather minor player at that, and the very fact that he had been able to get invitations for all of them had been the first miracle. It was more than Kelly could have hoped for to get even a glimpse of the star of the highly budgeted Evan Lambert film that was already slotted to be the season's biggest box-office smash. When he actually came over to her and started up a conversation, she was almost too star-struck to respond. Then Kelly had told herself she *was* star-struck. Now she knew it had been love at first sight. Somehow— Kelly was to this day not quite certain how— she had ended up leaving the party with David that night under Seth's disapproving scowl. They had had Mexican food along the coastal highway and before she knew it they were laughing and talking and having a thoroughly good time. She forgot that he was the fastest-rising star on the Hollywood horizon and saw him only as a devastatingly attractive young man whose company she enjoyed immensely. He tried to make love to her at the end of the evening, and it was instinct that caused her to refuse, even though it went against the nature of her own desires. He took her rebuff good-naturedly, but Kelly did not expect to hear from him again. She was ecstactic when he called her two weeks later.

For the last three weeks they had been together almost every free moment. The papers began to get the scent of a hot romance and it became a game with them to avoid the photographers and reporters, all adding to the excitement of a whirlwind romance. They had secret rendezvous in dark, out-of-the-way places. They met on the beach at midnight, then had champagne breakfasts at his highly secured hotel suite at dawn. But they had never been to bed together.

At first the reluctance had been on Kelly's part and mostly due to Seth. She was accustomed to listening to his advice and when he warned her that David Hampton was busily developing a reputation as an international sex symbol it made sense to move very carefully into a situation in which she could become no more than another scalp on his belt. Seth said that David was shallow and insincere, like all actors ultimately selfish, and that she was way out of her league. What Kelly discovered with amazing rapidity was that David was sensitive and easygoing, fun-loving but not wild. He was homesick for his native England and insecure because of his rapid rise to stardom. He liked simple pleasures and quiet times, and the tinsel and glitter was all a bit much for him. And Kelly was blindly, devoutly, head over heels in love with him.

But David had seemed to enjoy the intricacies of an old-fashioned courtship, and though his desire for her was obvious, it was carefully restrained. She loved him all the more for that. She saw it as a gesture of respect for her, an indication of the permanence of his feelings. She had thought they had all the time in the world, and she loved him for letting her set the pace.

They had not seen each other in three days—the filming had finally come to an end and David had been so busy with studio meetings and press releases and celebrations on the set that there simply wasn't time—and during that period Kelly had come to realize that, though there had been other loves in her life, this one was the real thing. She wanted to be with him forever. She wanted to belong to him utterly. And she wanted him to know.

"I don't know why I never realized it before," she managed in a somewhat more even tone but still unable to look into her friend's sympathetic eyes, "that he never said anything about love or—or permanence. I can't accuse him of leading me on. I guess the whole thing was in my imagination."

"Love does crazy things to people," Susan agreed sadly, and Kelly managed to send her a grateful glance. Susan would never have been so stupid. Neither would Trish, and least of all Seth. But her friends, though they had certainly had ideas of their own concerning the rash way in which she had rushed into a relationship with David Hampton, had been outwardly supportive and quietly encouraging, and—with the possible exception of Seth—they had never criticized her behavior.

Most likely they thought Kelly and David had been lovers all these weeks, for the strange hours they kept would certainly lead any moderately sophisticated person to that conclusion. And although Kelly cringed at the thought that they were laboring under that misconception, she was too embarrassed to enlighten them.

How could she admit her love affair had been *total* fantasy, and how could she explain a broken heart that was the result of nothing more than a strictly platonic relationship? Especially as that relationship had remained platonic purely through accident, a slip of the tongue, a fortuitous shift of circumstance.

She had left work early to meet David at his hotel. Their ardent reunion had completely precluded any notice of an unusual sense of disarray about the place — drawers open, closets emptied, suitcases and boxes half packed. He welcomed her lack of restraint with delight and surprise as she welcomed the heady sense of freedom her unreined passion gave her, and the knowledge that she was at last to possess and be possessed completely by the man she loved.

She was lying half undressed on his frothy bed, floating in a cloud of dreamlike happiness and intoxicating sensuality, and his eyes above her gleamed with desire and joy as he murmured, "You're going to make my last night here one I'll never forget. What a wonderful gift!"

And it was then that she noticed the suitcases, and some disturbance penetrated the gilded fog that surrounded her, though she was not yet ready to face the truth. "Last night?" she whispered, her voice unsteady as he planted warm, highly evocative kisses on the column of her throat. "Are you moving out of the hotel?"

He laughed throatily, his breath sending a new fan of heat to her face. "Of course, silly darling! My work here is over; I'm going home!"

And then the icy truth began to seep into her veins. "Home?" she echoed. "To England?"

"Where else?"

He began to nibble at her earlobe, but she turned her head desperately to look at him, her eyes wide with shock and pleading. "But, David, you don't mean forever? You'll come back?"

He seemed annoyed with her preference for conversation. "Of course, sweet," he assured her. "To promote the film, to make another...of course." He tried to claim her lips again, but she sat up, shaking as wave after wave of cold reality flooded her.

"But I—I thought—" she stammered. "You can't mean you were just leaving... without telling me...?"

"I just told you," he responded impatiently. "Whatever are you trying to say?"

"That—I thought—that I love you!" she whispered desperately.

A look of amused puzzlement came into his eyes as he answered simply, "You are a funny little creature!" And he took her chin between his thumb and forefinger and tried to kiss her again.


"So I just left," Kelly concluded to her friend. "It wasn't his fault, but it was obvious we were interested in two different things." She dropped her eyes again miserably.

"Poor Kelly." Trish had come out during the last part of her speech, and her voice was soft with sympathy and understanding as she sat on the redwood bench near the picnic table. "You left yourself wide open for that bastard, didn't you?"

"He's not a bastard," Kelly defended quickly and with vehemence. Even now his confused protests and the hurt in his eyes haunted her as she had fled his room without even a good-bye. "It wasn't his fault." She would never believe that he had been in any way to blame. He could not help it if he hadn't loved her back. "It was just one of those one-sided love affairs, no one's fault. He never understood...."

He never understood that he was playing with the emotions of a deeply vulnerable woman, one who was impulsive and steadfast and who simply couldn't help loving him.

"Well," suggested Trish tactfully, "it was all rather sudden. These things take time, for a man as well as a woman... maybe more so for a man."

"He might call you," put in Susan hopefully. "Now that he knows how you feel."

Kelly shook her head slowly. Even if he called, what could he say? That he was sorry? That he hoped they could still be friends? But he wouldn't call. She knew now, agonizing as it was to admit, that he had not even cared enough for her to want to continue a long-distance friendship. She had filled the space and reminded him of simpler times at home, that was all it had ever been. She had been a fool and he no longer needed her.

A heavy silence fell over the three women on the deck as the sun shed its last rays into a phosphorescent twilight. And then, as an almost welcome break to the gloomy spell, they heard Seth banging around in the kitchen. He called through the screen, "Anybody out there want a beer?"

Susan called back, "How about an orange soda?" But both Trish and Kelly shook their heads when her inquiring look passed to them. "One orange soda," she repeated.

It was another moment before Seth slid open the screen door and stepped out onto the deck, an open bottle of beer in one hand and the can of soda for Susan in the other. He was wearing a faded blue body-hugging tank top and equally faded denim cut-offs, his weekend "bumming around" clothes. Apparently he did not plan to go out tonight. He tossed Susan the drink and then noticed Kelly with some surprise. "'What light through yonder window breaks?''' he quoted melodramatically. He had taken to greeting her with Shakespearean references lately, possibly in subtle allusion to the folly of dating an actor. "'It is the east, and Juliet is the sun!'''

"Lay off, Seth," responded Trish shortly. "She's had a rough day."

Seth passed Kelly an inquiring glance as he sprawled out in one of the deck chairs near her, half sitting and half lying on it with his bare legs crossed at the ankles and tucked beneath the chair, knees comfortably wide apart. Kelly shrugged and avoided his eyes. "Go ahead," she answered his unspoken question. "Say I told you so. You have the right." Only he didn't. It wasn't David's fault that she had fallen in love with him. Not even Seth could have predicted that.

There was a short silence, and then he said quietly, "Tough luck, kid." There was no hint whatsoever of mockery in his tone. "You okay?"

She glanced at him gratefully and even managed a semblance of a smile as, after a moment, she nodded. It was amazing, the subtle transformation in atmosphere when they were all together. Nothing seemed quite so insurmountable anymore. It was something, Kelly had often reflected, that must have had its roots in early family life for all of them—the three women, separately, perfectly capable and self-reliant individuals, and together the best of friends, but always automatically looking to Seth for guidance and unity. He was the pillar on which their loose family unit was built, and everything would always be all right as soon as Daddy got home.

That made her smile again, although it hurt to smile, and she wondered how Seth would feel about being referred to as Daddy. If she had been in a better mood she would have teased him about it just to see if she could make him lose his temper.

"Seth." Susan absently called his attention to the fact that she was about to pull the ring on the pop-tab of her drink—another thing that had become such an automatic habit that none of them ever thought twice about it anymore. Seth had an unusual sensitivity to sound, and loud, sudden noises startled him into sometimes violent reactions. He had reduced Kelly to tears during her first week living in the house after she had accidently knocked a skillet off its hook and into the sink with an ungodly clatter; he had practically leaped down her throat. She had told him he reminded her of a gun-shy dog and they had had their first fight, but afterward he apologized so sweetly that their friendship was permanently cemented. And, in fact, Kelly came closer to understanding that particular idiosyncrasy of his than anyone else. She was the only one of them besides Seth to whom a slightly off-center radio transmission would grate like fingernails on a chalkboard, and who could spot the most infinitesimal lack of balance between stereo speakers and correct deficiencies most experts would have ignored. A television set that was too loud would drive her right up the wall. It was perhaps that tendency of hers that had made them almost immediate friends.

So they warned Seth about pop-tabs and made sure he was out of the house before blowing up balloons for a party, and they didn't giggle when he jumped and swore at a car's backfire because those were the automatic things a family did for one another. By the same token he was generous and understanding when Susan, who was particularly susceptible to such things, had her monthly bout of weepy eyes, or when Trish, most known for her absentmindedness, turned on the garbage disposal with a spoon inside, or when Kelly burned a meal.

Susan opened her drink and Seth sipped from his beer; Trish took off her glasses and combed her fluffy honey-streaked hair with her fingers; they settled back and relaxed. It was generally the time of day Kelly liked best, after work and before dates, when they talked about their individual days or solved each other's problems, or just took the time to let go and be themselves in the company of good friends. Today all she needed was a time of quiet to sort out her aching emotions and the comforting presence of the others around her. Sensing this, no one tried to solicit conversation from her. Susan was having troubles of a nonspecific nature at the ad agency at which she worked; Trish was working like hell in order to obtain a promotion that rightfully should have been hers years ago; Seth was worried about union problems. Kelly listened absently and let her mind drift back to the time she had first come here, three years ago.

She had, ironically, been running away from an unhappy love affair. She had placed applications with school boards all over the country, restless, needing a change, determined to do something positive with her life and to escape the solicitous domination of her family and hometown, filled with memories of the first time she had given her heart and had it returned to her badly damaged. The two letters of interest had come at approximately the same time: one from Nova Scotia and the other from Los Angeles. The salaries were comparable and it almost had been a toss-up. But then she had remembered Susan, her roommate in college, and written her on the off-chance that she might in some way be able to offset the unflattering things Kelly had heard about Los Angeles, which, at the time, were making the frozen shores of Nova Scotia preferable to poisonous smog and wall-to-wall traffic jams. Susan's letter had been so enthusiastic that Kelly was completely swept off her feet. Not only was her former roommate living in paradise at a standard of living twice that to which Kelly was accustomed, but she had a fantastic house in Topanga Canyon—the most beautiful area in all Southern California, according to Susan—*and* they were looking for a housemate. Obviously Kelly would be passing up the chance of a lifetime if she even considered Nova Scotia.

Susan neglected to mention until she met Kelly at the airport that one of her two housemates was a man.

Not, Kelly had tried to assure herself all throughout the drive to the canyon, that that should make any difference. Susan assured her that Seth shared the house and nothing else, and Kelly knew her friend too well to doubt her word. Susan went on to explain that Kelly would never find a comparable apartment for the price, and with housing the way it was these days an arrangement such as theirs was not so uncommon at all—even married couples were doubling up and sharing houses, for four people working was the only way they could afford the high interest rates and still have something left over for themselves. Seth had bought the house, overextending himself even before the time of inflation, and though it was possible he could afford to make the payments on his own he had seen no reason to live a cramped life-style when the house was big enough to accommodate housemates. So he had made the house available to Susan, Trish, and one other girl, who then got married. The absence of one housemate was putting a severe squeeze on their personal budgets, for even though Seth held the deed the house was run like a cooperative, everyone chipping in extra to make up the difference in the absence of one share's rent. And they were all desperately hoping Kelly would stay.

Kelly was uncertain. She was twenty-four years old at that time and she had never lived with a man—although she had come rather close on this last occasion. Her parents would have a fit. They had warned her of the type of decadent life-style she was likely to fall into in Southern California, and this would just prove them right. Three girls and a man living together! She wondered why the infamous Seth had not solicited male housemates and the reflection crossed her mind with a trace of cynicism.

"What did your parents say," she asked Susan, "when you told them you were moving in with a man?" She knew that Susan's parents lived in nearby La Mesa and she had met them once or twice while at college. They had not struck her as any more openminded than her own parents.

"Well," replied Susan, negotiating the narrow canyon roads in her red Torino, "first of all I didn't tell them until I had already done it. After all," she defended, "this is the twentieth century and I'm well above the age of consent." Kelly's eyes widened in admiration but Susan's bravado dissolved into an abashed grin. "They hit the ceiling," she admitted. "My mother said that she was well aware we were living in a liberal age and she had even learned to tolerate it, but that this was quite a different thing—I hardly even knew this man! So naturally they had to come up and meet him, and you know what?" She giggled. "They loved him! Of course, the fact that Trish is such a practical, level-headed girl didn't hurt a bit, and, I must admit, Seth was a sport about it—on his best behavior. So anyway, my father went away saying that it was probably the smartest thing I could have done and he would rest easier at night knowing there was a man about—for protection, you know. Can you beat that?"

Kelly thought it made perfect sense. She was quite sure that she would feel safer living in a house where the very presence of a man seemed to discourage the criminal element—providing he wasn't of that element himself.

Kelly had fallen in love with the wild beauty of the wooded canyon from the moment they entered it and when she saw the sprawling, cedar-shingled, multiwindowed house she thought she would have lived there with Count Dracula, providing there was a strong lock on the bedroom door. The setting was secluded and woodsy, and although there were neighbors all along the road they were only occasionally heard and rarely seen. The front yard was small and rolling, heavily planted in trees and shrubs, and the house practically tipped over the canyon on the back side, providing a spectacular view. They were planning to level out the side yard for a pool, Susan told her, as soon as they could afford it, and the way she said "they" gave Kelly the impression that Susan and Trish were as proprietorial about Seth's home as though they shared the actual deed, rather than just the rent. She went on to say that the women were all for purchasing a hot tub in the meantime, but Seth had heard they were dangerous and refused to allow it—which gave Kelly a clue as to who really had the last word in the management of the household.

It was a four-bedroom, two and three quarters bath house with a finished basement (an unusual feature for a Southern California home) that Seth had turned into a recreation room. It had a spacious modern kitchen, a combination family room/dining room and a separate laundry room. The proportions of the rooms were generous, allowing plenty of space for four occupants with no one feeling cramped. It was furnished with a combination of all the housemates' tastes and budgets, and the result was a charmingly mismatched, homey effect. Kelly loved it.

But she had yet to meet Seth and her nervousness mounted as, coming up from the recreation room, they heard the front door open and heavy steps cross toward the kitchen. "Oh, good," said Susan, "he's home."

Trish, who had accompanied them on the tour and whom Kelly had liked on sight, noticed her trepidation and reassured her. "Seth's a doll. In no time at all you'll be thinking of him as just another one of the girls."

Kelly giggled and doubted she would ever be able to go that far. When she saw him, she was sure she would not.

He was not one of those tall, ruggedly masculine, macho types, but there was certainly nothing effeminate about him. He was perhaps four inches taller than Kelly, leanly built, tightly muscular. He wore his sandy hair in the fashionably curly style, but Kelly learned later he would have done so even if it had not been fashionable—his hair was naturally curly, a fact his housemates often bemoaned as they spent hours at the beauty parlor or with messy home permanents. His tan was honey-golden, his eyes bright topaz. He looked as though he spent a lot of time on the beach. His face was surprisingly youthful—Kelly was amazed to learn later that he was five years older than she—or perhaps it was simply his lean form and the way he wore his hair that gave that impression, for there were deep lines about his mouth and eyes that hardly seemed to belong there and were most noticeable when he was in repose. At those times his face seemed to age and Kelly had often wondered whether the effect was due to the overuse of the outdoor life he loved so well—or whether those lines were marks of suffering.

He swept Kelly with one bright, assessing gaze that seemed to expose her entire life's story to him, and then, apparently satisfied with what he saw, he turned back to the refrigerator, pulling out the components of a sandwich. "Your share of the rent is three hundred dollars a month," he informed her without further preliminaries, "payable to a joint account no later than the twenty-fifth of every month. We rotate bookkeeping duties in two-month hitches, and your turn will start the first of December. We each contribute forty dollars a week to the grocery fund and split the utilities equally. You're responsible for your own long distance telephone calls and you'll pay whoever happens to be treasurer that month as soon as the bill arrives."

Kelly did some rapid calculation in her head. She would have been appalled had anyone mentioned such sums to her back in Springfield, Illinois, but now she understood why Los Angeles County teachers were among the highest paid in the country—they needed it to keep up with the cost of living. She had not considered Susan's offer without first doing some checking on her own, and she had discovered that she was not likely to find an apartment in a decent neighborhood for under five hundred dollars a month. Surely four people splitting the utilities would be cheaper than trying to maintain a place on her own. At the time the food budget seemed a little outrageous, but that was before Kelly visited a supermarket. She thought she could manage on what the county was offering with plenty to spare.

"You'll be sharing a bathroom with Susan and you'll have to work out your own schedule for keeping it clean," Seth continued, moving back and forth between the refrigerator and the counter in the process of building one of the most incredible sandwiches Kelly had ever seen. "Your bedroom is your own responsibility. Your laundry day is Thursday. We all pitch in on Saturday mornings for a floor-to-ceiling housecleaning party. We don't do dope," he went on, adding two thick slices of pastrami to an already nauseating concoction of peanut butter, mustard, rye bread, and bell pepper, "and we don't bring anybody into the house who has the stuff on him—and that includes any kind of cigarette you can't get out of a machine, so keep that in mind at party time. You can entertain in your room any time, but there's a schedule of date nights for the use of the other parts of the house—kitchen, rec room, family room, et cetera. We alternate cooking duty for dinner, but breakfast and lunch are your own responsibility. The stereo goes off at eleven thirty at night unless otherwise agreed upon by all members present— we're all working people here. Parties require a two-week notice, but overnight guests are okay as long as they don't disturb the routine. And another thing," he added, picking up the sandwich and starting for the door, "I don't like playing bouncer, so be careful about the type of man you bring home."

"He's worse than a father," murmured Susan in an

aside to Kelly. "He has to give the third degree to every guy we bring in."

"I heard that comment, Susy," he responded, shrugging into his jacket. "Fortunately for you, I'm late." And without another word, he bit into his sandwich and left the house.

Kelly watched him go with a mixture of amusement and indignation and was very nearly prompted to follow his example. It was obvious this would never work out. If it was independence she sought, she would be better off going home to live with her mother, and she had a feeling Seth Mason would tolerate far less in the way of infringement of the rules than her own loving parents would have. Surely it would be less complicated to try to run a household on her own than to live up to his standards of almost military precision. Besides, no matter how the other housemates felt, she would never be able to look at this arrangement as anything other than the fact that she was living with a man, and a man she did not know, and that made her very uneasy.

It was Trish who once again zeroed in on the real reason for Kelly's reluctance. "Poor Kelly," she said with a sympathetic laugh. "You must feel like you've just been welcomed to the harem! I know it must seem kind of odd, the two of us living here with him, but take my word for it, it's a strictly hands-off situation. Seth won't even *look* at you like you're a woman, and as far as we're concerned he hasn't a lecherous thought in his head."

Kelly was not certain whether it was relief or trepidation she felt. "Is he, er—" She paused delicately over the word, but the other two got her meaning and burst into uproarious laughter.

"Hardly!" gasped Susan at last. "As a matter of fact, although he raises all sorts of hell with us if we're in the least bit 'indiscreet' with our boyfriends, you have to be double-sure to knock on every door in the house before entering when he has a date over. He doesn't waste any time, and he's not always very particular where either!"

"He has a very normal and very active social life," Trish put in more tastefully. "But to us he's just a big brother, no more, and if he likes you, which I think he already does, you couldn't ask for a better friend."

"At least," persuaded Susan, "stay with us while you're here, and get to see how things operate. You don't have to make a firm commitment until you know about your job."

So during the two days she was interviewing for the position of physical education instructor and coach to eighth and ninth grade girls at a nearby junior high school, she stayed in the house with Susan and Seth and Trish, observing the situation carefully, making her decision cautiously. She found it to be exactly as the two women had predicted. Living with Seth was easy and fun, and he was at all times in her presence a perfect gentleman. Although she suspected he might have been on his very best behavior for her sake, going out of his way to entertain her with amusing stories and taking them all to dinner and arranging tours of some of the most prominent must-not-be-missed-at-any-cost sights of Los Angeles, he never at any time treated her with anything other than an impersonal brotherly regard. Within two days she was laughing at her initial prudishness. After all, men were no more slaves to their animal lusts than women were, and just because people of the opposite sex shared a roof did not necessarily mean that orgies were the inevitable result. It was the twentieth century and she may as well relax and enjoy it.

She accepted the position with the L.A. County School Board to begin in the fall, telling herself that the proximity of her school to the house was another reason for deciding to stay there. She found a job teaching aerobics at a ladies' salon during the summer, with the added bonus that she could return to that position every summer if she wished, and from that point her life fell into a settled, contented, perfectly agreeable routine.

It was easy to see why Trish and Susan had considered this to be an ideal situation. The four of them living together had the best of all possible worlds. They were free of most of the financial worries that afflicted the rest of the population, they could regulate their social lives to please themselves, and none of them would ever be tempted into marriage or an unsatisfactory romance for any of the less than worthy reasons—security, companionship, financial stability. Kelly could easily imagine them all growing old together and never complaining. For the women's part, it was very comforting to have a man around the house. If their cars broke down or minor repairs were needed on the house, Seth was there. To fend off unwelcome advances from an overanxious date or to fill in a party, Seth was there. And it was obvious he did not mind the arrangement either. If he needed a button sewn on or advice on a failing romance or a blind date for an out-of-town friend, he knew where to go. There was always someone to talk to; no one ever had to come home to an empty house. Oh, they had their spats and disagreements like everyone else, but the miracle was they all liked one another. It might not have worked with any other four people in the world, but they were a winning team. Yes, it was a totally satisfactory arrangement all around.

It did not take long for Kelly to see what Trish had meant when she said that soon she would be seeing Seth as "just another one of the girls." It was easy for Kelly to imagine him having grown up in a houseful of sisters, because he seemed perfectly at home in such an environment. He did not mind pinning up a broken strap or fixing the zipper on a low-backed evening gown, nor wading through piles of lingerie in the laundry room. Unself-consciously the girls sat around in their pajamas with him over Saturday morning breakfasts or late-night snacks, and even Kelly got used to seeing him coming out of the bathroom with nothing more than a towel wrapped around his waist or, occasionally, pulling a robe over his seminude body as he rushed to answer an early-morning phone call. He was so much a part of the family that often they forgot his presence and launched into intimate female discussions, which did not embarrass him either. He appeared to be used to it. Eventually Kelly grew used to it too, to some extent. But she did not seem to be able to forget, as the others so easily did, that, when all was said and done, he was still male and she was still female. She rather liked it that way.

A heavy plop on her soft abdomen startled her out of her reverie, and she gave an involuntary cry that broke up the indolent conversation around her. It was Fleetwood, the enormous orange tomcat who had ruled the house since Seth had given him to Kelly on the first birthday she had celebrated here. No one could have guessed that the cuddly little kitten would mature to a size rivaling that of a mountain lion and weigh almost twenty pounds—he was undoubtedly the largest cat any of them had ever seen. Kelly had loved him at first sight because he had been Seth's gift to her; it meant that she had finally and irrevocably been accepted into the family. She had spoiled her pet and so had everyone else, with the inevitable result that he was temperamental and arrogant, domineering and jealous of attention and, because of his size, he generally got what he wanted. What he wanted now was petting, and with a resigned sigh Kelly shifted his weight more comfortably onto her thighs and began to stroke his fur.

"My goodness," exclaimed Susan, glancing at her watch. "Will you look at the time? I'm being picked up in fifteen minutes!"

She scurried inside and Trish rose, rather reluctantly, to follow her. "From the look on your face," commented Seth, finishing his beer, "he must be a real winner."

Trish wrinkled her nose at him and replaced her glasses, without which she could not see her hand in front of her face. "Don't I wish. Boring business dinner. Boring, boring, boring. I'll be home early."

As she closed the screen behind her Kelly glanced at Seth and remarked, "What's this, Friday night and no date? Must be the slow season."

"Everyone needs a rest every now and then," he retorted.

"Struck out again, huh?"

He grinned and shrugged, and Kelly pretended to commiserate. The latest object of his pursuit was Melissa Hollander, a producer at the television studio at which he was a sound engineer, and since he had set his sights for her he had had eyes for no one else. One thing had to be said for Seth, he was relentless—and strangely loyal in his own way. But so far his efforts toward his latest ideal had been fruitless.

"So here we sit," she said, but her effort at flippancy came out as more of a sigh. "Two lonely hearts on a Friday night...." And she had to swallow on a sudden lump in her throat.

Seth's face sobered as he drew his chair up to hers and said quietly, "Look, Kelly, I'm sorry, not because you got rid of the two-bit phoney, which is probably one of the best things that could have ever happened to you, but because of what he put you through in the meantime. Does it hurt very much?" he inquired gently.

She stared unseeingly against the film of tears at a

stand of trees in the distance and all she could see was David's face—kind, thoughtful, gentle. Beautiful. She nodded.

"Poor kid." He cupped his hand against the back of her neck in a gesture of comfort, and Fleetwood, jealous of anyone touching Kelly but himself, immediately jumped off her lap and pushed his way through a crack in the door into the kitchen in search of something to eat. "You don't exactly have the best luck in the world with men, do you?"

She was trying very hard not to cry. "This was different," she gulped.

"Not like old Sherman, heh?" he said with a faint smile, trying to cheer her with the reminder of past follies.

"He even had you fooled," she responded through her tears, trying to follow his mood.

"Yep. If it hadn't been for that private eye his wife hired you might at this moment be committing bigamy." She managed to smile because she had never been that serious about Sherman. "And who can forget," he went on airily, "the inestimable Mr. Lakewood?" The mention of that particular suitor never failed to bring a laugh all around, mostly from the memory of the look on Seth's face when he had discovered that, as lovers go, the innocent-looking young man was far more interested in Seth than in Kelly. Even through her misery Kelly felt a giggle rising, but it dissolved unexpectedly into a hiccoughing sob. She covered her face helplessly and let the pain and the tears wrack her, and she wanted to die.

His arm slipped around her shoulders and tightened affectionately. "It's okay, babe," he said softly. "Just let it go. It's a rotten deal, I know."

She couldn't stop crying, great, violent, tearing sobs that shook her entire body as he drew her gently to him so that her face rested against his bare leg, stroking her hair in steady comfort. "Poor Kelly," he said quietly with a gentle sigh. "She loves not wisely but too well."

She clung to him and buried her face against the solid muscles and soft hairs of his thigh and let him comfort her until, at last, the sobs had spent themselves.

## Chapter Two

Exhausted and drained, she lay against him a long time after the tears had stopped, liking the feel of his warm skin against her wet cheek and the way his hand played with her hair. The hairs of his leg were silvery gold against the honey tan and to her absently stroking fingers they felt like silk. She felt so relaxed with him, so comfortable and comforted. She never wanted to move.

But at last she stirred, drawing slightly unsteady fingers over her ravaged face and murmuring huskily, "Well, I guess I'd better start dinner." It was her week to cook. "Steak and salad okay?"

He reached into his back pocket and produced a handkerchief, which she gratefully rubbed over her mascara-stained face, mumbling, "I hate to cry. It makes me look like a toad." Then, for good measure, she wiped the portion of his leg that her tears had dampened and returned the handkerchief to him with a little smile. She did feel better.

But as he accepted the handkerchief she surprised an unusually reflective look on his face, enigmatic and strangely guarded. It was only for a second, but it left her puzzled as he quickly replaced it with an easy smile and suggested unexpectedly, "Look, there's no point in both of us sitting at home tonight feeling sorry for ourselves. Let's go out—dinner, dancing, the works."

She hesitated, reluctant to refuse his offer after he had been so understanding and patient with her, but knowing she would do him no favor by accepting. She dropped her eyes to study her interlaced fingers. "I really don't feel like going out," she said. "I would be terrible company."

"I know you don't feel like it," he replied firmly, his mind apparently made up, "which is exactly why you're going to do it. Hey." He lifted her chin gently with his finger, compassion and sincerity softening his voice. "He's not going to call, you know."

She swallowed hard and dropped her eyes again. She knew. And it hurt like a knife twisting inside her whenever she thought about it. He would never call again.

"All right." He grasped her wrist firmly and pulled her to her feet. "We'll go out, get sick on expensive gourmet food, get smashed, dance till dawn and make perfect fools of ourselves. To hell with the David Hamptons and Melissa Hollanders of this world!" She gave an uncertain little laugh and he pushed her toward the door with a playful slap on the bottom. "Go on. Take a hot bath, put cold compresses on your eyes, and wear your sexiest dress. I'll give you an hour."

She hesitated at the door for only another minute. How could she refuse when he was going out of his way to cheer her up? Besides, it was really he who did not want to sit around the house tonight, and she owed him a favor if for no other reason than for the remarkable restraint he had shown in not saying "I told you so." She shrugged and opened the screen door. "All right; you know what you're letting yourself in for."

"A good time," he called defiantly after her, and she even managed a laugh.

She dressed as though going into battle—and in a way she was. It was a battle against depression and self-pity and she would go armed to the teeth.

Seth was right, of course. She was not known for her

wisdom where relationships with the opposite sex were concerned, and this was not the first time she had put her heart above her head and taken a nasty fall for it. It only seemed like the first time because it hurt so much.

The cold compresses did wonders for the swelling and redness of her eyes, and after her bath she did feel a bit more like facing the world. Seth liked his women to be well-dressed, and his criticism could be merciless when the female he was escorting fell short of his expectations, so she chose her outfit with care. She finally decided on a white crepe dress, simply styled with spaghetti straps and a dipping bodice that loosely hugged her figure, slit up the side from hem to midthigh. She cinctured the waist with a wide turquoise silk belt fastened with a silver buckle, and completed the outfit with a heavy strand of turquoise beads at her throat and matching dangling earrings. The color of the jewelry brought out the highlights of her aquamarine eyes, which were crystal clear now and very bright, possibly the result of the cold compresses or lingering distress. The clinging white material lay in smooth contrast to her own light tan and her cocoa-colored hair as she lifted the hairbrush to free her locks from the tangles of its customary braid. Her hair was smooth and straight, and she generally wore it in a French braid from midcrown to the small of her back. But tonight she brushed it free and let it shine against her smooth shoulders and the contrast of the white dress, fastening it at the sides with silver combs because Seth liked it that way. She brushed her lips with a pale coral lipgloss, highlighted her cheekbones in the same color, and darkened her lashes with mascara. Then, as a final daring touch, she swept an arch of glittering silver powder over her brow bones and onto the temples and stepped back to observe herself critically in the mirror, pleased with the effect.

Seth reflected her opinion as he met her in the hallway. "Now that," he said, sweeping her with his eyes once from the tips of her turquoise sandals to her nearly bare bosom, "is what I call a sexy dress."

He was wearing a casual suit of an almost coral-colored beige, and an open-necked, pale blue silk shirt. She thought as he slipped his arm naturally about her waist that they made a very nice-looking couple.

He took her to an Indian restaurant on the Strip, where they did, indeed, overindulge themselves on spicy dishes and curry. She remembered the first time she had come here with Seth, Susan, and Trish. Unused to approaching a meal with caution, Kelly had taken a large forkful of a particularly spicy dish over the protests of the other women and under Seth's mildly watchful gaze. It had burned all the way down, and gasping with her eyes streaming, she had accepted the glass of ice water Seth had pushed into her hand, not noticing the mischief in his eyes behind the bland mask of concern. She had gulped half of it before realizing that water was only turning her throat to fire, and before learning, through Trish and Susan's unforgiving scolding of Seth, that cold water was the worst antidote in the world for a spicy meal. She was wiser now and drank copious amounts of the exotic beer served with the meal between samplings of the hot dishes.

"Go easy on that," Seth warned. "The food alone is enough to give you a hangover."

"It's good for what ails you," she retorted, lifting her glass to him. But Seth did not have to worry; they both knew she was not a very good drinker and she was extremely careful not to overindulge.

"Not for what ails me," Seth replied with an exaggerated look of glumness.

"And what is that?" she replied lightly, trying very hard to put the day behind her and relax for a few hours. It would all come flooding back too soon in the lonely dark hours of the night and the ache would settle inside her like an obscure disease, haunting her the rest of her life. While Seth offered distraction she would seize it gratefully, for she knew too well the torment that lay before her in her empty bed.

"Lack of a good woman," Seth said, again with an exaggerated sigh.

"Nonsense," she retorted, lifting her fork. "You have three of them right under your own roof."

He grinned. "Not exactly," he pointed out, "what I had in mind."

"You know what your real trouble is," she told him sagely, touching her napkin to her lips as she finished her meal. "You need to get married and settle down. Find yourself a pretty little thing in a pink gingham apron, have two or three kids, give meaning to your life. You're thirty-two years old. It's time to start thinking about those things. You don't want to be an old man leaning on a cane by the time your oldest graduates from college, do you?"

Of course she said it purely to tease him. The last thing she wanted was for Seth to get married—it would ruin all their lives. And it was also the last thing any of them could imagine, a fact that Seth confirmed with an easy laugh and a sparkle in the golden depths of his eyes. "Now why would I want to do a foolish thing like that? I've got all the conveniences of marriage without the problems as it is."

"Not all," she reminded him coyly, and he sobered just a fraction.

"That," he told her, "is a suicidal reason for getting married. I don't deny my sex life could use some improvement, but I'm not about to go to those lengths for it."

"What about kids?"

"Not interested," he replied briefly, finishing off his beer. And then he chuckled. "God, can you see me changing diapers and warming bottles? I'd go screaming into the night within a week. Little people get on my nerves, you never noticed that?"

"I've never seen you with children before," she replied. "At least not to the point where you ran out of patience with them. But I must say, I'm surprised. I always pictured you in a family filled with children. I thought you had plenty of experience." And it also surprised her how little she really knew about Seth's background. For the past three years they had shared everything from a breakfast table to head colds, but he rarely talked about himself. Suddenly she was curious.

"I was an only child" was all he would reveal, and then he turned the tables on her. "Now, you," he declared, "are the one who needs to get married. Find yourself some nice level-headed guy and settle down before you ruin your life."

She dropped her eyes, caught off-guard by the sudden stab that seemed to go right through her heart. She had not realized until this moment how far her daydreams about David had progressed.

"Sorry," he said quietly.

She searched for a smile as she straightened her shoulders, trying to regain the equilibrium of the evening. "That's all right. I can't picture myself as an appendage to an international superstar, anyway. It was probably all for the best."

"You will never be anyone's appendage," he told her seriously. "And don't you ever let me hear you talk about yourself like that again. Hampton was a fool for letting you go and you just remember it was his loss, not yours."

Now she could not help smiling at him. The look in his eyes was just like the one that came over him when anyone threatened one of "his girls"—defensive, proprietorial, valiantly supportive. She was grateful for his concern, but this time he was wrong. "You never liked David," she pointed out. "But you never knew him. You just slotted him with all the other actors and bad breeds you know and he really wasn't like that, Seth."

"Oh, no?" He leaned back in his chair, toying with his glass, issuing her a mild challenge.

"No," she insisted, and her eyes shone with earnesty as she tried to convince him. "He was sensitive and kind, easygoing and fun to be with...a lot like you, in a way."

"Thanks for small favors," he drawled dryly, but she was undeterred.

"He didn't like the image the studio was building for him," she went on, "and he wasn't really like that at all. He was just a simple man from a small town, very serious about his art, but afraid of going overboard, you know, of starting to believe his own publicity. There was never any real danger of that," she added softly, almost to herself, as she let herself be wrapped again in all the things she loved about him. "He was practical, sensible, generous...level-headed, and— what's the word?—empathetic. He cared more about what I felt or wanted than about himself and it was just a natural thing to him. He was a very *genuine* person, Seth, a good man," she concluded, looking at him, almost begging him to understand, to agree.

There was a strange expression on his face and she thought she had him convinced. "Sounds too good to be true," he admitted.

"I love him," she answered simply.

His eyes were very steady as he looked at her. "The real thing?"

She nodded, slowly.

"Then why...?"

She shook her head sadly, her hair rippling across her shoulders and gleaming in points of multicolored candlelight. "He never knew how I felt." Again she was speaking almost to herself. "I moved too slowly, I didn't make it clear...we had two different ideas of what our relationship was."

"You thought it was forever," supplied Seth, "and he thought you were just another cute trick to warm the sheets at night."

She drew in her breath on a horrified gasp. "No!" He did not understand at all!

He lifted light brows in mock surprise, and she could not tell whether the rankling disapproval she felt from him was over her own behavior or David's. She only knew that above all things she hated Seth's censure and she would have done anything to avoid it. "It—it wasn't that way at all," she stammered hotly. "And if you're going to insult me—"

"I'm not insulting you," he said patiently. "Just trying to understand. You're telling me that the two of you have been lovers for almost a month—you practically lived together in that time—and he had no earthly idea how you really felt about him? Come on, Kelly, that's no defense. Any way you put it, he comes out a bastard. No woman can hide her feelings that well and no man can be that stupid."

Her cheeks were burning. "I—I never said we were lovers for a month." And how he would laugh if he knew the truth!

"For whatever length of time, then," he conceded mildly. "Let me tell you something, Kelly. It's going to sound crude and you're not going to like it, but you need to hear it." His lean dark fingers absently caressed the slender glass, but his eyes never wavered from hers and the steady confidence there was intimidating. "You can't make love without leaving something of yourself behind—and that's as true for a man as it is for a woman. There's no such thing as free sex, you know, and there is a point when a man is making love where he becomes very vulnerable, where he wants to hear, and wants to believe, that he is loved, just like a woman does. So don't tell me he didn't understand how you felt. Tell me he didn't care, but not that he didn't know. It's impossible," he concluded flatly.

For a moment she looked at him, amazed by his philosophy and wondering at the truth of it. It flashed through her mind that because she and Seth could talk so easily and frankly to one another she had learned more about men in the past three years than most women were likely to learn in a lifetime, and that it would seem she would have stopped making the obvious mistakes by now. But then she dropped her eyes, because Seth's observations did not really apply to her situation. Perhaps that was the basis of her entire problem. If she had not been so hesitant about committing herself to David sexually—if she hadn't paid quite so much attention to Seth's opinion about him in the first place—David would have known how she really felt about him, and by now they would have worked themselves into a meaningful relationship with a basis of permanence instead of a casual good-bye. She should have told Seth that. She should have told him exactly what her relationship with David had been and that it was he, Seth, who was basically to blame, who had caused her to waste precious time trying to decide whether or not to commit herself to the man she loved. But she couldn't. While she did not consider Seth particularly sophisticated, she knew that he did not consider any relationship serious unless it was also sexual, and Kelly was accustomed to moving more carefully. He simply would not understand how she could give her heart without giving her body—nor how she could expect a man to accept her on those terms.

So she simply said lightly, "Wow. Advice from the expert. I'm honored."

He replied with an easy grin as he signaled for the check. "And it didn't cost you a cent."

"So what's with this Melissa person that has put you

in a blue daze for the past couple of weeks?'' she inquired as they walked out into the warm night air.

"I have not been in a blue daze," he defended mildly and opened the car door for her. They had taken her Toyota because Seth drove a Jeep and Kelly did not feel comfortable in evening clothes in a Jeep. "Anyway," he added as he got behind the wheel, "who's to say what attracts one person to the other? Maybe because she's so damn unobtainable."

"So," she suggested, slanting her eyes toward him as she repaired her lipstick, "the attraction is not at all mutual?"

He smiled enigmatically and did not reply.

"Oh-ho," Kelly teased him. "So the iceberg is finally beginning to melt under the old charm, huh?"

"Could any woman resist this gorgeous face forever?" he asked of her reasonably.

"I've known a few who have," she retorted, her eyes beginning to twinkle beneath this familiar banter. "She's doing a number on you, Seth. It's the oldest trick in the book. Play hard to get, pretend not to be interested, and it drives a man wild. Then you give— just a little, then a little more, and before you know it, he's hooked."

"Free advice from the expert," he retorted.

"In repayment for yours." Then she glanced at him mischievously. "I've never known you to wait so long for anyone before. You must have it bad."

"She's special," he admitted.

"Could this be the real thing?"

"If you're going to start that marriage talk again, we're going home."

"So speaks the confirmed bachelor."

"I suppose," he answered with surprising thoughtfulness, "if there is such a thing, I'm it. I mean, you may not have noticed, but when you were talking about wives and children awhile ago, my palms were sweating." She laughed, but then he added seriously, "Some people just aren't cut out for that sort of thing and you're lucky if you realize it before you make a mistake. I'm one of them."

"There's someone for everyone, Seth," she assured him. "One day you're going to find your soulmate."

"That," he replied with confidence, "is nothing but an old wives' tale."

But then she wondered over how easily she gave to Seth advice she should have taken herself. If she really believed there was someone for everyone, why did she keep risking her heart on foolish encounters? Why was it that she believed every man she met was that "special someone"... just as she had believed it of David?

They drove to a local nightclub and the beat of the music drew them together. Seth was a terrific dancer and Kelly threw herself fully into the physical exercise—the best way she knew to blot out depression. She drank her limit of champagne cocktails, two over a period of three hours, which was not enough to make her feel high but just enough to make it easier not to think quite so much about David. Seth made that easier too. He took her on the floor for every dance until she begged to rest, and as they sipped their drinks he vacillated between ruthless teasing and exaggerated flattery, making her feel amusing and witty one moment and feminine and beautiful the next, making her laugh, sharpening her wits trying to keep up with his mood. The evening sped by and she grew tired, but she was reluctant to go home and face the inevitable memories and heartaches that would assail her as soon as she was alone. Seth sensed this and did not suggest they leave.

As the hour grew late the dance music wound down into slow ballads, and they danced together with the intimacy of all the other couples on the floor, wrapped close to one another, hardly moving at all. Exhaustion was making her somewhat soporific and she liked the feel of his body next to hers, her arms around his neck, her face against his shoulder, and his breath on her hair. It was relaxing to be with him like that, and comforting, and mildly, innocuously sensuous. She enjoyed the clasp of his arms around her waist, the spread of long fingers against the small of her back, and the upper part of her hips, reminding her of her own femininity in a delightfully pleasant way. She liked the feel of his thighs brushing against hers in the slow, undulant motions of the dance. Then gradually, with an increasing disturbance, she became aware of something else. She did not know whether to be alarmed or embarrassed, but all signs of lethargy left her as her own body quickened in automatic response to the unmistakable signs of his sexual arousal. She took a quick step backward, so that they were no longer touching at all points, and glanced at him quickly in some confusion.

The grin he gave her was endearing and not the least bit abashed. "Should I apologize?" he inquired. "I told you that was a very sexy dress."

Her cheeks flushed scarlet as she gave a choked sound of reprimand and laughter, and he pulled her firmly into his embrace again. "Relax," he murmured against her hair. "The dance floor is too crowded to do anything about it if I wanted to."

She thought he must have had more to drink than she realized, and she tried to tease him out of it while at the same time maneuver herself into a less awkward position by once again stepping back and challenging him. "Which means you don't want to?"

He pushed her head firmly back onto his shoulder and held her tightly. "Tease," he said. "You have a very touchable body."

Now she was really uncomfortable, but more at her own reaction than his. Every part of her was alert and fluttering with anticipation. She felt a fine flush spread through every fiber, and her breath quickened to the tripping rhythm of her heart. "No more talk about my body," she murmured, burying her face in his shoulder and trying to keep the conversation light so that he would not guess how he had disturbed her. "You're embarrassing me."

"No need," he assured her, caressing the silky material that covered her back with long, gentle strokes, causing her to subdue a shiver. "You should be flattered. You have a perfectly acceptable body and it's doing to me exactly what it was designed to do."

To her great relief the music ended and he slipped his arm easily around her waist to lead her back to the table. Her cheeks were flaming—although she was no longer certain it was from embarrassment—and he only made it worse by peering at her in amusement and exclaiming, "You really *are* embarrassed, aren't you?" He laughed and squeezed her waist affectionately. "I never claimed to be a monk," he told her, eyes sparkling, "just a tower of self-control." And then he whispered in an exaggerated imitation of a lecher, "Don't worry, baby, you're safe with me."

She laughed at her own foolishness as they reached the table and reflected again how much she had learned about men while living with Seth. Tonight's lesson was just a reminder of what she had thought she had learned before—that he was no more than human and just as vulnerable as she was. The alarm she had felt at the possibility of a changing relationship a few moments ago dissolved into nonsense, and she felt closer to him than ever.

She finished her cocktail, which had by now gone quite flat, and Seth watched her thoughtfully, the incident on the dance floor apparently completely forgotten. "I've been thinking," he said at last, his expression and his tone surprising her with its sobriety, "about what you said before—about there being someone for everyone." Her eyes flew to his in question and amazement, and far away an inexplicable pulse throbbed, too quick to be defined, too subtle to register alarm. "And, honey, if it's Hampton you really want, if you're really sure"—he reached for her hand and squeezed her fingers tightly—"then don't give up. Don't get yourself into a depression thinking you'll never see him again and you've lost him forever, because you *will* see him again, you know. He's not exactly invisible and he'll be back. In the meantime write him, call him, make sure he knows how you feel. Give him a chance to think about it, and if he's half the man you say he is, he'll see that he's passing up the chance of a lifetime if he lets you go. I don't know much about the real thing," he admitted, lowering his eyes just briefly to study their entwined hands, "but it seems to me if it's really love, there's always a way. So don't give up, okay?"

Her eyes stung with tears of gratitude and overwhelming affection, and it was a moment before she could speak. "Give Melissa another week," she advised, smiling at him gently through bright, radiant eyes. "Play it cool, let her squirm. Then ask her out again and see if she doesn't leap at the chance."

They shared the moment of gratitude and silent understanding and then, releasing her hand, he said, "Are you ready to go?"

"Do you want me to drive?" she inquired dubiously, getting to her feet as he placed a number of bills on the table.

"Haven't been counting my drinks, have you?" he teased as he guided her carefully through the crowd.

"No," she admitted, "but—"

"I didn't think so. If you had, you would have noticed that I only had one Tom collins. The rest were soda water." He grinned at her in the strobing multicolored lights of the dance floor. "You don't really think I'd take any chances with such valuable cargo in the car, do you?"

She laughed, feeling strangely and wonderfully happy when she had every right to be the most miserable person in the world. She even thought she would sleep tonight and the heavy ache that had settled in her chest that afternoon no longer seemed quite so noticeable. In fact, it hardly hurt at all. Friends, she decided, made all the difference. How could she make it without them?

Outside she stopped and stood on her toes to kiss him on the cheek.

He looked surprised. "What was that for?"

"You," she told him and smiled, and they walked hand in hand to the car.

# Chapter Three

In a house such as theirs it was very difficult to find time to feel sorry for oneself. As often as Kelly had complained about the lack of privacy, the nonstop activity, and the constant bombardment of conversation, she was grateful for it in the week that followed. The yearning ache that had coiled deep within her only made itself manifest in odd moments of solitude; it was the only thing she took to bed with her at night and the first thing she faced every morning, but during the times in between she kept it at bay with the help of her friends.

During the school year Kelly was usually the first one home from work, followed closely by Seth and then Susan and Trish at five and five thirty, respectively. For four single, unfettered people, they led surprisingly well-ordered lives. They were each old enough, and mature enough, to know the value of a stable home life in the background of their sometimes frantic lives, and the obligations of maintaining that environment were a pleasure rather than a chore. They knew the havoc midweek dates could create with their ability to function on the job the next day, and for that reason such occurrences were very rare. Family-style meals during the work week were the rule, not the exception, and those quiet times unwinding together and sharing their days were something to which they all looked forward equally. It was quite un-usual, therefore, that, as Kelly and Susan helped Trish set the dinner table at a quarter to seven, Seth was still not home. "You'd think he could call," complained Trish, but there was more concern than annoyance in her voice.

"You know he always does." Susan filled the water glasses and Kelly placed them on the table. "He'll be here."

"Probably some sort of trouble at work," suggested Kelly. "Or another union meeting."

"No, that's not until Thursday—" And then relief crossed Trish's face as they heard the front door slam, and it was quickly replaced by a frown of irritation as she exclaimed, "Well, it's about time! He almost missed the best lasagna I've ever made." She bent to take the casserole from the oven, a look of maternal satisfaction on her face.

"Hello, my beauties!" Seth sailed into the kitchen, tossed his jacket toward the chair, and deposited a bottle of Chianti on the table. His eyes were sparkling and his step bright as he declared, "I could smell it all the way downtown, that's how I knew what kind of wine to bring."

Trish glanced at him suspiciously. "Did you bring a whole bottle, or did you drink half of it on the way home?"

He laughed and slapped her on the bottom as she bent to place the casserole on the table, then impulsively grabbed Susan, who was balancing two salad bowls, and kissed her on the lips. Susan, barely escaping with the bowls still filled, agreed, "He's been hitting something, all right."

"Pick up your jacket," Kelly scolded and turned to take down the wineglasses.

He caught her from behind and hugged her hard until she squealed for breath and demanded, prying his hands from around her waist, "What in the *world* is the matter with you?"

He laughed with boyish pleasure as he moved her aside and retrieved the glasses himself. "I thought you'd never ask!" He placed two glasses in her hands and reached for two more, his eyes dancing as he announced, "She said yes. And I owe it all to you."

Trish and Susan, uncomprehending, said, "Congratulations!" and "Who?"

Kelly inquired, "Melissa?" And he nodded, opening the wine with a flourish. His excitement was contagious and his pleasure so ingenuous that Kelly could not help sharing it. Her sentiment was genuine as she exclaimed, "Oh, Seth, I'm so glad!"

Susan laughed, "Well, good for you, stud!" and Trish, astonished, said, "I've never seen you so excited about a girl before! This must be serious."

He filled the glasses and served them in turn, answering, "The old hard-to-get routine works two ways, you know. She was putty in my hands." And then, assuming sobriety, he raised his glass and declared, "A toast. To the sweet flower of romance. May it bloom forever."

They sipped the wine, returning his toast, and then took their seats as Seth enthusiastically began serving their plates. "We had coffee this afternoon," he explained. "Got to talking, completely forgot about the time. Nice girl," he pronounced in modest understatement. "Real nice. We're going out Friday night."

Though the girls couldn't help giggling at his childlike satisfaction with himself, they shared his pleasure and his enthusiasm, as it was natural for them to do. "Coffee," murmured Susan in an aside to Trish. "Sounds like a pretty tame beginning to me."

"That's a sign that it's *really* serious," Trish told her soberly.

"Could just be," agreed Seth enigmatically, and Kelly felt a perfectly uncalled-for twinge of disturbance.

"Where are you going to take Melissa?" she asked quickly, spearing her salad.

"Now, that's the problem." Seth tasted his lasagna, made an appreciative sound, and told Trish, "You outdid yourself, babe. Fantastic. This situation," he continued to all of them, but turning to Kelly, "calls for a special touch. I want to give just the right impression. Any suggestions?"

"What kind of impression do you want to create?" inquired Trish.

"Swinger, home-and-hearth, intellectual..." suggested Susan, and Seth made a face at her.

"You make it sound as easy as picking out a suit."

She shrugged, "It is. We all play those first-date games."

Kelly let the conversation go on around her as the depression unexpectedly crept up on her. There was no reason for it, she really was happy for Seth, but she just felt suddenly lonely, as though she were losing David all over again. Perhaps it was because Seth was no longer giving her his full attention, or even partial attention. He was no longer available for comfort or advice. Perhaps because she needed him and she wished Melissa had held off another week or two, until Kelly had gotten her own life straightened out. Jealous? she thought dryly, and had to admit she was—of Seth's attention, not his affection. He had spoiled her.

They had decided dinner and drinks at a quiet, richly atmospheric place would make a perfect first date. Now the only question was where. Seth was all for an exclusive dinner club with prices to match, but Susan immediately vetoed that idea.

"Talk about your bad impressions!" she scoffed.

"Do you want her to think you're some kind of Diamond Jim or something? Start off like that and she'll be expecting it every night."

"Sure," agreed Trish, teasing him. "You don't want her to marry you for your money, do you?"

And maybe it was because Kelly was afraid Seth might really be falling in love... but she dismissed that idea immediately. It was ridiculous. He hadn't even gone out with the girl yet! Besides, hadn't he just gone to great lengths the other night to convince her he was *not* the marrying type—even if she had had her doubts before. No, that was certainly nothing to worry about.

They went through the list of ethnic and continental cuisines, and Kelly watched Seth's face carefully as he devoted his attention to conjecture about what his date would and would not like. *Smitten,* she thought, and began to relax in some amusement. *That's what he is. Just plain, old-fashioned smitten.*

They decided on a nice restaurant featuring French cuisine, elegant but not overstated. "And now," Susan said, her eyes twinkling, "for the big question. Your place or hers?"

"No," Kelly said, and they all looked at her in some surprise. She realized that was the first contribution she had made to the conversation. "Don't make your move too soon," she advised him, "or you'll blow the whole thing."

"That's right," agreed Trish wisely. "There's nothing a woman hates worse than being rushed."

"That's not rushing," complained Seth. "That's just being polite."

"Typical male chauvinism!" exclaimed Susan, throwing her napkin at him as he dissolved into laughter. "'Thanks for a wonderful evening; would you care to come to bed with me?' Just being *polite*!"

Seth retrieved her napkin and tossed it back to her, his eyes dancing. "Most girls I know would be disappointed if I *didn't* ask," he pointed out. "It's a two-way street, you know."

"But I thought Melissa wasn't 'most girls,'" suggested Kelly.

He seemed to consider this. "All right," he agreed after a moment. But there was a hint of dryness in his voice as he inquired, "May I kiss her good night?"

"No," pronounced Kelly, and his light brows flew up in surprise. "Don't you see," she explained, "that's exactly what she'll be expecting—the old octopus-wrestle at the front door. Catch her offguard. Let her know that you want to, but then don't. She'll be so fascinated—and so stunned—she won't be able to refuse when you ask her out again. And better yet, you'll be different, you'll be special in her book from then on. She'll be hooked, and that's the start of something big."

The other girls looked at her in admiration, agreed it was the absolutely perfect approach, wished they could find dates like that, and told Seth he did not know how lucky he was to have them advising him. After a moment he seemed to agree, reluctantly. But then he asked innocently, "What if she tries to kiss me?"

Kelly's lips dimpled with a repressed smile as she began to relax. "Tell her you're not that kind of boy," she retorted.

"And then come home and take a cold shower," concluded Susan, and they all laughed.

"Cheesecake for dessert," announced Trish, beginning to clear the table.

"Not for me," replied Seth, and got up to pour himself a cup of coffee from the ever-ready coffeemaker on the counter.

Susan, groaning, pushed herself away from the table and complained that just looking at one of Trish's meals made her fat. But Kelly was feeling reckless and she cut herself a large slice.

"Four hundred and fifty calories," warned Seth, sitting beside her again, and Kelly ignored him. Trish served herself and then, as Susan mentioned a television program they wanted to watch, took her plate over to the family room area, promising to do the dishes later.

For a while Seth sipped his coffee and absently watched the television across the room, and then, under the cover of the background noise, commented, "You strike me as a girl suffering a delayed reaction from a broken heart. And cheesecake is a very bad prescription."

She shrugged, not looking at him. "There's nothing delayed about my reaction."

"Have you written him?"

She hesitated and shook her head. How could she write to him? What could she say? It had all been a rash and foolish mistake; it was not David's fault, he owed her nothing. Yet she could not close her eyes without seeing those soulful dark eyes and that gentle smile... yearning for him, wishing things could have been different... wishing. That was all there had ever been between them, but she couldn't expect Seth to understand that.

He watched her thoughtfully for a moment and then he said abruptly, "There's a new guy on cameras down at the studio. Nice fellow, about your age. Why don't you—"

"Oh, Seth, for goodness' sake!" She pushed the half-finished cheesecake away impatiently. "That's the last thing I need."

"Well, sitting around here and moping isn't doing you any good," he retaliated. "The only way you're ever going to get over that turkey is to get out and start enjoying yourself, meeting new people—"

"Turkey!" exclaimed Kelly incredulously. She had really thought they had reached an understanding about David, and his last words on the subject had been so kind and understanding, she felt betrayed. "But last week you said—"

He gave an impatient shrug and picked up her fork, helping himself to the remaining cheesecake. "I know what I said, but he's still a turkey. I just want you to be happy and if you really don't think you can live without the jerk, I say go for it. But"—he pointed the fork at her accusingly—"if you're not going to give it everything you have, then you may as well forget it. The only way to get him out of your system is to shop the competition. You'll see quick enough what a mistake you almost made."

Susan overheard the last part of the conversation and commented, "Don't listen to him, Kelly. You know he'll never like any man you date."

"That's not true," defended Seth mildly, finishing off Kelly's discarded dessert. "I just now offered to fix her up with someone and it's not the first time either, if you'll recall."

Susan gave a hoot of laughter. "And the type of men you pick out for her! They make my south Georgia grandpa look like a swinging liberal. I never knew there were so many dull, unimaginative stick-in-the-muds living in Southern California. I think you have them imported."

Kelly resented having her social life discussed as though it were an amusing magazine piece. "I don't see," she put in, bristling, "why anyone has to fix me up with anyone. I can manage my life quite well on my own, thank you."

"The hell you can." Seth got up and poured himself another cup of coffee, and Trish shushed them loudly from the other side of the room as the program resumed. "You need a lot of taking care of when it comes to the opposite sex," he continued as he returned to the table, lowering his voice so as not to disturb the television viewers. "And careful management on the part of someone in the know."

"Yourself, of course," she interrupted sarcastically, draining her wine.

He lifted an eyebrow mildly. "Of course. Who knows you better than I do—your strengths and weaknesses, your needs and vulnerabilities? You have this fatal tendency to leap first and look later," he said, launching forth onto one of his favorite subjects, "especially where matters of the heart are concerned. You need protecting from your own mistakes."

"You're not my father," she said irritably, hating his patronizing tone.

"No," he agreed equitably, "but I'll do in a pinch. Kelly." He touched her fingers and she pulled them away, scowling at him, but his tone was very serious, not accusatory or disparaging. "You're not so different from the rest of us, you know. You're looking for that one and only special lifetime love, and I guess that's an affliction common to the whole human race. But you look a little too hard, so that you're always seeing things that aren't there. Maybe if you'd just relax a little, it would find you." He smiled slightly, trying to win back her good favor. "The way you've been going, by the time your prince does come you'll be married to some guy with an ex-wife, a girl friend, and three kids to support, wasting your pretty young life darning his socks and wishing you'd listened to old Seth."

She gave an impatient snort and took the remaining dishes to the sink. "You're impossible when you're charming."

"But I will do you one favor," he said, looping his arm negligently over the back of the chair and watching her as he sipped his coffee. "You don't like the guys I pick out for you—I'm open-minded. Tell me what you want and I'll have a list of ten possible suitors for you first thing tomorrow morning."

"Don't be ridiculous, darling." The television program was over, and Trish came into the room to start the dishes, brushing his hair lightly with a kiss. "You've spoiled us all for other men. That's why we're such contented and consummate spinsters."

Seth grinned and Kelly said derisively, "Ten! You must think I'm pretty easy to please."

"Just giving you a wide open field, babe," he replied. "I've got to find something to cheer you up." Then he stood. "Hey, Susy, how about beating me at pool? This is your last chance to break even."

The two of them left and as Kelly absently helped Trish with the dishes, she thought about what he had said. He was probably right. She loved not wisely but too well—and too quickly. And the pain she was feeling now was the inevitable result. But the last thing she intended to do was to rush into another romance or even risk a meaningless and nerveracking encounter with the men Seth was all too eager to supply her with. She simply wasn't interested, not now when her heart was in England with a man who did not want it... perhaps not ever.

Besides, she thought with a rather vague sigh as they turned off the kitchen light and went to join the others downstairs, Trish was right—Seth had spoiled her for other men, in a way. She had gotten so used to living with him that the ordinary men she dated—David excluded, of course—all seemed to fall short in some way. And she found some small satisfaction in deciding that, once again, her troubles were all Seth's fault.

Friday night the girls saw Seth off as though he were a crown prince on his way to a coronation. Susan and Trish both had dates, and Kelly was left home alone, a fact of which Seth did not approve in the least. As male protector of the house he did not like any of the girls to be alone at night in the relatively secluded place, but the fact that it was Kelly, whom, he assumed quite correctly, would spend the evening nursing her broken heart, seemed to make him so uneasy that it actually threatened to spoil his evening. She finally mollified him by promising to call one of her friends and go to a movie, but when they had all left she actually relished the silence and enjoyed having the house to herself . . . for about twenty minutes.

Despite Seth's opinion to the contrary, Kelly was not really a girl who was prone to feeling sorry for herself. She had had heartbreaks before and she had gotten over them, it just seemed as though this one would take a little longer. It was like Seth had said, with every love you leave a little of yourself behind until eventually there was less and less solid fabric with which to piece back your heart. It would take time, that was all. For there was nothing she could do about David. She came to see that on that one quiet evening when she was all alone and had plenty of time to think. She was no longer certain she even wanted to. Seth's idea about not giving up had been noble and generous and probably would have applied in any other situation, but not hers. Seth did not really know the facts; it had not been a love affair even in the loosest sense of the word. David owed her nothing. She would never be more than a friend to him, a light encounter to ease the turmoil of his life during a lonely phase. Certainly he did not deserve to be burdened with more of her declarations of undying love, which in themselves were a veiled reproach. He had made her no promises, told her no lies, and she had brought her hurt upon herself. Looking back, she knew she should be grateful that his integrity had kept their relationship on a purely friendly basis. He had to be admired for that.

She was so tired of being everyone's friend and no one's lover.

With a mental sigh she squared her shoulders and

resolved to put the past behind her. Oh, it would hurt. It would take time to get over. But she would recover, and in the meantime she would not drown herself in self-pity. And she would be so very, very much more careful the next time. If there was a next time.

Even in ordinary circumstances, Kelly did not date much. She did not feel desperate if she did not have a date for Saturday night, and months at a time would go past without her seeing anyone steadily. She had her friends, she had Seth to fill in on last-minute social occasions when an escort was required, she had a rewarding career, and very little was lacking in her life. It was only that, as Seth had pointed out, she had a tendency to fall head over heels in love with every man she did meet who was even remotely compatible, to give her heart with the first kiss and mourn it later. Perhaps the best solution would be to see no one at all. She did not think she would mind that very much. After all, as long as Seth was around she hardly lacked for male companionship, and she thought it would simplify her life all around if she just stayed away from other members of the opposite sex for a while.

After a time, feeling her personal life fairly resolved and having had as much as she could take of the silence, she turned the stereo on in the basement, opened the remote speakers in the family room, and sat down to write her parents a letter. Of course she had told them about the living arrangement—to do otherwise would have been folly—but she had waited until she had safely made the permanent move. She had phrased it in a letter very carefully, so carefully that it had taken all four housemates two days to strike the exact note of negligence and confidence she had been trying to achieve. She described the house at great lengths, reminded them how much they had liked Susan when they had met her, and assured them that Trish was just as nice, that all had steady jobs and none

were prone to wild parties, and then, almost as a post-
script, she had added, ''By the way, the fourth housemate is a man, so tell Daddy he doesn't have to worry
about me living alone in such a remote place, as there
is always a male around for protection.''

Her mother's letter had shot back with the speed of
light. Which one of the girls was the man married to?
How old was he? What did he do for a living? And on
and on. Why would a married couple want to share
their house with two single girls? Surely Kelly could
see that such an arrangement would never work out....

She had been obliged, of course, to explain the situation in full. And of course her parents had simply not
understood. Her mother had affected a broken heart,
quietly bemoaning her daughter's fate and wondering
where they had gone wrong, but concluding with a
staunch air of martyrdom that Kelly was over twenty-
one and if she chose to ruin her life it was certainly
none of their concern. Her father was a different story
altogether. A career army man and an elder in his
church, he was conservative to the core, almost fanati-
cal in his support of God, Country, and Morality. He
took Kelly's behavior as a personal affront, and outrage
was too mild a word to apply to his reaction as he condemned her to everlasting purgatory and then threatened to come to California and remove her from the
den of iniquity by bodily force. His letter had horrified
her. When she called him, his sermonizing and angry
accusations had reduced her to tears. Though she had
never been particularly close to her father, this had re-
sulted in an open breach. She was hurt at his lack of
trust and righteously insulted by his veiled insinua-
tions, wholly embarrassed by the issue he was making
of a perfectly innocent situation. Through her tears of
anger and humiliation she had confided in her housemates, and it was Seth who had helped her see the
problem from her parents' point of view. He explained

that while most people could understand a living arrangement involving a male and a female who were in love, there was something altogether different and undeniably suspicious about a man and three women sharing a roof. He pointed out that she had been raised with her parents' moral values and should be more understanding of their reaction. He persuaded her to try to make peace.

The rift between her and her father had never completely healed, but Kelly made a conscientious effort to write her mother twice a month and she received prompt, chatty, if somewhat impersonal, replies. Her father never wrote her, or called her—possibly for fear Seth might answer the phone—or even sent a personal regard via her mother. But twice yearly, on her birthday and Christmas, she would receive a signed card and a check for fifty dollars—a symbol, she supposed, that she had not been completely disinherited.

She still thought her parents were being unreasonable and it still sometimes hurt her to think she had lost them, but she was almost thirty years old and they surely could allow her the right to make some decisions for herself. Sometimes it made her sad to think of their disapproval, but she had in effect only traded one family for another and she did not regret the bargain.

Trish and Susan came home early. Neither one was particularly thrilled with their dates and both were anxious to hear about Seth's. At twelve thirty precisely he came in, looking satisfied, annoyingly mysterious, and enormously pleased with himself. They clamored for the details, but he simply raised a hand mildly and said, "No interviews tonight, ladies, it's been a long evening." And he started for his room.

They accosted him bodily and dragged him into the family room, where he laughingly conceded to their demands for information as Kelly made coffee and tried to look suitably impressed while he sang Melissa's praises. He was, without a doubt, completely under the woman's spell and enjoying it thoroughly. He informed Kelly that her strategy had worked perfectly and that he had another date with Melissa Saturday afternoon to go sailing. They would spend the day at Catalina Island and probably would not return until late in the evening . . . if, he told Kelly with a wink, even then. He had never looked happier, but for some reason Kelly could not share his enthusiasm.

But Saturday morning Seth looked awful. He mumbled something about not having slept well, and Susan and Trish teased him about the first signs of a serious case of love at first sight. Uncharacteristically, he did not respond. He was subdued and rather grumpy as they all went about their Saturday-morning chores, and after a while they realized he was in no mood to be teased.

"Like a bear with a sore paw," whispered Susan to Kelly when his back was turned. It wasn't the first time Seth had had bouts of moodiness but Kelly could not help thinking it odd, following so closely on the crest of his triumph with Melissa. When he returned from his date that evening at ten o'clock, he went straight to bed, and Kelly wondered whether the brief-lived love affair had burned itself out. She should have felt sympathetic but actually she felt a strange and completely inexplicable sense of relief.

On Sunday the women all slept late and when they awoke, Seth had already left the house. They spent the day doing their nails, setting their hair, giving themselves facials, and gossiping about Seth. He returned at eight o'clock that evening, looking hollow-eyed and exhausted, and once again went straight to bed without enlightening them regarding any of their speculation. It was all very strange.

On Monday afternoon Kelly had basketball practice

and Seth was already home by the time she arrived. The stereo was on and he was sitting at the dining room table, writing checks with the help of Fleetwood as a paperweight—and smoking a cigarette.

"I thought you quit!" she exclaimed in automatic astonishment, dumping her books and her briefcase on the table. Fleetwood gave an annoyed yowl, stretched himself out over Seth's papers, and Kelly ruffled his ears absently.

Seth glanced at her with an easy grin. "Temporarily," he replied.

She peered at him suspiciously as she kicked off her shoes. "You feeling okay?" she inquired.

He put down the pen and leaned back against the chair, the muscles of his arms straining against the blue denim fabric of his shirt as he stretched his arms overhead. "As well as can be expected after just having spent two thousand dollars in ten minutes with no end in sight. Why do you ask?"

"Well," she ventured, taking a canned drink from the refrigerator, "you weren't exactly God's gift to humanity this weekend."

He shrugged, took the can from her, and opened it silently. "I must have picked up a bug. I'm okay now."

She took her drink over to the sofa and sat down. "Everything okay with Melissa?"

He took a final draw on the cigarette and crushed the filter in the ashtray before beginning to gather up his papers. "Terrific. That is, I guess so. I didn't see much of her today."

And just as she was beginning to think everything was getting back to normal, as she curled her feet beneath her and sipped her drink and prepared to unwind from the day, Susan came in. Immediately they knew something was wrong. She entered quietly and did not say anything but she looked tense, drawn, distracted. Her lipstick had been chewed off and she looked pale, her eyes were wide with distress. Seth inquired, "What's wrong, Susy?"

She glanced at him nervously. "Oh, nothing." She sank to the love seat opposite Kelly, absently biting her lip. "Just a little problem at the office."

"Some clown make a pass at you?" Seth got up and came to sit beside her, resting his arm across the back of the love seat, inviting confidence.

She glanced at him worriedly, then at Kelly, and she seemed to make a decision. She opened her briefcase and took out a stack of magazines. "Look at this." She opened one of the magazines to a full-page color ad and passed it to Seth. "What do you see?"

Kelly, definitely curious, leaned forward to see what there could be about a magazine ad to upset Susan so. It was nothing more than a familiar layout for a new automobile, and apparently Seth was just as confused as she was. "A girl in a slinky evening gown selling cars," he replied. "Why?"

Susan shook her head firmly. "Sex. That's what you see. And that's what you're buying. But at least there you know it." Seth glanced at Kelly in amused puzzlement as Susan frantically turned the pages to another ad. Obviously she was upset, but about what neither of them had the faintest idea. "There." Susan slapped the page of another ad. "Now what do you see?"

Patiently Seth played her game. "Party in the background, nice cool drink in the foreground. More girls in slinky evening gowns."

"Look again," commanded Susan. "Especially at the ice cubes."

Another amused look passed between Seth and Kelly, and he looked back down at the page. He studied it for a long time. Slowly his eyes widened. He began to chuckle. He said softly, "Well, I'll be damned." He laughed out loud. "It's a naked woman! Look at that!"

He flipped the page toward Kelly, but too quickly for her to see.

She got up and came over to him, demanding, "Let me see!" but Susan was already reaching for another magazine.

"It's subliminal advertising," Susan explained briefly. "Little hints of sex tucked away into very ordinary-looking advertising spreads. Your conscious mind doesn't see it, but your subconscious does, and bingo—you buy the product without really making an intelligent decision."

Kelly studied the page in amazement as Seth laughed. "Oh, come on! Just because someone plants a pretty nude in an ice cube doesn't mean I'm going to rush out and buy a fifth of booze. Give us a little credit."

"Oh, no?" Susan held his gaze steadily. "What brand of rum do you buy?"

He looked from her to the advertisement in Kelly's hand, looked slightly uncomfortable, and did not answer. Susan opened the other magazine to an ad for a popular household cleaner. In the foreground was a rather ordinary-looking model in slacks, holding the product. Behind her a spotless kitchen and walls papered in an intricate pattern. "Look closely at the wallpaper," she suggested.

Seth did, and to Kelly's amazement he actually began to flush. He closed the magazine abruptly, no sign of amusement on his face at all. "That's disgusting," he said briefly.

"Ha!" Susan gave an impatient sound of exasperation. "When it's a female, it's funny, but when it's a male—"

"That's not even decent," declared Seth, and Kelly tried to wrestle the magazine from him. He held it firm.

"There's something decent about naked women in ice cubes?" countered Susan incredulously.

"But this isn't even erotic, it's—"

"It may not be erotic to you, but to the thousands of women who buy household cleaners—"

"Oh, for goodness' sake!" exclaimed Kelly. "Let me see!"

"You're too young," replied Seth, pulling the magazine away and tucking it under the cushion on which he sat. Kelly made an impatient sound of exasperation mixed with amusement, but Susan looked far from amused.

"It's been going on for years," she said heavily, "in national publications, family magazines, only now it's just beginning to come out and, oh, Seth!" Her eyes were wide with distress. "We're being investigated for it!"

"You!" Kelly sat back on her heels, her interest in the pornographic wallpaper fading. "Why you?"

"I thought most of this stuff came out of New York," added Seth.

She nodded wearily. "But *our* Senator Apling is drafting a bill for the California legislature against it, and since we're the biggest agency in the state...."

"And since," Kelly understood slowly, "your agency is guilty of the practice...."

Susan nodded, abashed, as though she personally had been responsible.

Seth leaned his cheek on his fist, shifting his position to look at her. "So what's all this got to do with you? You didn't design any of the ads; you don't even handle big accounts. Your job's not in jeopardy, is it?"

"It could be," she answered dolefully, "if I don't keep Senator Apling happy." For a moment Kelly was completely baffled. Susan was the assistant to the chief account executive. She sometimes handled small accounts on her own but never made executive decisions regarding national campaigns. How could this all fall back on her? Unless...

"You don't mean..." began Kelly incredulously.

Susan nodded bitterly. "*I'm* the liaison between Apling and the agency. And why?" She mimicked her boss's gruff voice sourly. "'Because you have a better figure than I do, my dear!' He refuses to touch it and he made it very clear that *my* future, as well as that of the agency, is at stake." Her voice rose in outrage and despair. "What does he expect me to do, sleep with the man? Wouldn't that be the final irony? We're dragged before the legislature on a sex scandal and how do we solve it? With prostitution!"

"Oh, but surely—" exclaimed Kelly, and Seth's brows drew together ominously.

The front door slammed and Trish flew in. Her hair was wild and her face tear-streaked; she threw down her purse and flung her glasses on the table, then stumbled into a chair and buried her face in her hands, sobbing.

For a moment the three on the other side of the room were frozen with shock, and then it seemed they all moved at once. "What is it?" demanded Susan, her own problems completely forgotten as she rushed to her friend. "Were you in an accident? Are you hurt?"

Kelly exclaimed softly as she got to her feet, "My God!" She felt as though the entire house were falling in about her, pillar by pillar. She went quickly to Trish's aid.

Seth poured her a glass of water and placed a hand on her shoulder, urging, "Come on, sweetheart, don't keep us in suspense. Out with it."

"I'm just so—*mad*!" gulped Trish at last. She dropped her head to her folded arms and beat her fists against the table, once and hard, as though gripping her self-control with both hands. At last she lifted a red and ravaged face to them, choking back sobs and trembling with the effort as she pushed back her hair. Her eyes were enormously bright blue and brimming with tears. "That job was mine!" she exclaimed furiously. "You know it was! I've worked for it for five years, I'm the only one qualified. It was practically promised to me."

"The promotion," Kelly said sympathetically. "You didn't get it." Trish had been office manager at her firm for five years, and the position she had worked so hard for had finally become available this month when her department manager had retired. She was the logical choice. She had been so certain she would get it.

Trish took the water glass in both hands and gulped half the contents while Seth patted her shoulder reassuringly. In a moment she seemed better able to speak. "A man," she said brokenly, fury shaking in her voice. "They brought in a man from the outside, a thirty-five-year-old junior-executive type with *no* experience, *no* qualifications... except that he's a man! And wait, here's the kicker!" She gave a short, hysterical laugh. "*I'm* supposed to train him!"

Kelly's eyes met Seth's over Trish's head in helpless sympathy. She suddenly felt very lucky—and at the same time in as much turmoil as though her friends' crises had been her own.

"You could file a sex discrimination suit," suggested Seth. "If you're sure—"

"Oh, I'm sure all right," replied Trish bitterly. "It's crystal clear. But if I take any action I'll lose my job and I'm in no position to wait two or three years going through the courts to collect back pay. Oh, damn!"

"Sex," said Susan glumly, drawing up a chair and slipping an arm about Trish's shoulders comfortingly. "It all boils down to sex. Eliminate sex and you could solve all the world's problems in one blow."

Seth's eyes twinkled as he perched casually on the edge of the table near Trish. "Sure," he agreed. "We'd all die of boredom." And then he added lightly, "Well, I guess this is as good a time as any to tell you my news. Maybe it will cheer you up. I'm on strike."

Once again, as one, their attention shifted from their

own problems to that of their friend. Dismay and sympathy filled their eyes with exclamations of concern, but he shrugged it off. "I could use the vacation, and at seventy-percent salary, who's complaining? It won't last long. And the best part"—once again his eyes twinkled with amusement as he swept them all in consideration of their various problems—"is that it has nothing whatsoever to do with sex."

That drew a reluctant giggle from Susan and then Kelly joined in and soon they were all laughing, relaxing, feeling better about their problems and their ability to face them. It was always that way when they were together. Eventually, somehow, everything seemed to work out right.

"What this household needs," declared Kelly, "is a distraction. Something different and exciting to keep us all from smothering in self-pity or having a collective nervous breakdown or both."

"Let's have a party," suggested Susan immediately, already considerably cheered.

But Seth said suddenly, "No. We'll go camping. We haven't done that all year. How about this weekend? Is that good for everybody?"

After a moment's thought, they all enthusiastically agreed. It was exactly what they needed: the fresh air, the barren desert landscape, the freedom, and the quiet times with good friends. It was one of Kelly's favorite recreations and she was amazed she had not thought of it herself. She slipped her arm around Seth's waist and hugged him in gratitude.

Afterward Kelly would look back many times on that afternoon. She would see them all gathered at the dining table, enthusiastically making plans, turning a day that had started out in disaster into one glistening with promise. She would see herself and Seth with their arms around each other and their heads close together, laughing and talking just as they always had.

But in looking back it would all be different, seeming somehow to hold a tabloid of the past and foreshadow the future with changes she never would have guessed and, at that time, would not even have wished to know.

# Chapter Four

As the week progressed it became obvious they were all even more desperate for a holiday than they had first realized. Susan dragged herself to work each day and hurried home at night, dreading the inevitable personal confrontation with the infamous Senator Apling. Trish stormed out of the house with fire in her eyes and worked late at night, usually forgoing dinner in favor of antacid tablets that she gulped by the handful. Seth continued to see Melissa, but it did not seem to improve his spirits much. He got his bout with picket duty out of the way, cursing and complaining the whole time, and was restless and at loose ends during the day. He changed the oil and spark plugs in all their cars, fixed sagging shelves and squeaky doors, repaired the hole in the screen door Fleetwood had created in a fit of temper with his inattentive mistress, and wandered about the house looking bored and disgruntled, trying to find something to do.

He was not sleeping well at night either and Kelly at last thought she knew the reason why. "Melissa is in management, isn't she?" she asked him one early evening as he drove her home from a basketball game. Seth usually attended all of her games when he could, much in the same way the proud parents of her girls' team did, and they had won, which had put Kelly in an extraordinarily good mood but left his untouched.

"Yeah," he answered vaguely, lighting a cigarette. "Why?"

"What," she inquired shrewdly, "would the union do if they found out you were in league with the enemy?"

He shrugged carelessly. "Break both my arms probably."

"Seth!" She laughed at the exaggeration.

"What's going on with Melissa and me has nothing to do with work," he explained. "Besides, they can't do anything if they don't find out."

Kelly was burning to know what, exactly, was going on between Melissa and him, but in the mood that had prevailed this past week she did not dare ask. She simply suggested, "But it does put a strain on your relationship?"

He grinned suddenly. "When you were a teenager," he replied, "didn't you ever sneak into the backseat of a car with some boy and do something you knew was wrong, scared to death you'd get caught, but the element of risk making it all that much more exciting?"

She tingled with embarrassment. "Don't be ridiculous!"

"Same thing here. Breaking rules always makes the adventure more tempting." And then he glanced at her in curious amusement. "Didn't you really ever—"

"My parents didn't even let me out of the house with a boy until I was eighteen," she interrupted him quickly, uncomfortably. "By then, backseats were out of fashion."

"Poor baby," he exclaimed in genuine astonishment. "No wonder you're so ignorant about the wiles of the opposite sex. But," he mused, "I suppose there is a lot to be said for old-fashioned morality. After all, it's kept you safe and sound all these years."

She did not know how he had switched the subject so

deftly from his personal life to hers, but she did not like it. She quickly launched forth into a more neutral topic.

When they walked in the door Trish greeted them flatly with "I can't go." At their questioning looks, she explained resentfully, "Camping this weekend. I can't go. I have to fly to San Francisco with Mr. Know-it-all Junior Executive to show him the ropes of the home office. I won't be back until Tuesday."

They were all visibly disappointed, and Susan moaned that she didn't know how she would make it through another week if she didn't have some relaxation. Seth suggested, trying to be a good sport, "We'll just have to make it next weekend, then. No big deal."

Trish shook her head. "Next weekend's no good, either—sales conference. As a matter of fact, I'll probably be working a lot of weekends until I get this guy straightened out. It will be impossible for us to all get together. You just go ahead without me and have a good time. Don't worry about me." Her eyes narrowed bitterly. "I'm going to enjoy every minute of carving up Mr. Self-confidence before the home board. He'll curse the day he ever saw me before this weekend is over, you can bank on that."

They all made the proper noises of regret and reluctance, but Trish seemed to be savoring her anticipated revenge with such relish that there really wasn't much guilt about leaving her behind.

On Thursday afternoon they packed supplies for three, rather than four, as they planned to leave as soon as Kelly got home from school on Friday. Susan had arranged, by hook or by crook, to take a half day off and Kelly's last class on Friday was over at one o'clock. They planned to leave by two.

Susan, looking drained, a little pale, and badly in need of a vacation, went to bed early on Thursday. Kelly stayed up with Seth and watched television until after the late news, then went to bed herself. At two thirty she awoke suddenly, not knowing why, but fully alert. Try as she might, she could not go back to sleep. At last she got out of bed, pulled a light wrap over the short one-piece sleeper she had worn to bed, and went into the kitchen.

A pale yellow light shone under the door and as she pushed it open the aroma of coffee greeted her. Seth sat at the kitchen table, wearing a pair of low-slung jeans with the belt unbuckled, his torso and his feet bare. His shoulders sagged as he sat over a cup of coffee and there was an ashtray littered with cigarette butts at his elbow. Kelly moved into the room cautiously, almost afraid to disturb him.

He looked up, and the glimpse she caught of his face caused sudden alarm to tighten within her. It looked haggard. His eyes were haunted and, for just that brief moment before he masked his expression, she saw a raw pain there she would never before have believed could belong to Seth. It frightened her. She wanted to creep away and leave him alone, and at the same time she wanted to run to him and put her arms around him and soothe away whatever was torturing him so. Her heart began to thud in her chest as she wondered whether Melissa could possibly be the cause of his suffering, and she briefly hated the woman she had never met.

Then he managed a vague smile and gestured her to come in. "What are you doing up this time of night?" he asked.

"I don't know." She came slowly into the room. "I just woke up."

He smiled a little into his coffee cup. "We've always been able to do that," he said softly. "Did you ever notice? You and I always seem to be able to tell when the other one needs to talk, or be left alone, or just sit quietly together. Seems like whatever I need, you always have."

She looked at him, an alien and not totally unwelcome emotion tightening in her stomach. In the quiet intimacy of the soft kitchen light he looked so vulnerable and alone, and she always wanted to be there when he needed her, for hadn't he always been for her? But this time was different. There was something about the lateness of the hour and his half-undressed state, the pain she had surprised in his eyes, and the strange way in which he had spoken to her that seemed to draw her into another dimension of caring for him. She said softly, "Do you need to talk?"

Absently he fingered the half-empty cigarette package, not looking at her. "I guess so. I suppose I'd better, but it's not going to be easy."

Concern and a little dread slowed the racing of her pulse. She turned quickly to the refrigerator. "You shouldn't be drinking coffee. It will keep you awake all night."

"That's fine with me." It was said heavily, on a sigh, and he leaned back in his chair, rubbing the back of his neck wearily.

"Have you been to bed at all?" She removed his coffee cup and replaced it with a glass of milk, then poured one for herself.

"For a while," he answered absently. "Couldn't sleep."

"You haven't been sleeping the past couple of weeks," she pointed out gently, sitting across the small table from him. "Are you worried about the strike?"

"Not really." His restless fingers played a light rhythm on the glass, reached for the cigarettes, returned them to the table. He still did not look at her. "I mean, no one likes to be out of work, but it's not as though I'm hurting for money or anything. And it won't last forever."

That was exactly as Kelly had thought. Seth's was a highly specialized profession and he was paid accordingly. Even without the help of three housemates he would have had no financial problems. As it was he had the freedom to make investments and savings, and money should be the least of his problems. A sort of cold disappointment crept through her as she realized it could only be—

"Melissa," she said dully. It must be really serious if Melissa could put him into this state, and low panic stirred within her as she realized the full consequences of this.

But his rather strained smile immediately allayed her fears. "Way down at the bottom of my list," he assured her. "As a matter of fact, that seems to be the only thing in my life that's going right lately." And then the smile widened into a slow grin as he looked at her. "You know what?" he suggested softly, with a trace of amusement. "I think you're jealous."

"Of Melissa?" She swallowed back an unexpected blush and took a quick sip of her milk. "Don't be silly."

He looked at her, and the way his eyes traveled slowly over her made her suddenly aware that she wore nothing but the brief cotton sleeper beneath the almost transparent robe, and grateful that the table hid the way the robe parted at her thighs. Still, she made discreet movements beneath the table to cover her bare legs, an automatic gesture that Seth probably did not even notice. He did not seem to affect either of the other women that way, but still there were too many times when Kelly forgot to think of him as her landlord and housemate and saw him simply as a man. It was nothing he did deliberately, she was certain, but she just couldn't seem to completely put aside the constant awareness that he was a man and she was a woman. Maybe, she thought for the first time, that was what made their relationship different. She was not at all certain that was a good thing.

But then he reached for her fingers and squeezed them gently. "You don't have to be," he told her with a smile. "Melissa is just another pretty face, and you— you're my very best friend."

Somehow there was a happy reassurance in that, but also a little uncertainty. She had to ask, "Is she?" It suddenly seemed very important that she know. "Is she just another pretty face?"

His eyes wandered; he released her fingers. "I don't know," he said after a moment. "Maybe more than that; it's too early to tell. I really don't want to think about it tonight."

So she gave him the silence, did not reprimand him when he lit another cigarette, and allowed him to take all the time he needed to relax and put into words what was really on his mind. And in the comfortable quiet between them she let her own mind wander, aimlessly, absently, feeling nothing but the tranquillity of the time they shared. It was good, sitting with him in the cozy warmth of the kitchen while the house lay still and shrouded around them. It was a private time, a restful time, one of those all-too-rare moments that belonged exclusively to them, and it always felt right when they were together like this. The smell of coffee and cigarette smoke was intimate and familiar, just as was the easy, unspoken rapport between them. She liked the way the light fell on the smooth dark skin of Seth's shoulders and the movements of the sinewy muscles of his arms as he leaned back in his chair and stretched for the ashtray. She observed in distant fascination the pattern of golden-brown hair on his chest and the way it narrowed into a darker triangle across his firm abdomen to the point where it met the open belt of his jeans low on his pelvis. The effect registered as vaguely, somewhat disturbingly, erotic. But Seth was a nice-looking man, this was not the first time Kelly had realized that, and it was inevitable that his nearly naked presence in the close atmosphere that surrounded them in the after-midnight hours should cause some stirring of emotions within her. She tried not to dwell on it, and it was obvious Seth's thoughts were very far from taking any turn in that direction.

He said abruptly, crushing out the cigarette, "Have you ever heard of Delayed Stress Syndrome?"

The sound of his voice breaking into her private reverie was enough to make her start, bringing her back into a reality that embarrassed vague daydreams for the adolescent wanderings they were. A moment later his actual words registered, along with the tight, strained look on his face, and her heart began to pump adrenaline that was a mixture of surprise and concern. Her senses were alert and keyed up for a challenge, scanning everything about his posture and tone—the reserved, nervous look in his eyes, the absent fidgeting his fingers did with the untouched glass of milk, the tautness of his bare shoulders and the stiffness about his mouth—ready to interpret and act upon his signals, straining to understand, knowing instinctively that he was about to ask something very important of her and hoping desperately that she would be equal to the request.

"Yes," she admitted slowly, casting around desperately in her mind for the connection. "But I'm not sure—"

"Vietnam," he said briefly, not looking at her, and that one word was all the clue she needed to bring it all together. She stared at him, hardly believing it.

"You were there?" Her voice was softened with incredulity, her mind was racing. She thought she knew him, but she had never guessed— Once again she was reminded of how little she really knew about Seth, beginning with this one enormously important part of his life he had never told any of them. Her eyes were wide and still somewhat stunned as she stammered, trying to adjust to a radically new view of him, "But—but I didn't think you were old enough! I mean—"

He gave a short, dry laugh and glanced at her briefly. "I wasn't, believe me." Nervously he lit another cigarette, narrowing his eyes against the flare of the match and the sulphuric smell. "I went straight from high school, didn't wait to be drafted. Thought it was the thing to do."

"I never knew," she said softly, looking at him with entirely new eyes. The emotions that assailed her were those that appear unexpectedly when something old suddenly seems new—confusion, hesitance, a sense of mystery and adventure, and the uncertainty that accompanies a radical readjustment of viewpoint.

The glance he gave her was briefly bitter. "Well, I learned on my first day back in the States it wasn't something you're supposed to be proud of." He drew on the cigarette, looking away from her. "I don't talk about it much. I try not to think about it."

And suddenly so much was becoming clear. Walls he had built between them without her ever having been aware of it gradually came tumbling down as she began to understand. "That's why sudden noises upset you," she said slowly. "And thunderstorms...."

His look was of quick, silent gratitude at her easy grasp of the details, and something warm and yearning tightened in her chest for him—the need to share, the desire to understand, and in understanding to draw closer to him. "Noises," he agreed mildly, though his gaze slid uncomfortably away from hers, "dark rooms, closed doors, things I can't see over or around...and rain." His voice dropped to a tone of ragged despair and it was almost a whisper as he inhaled quickly and deeply on the cigarette. "God, I hate the smell of rain." Again his glance flickered quickly over her face, as though to reassure himself of her reaction before going on. "That's why I moved to L.A. To get away from the jungle smells on the east coast."

She inquired softly, "Where are you from originally?" And she was reminded in that moment of almost mystical confidence of another thing she had never known about him, how many secrets had stood between them, how many closed doors had separated what she thought she had known of him from the real man. And now those secrets were falling away, those doors were opening....

He responded automatically, his attention fixed upon the curtained window above her shoulder. "Newport News, Virginia. A navy town. Shipbuilding actually, but it seemed as though the military was a way of life there. Eighty percent of my graduating class went into the service." Again his voice fell. "I wonder how many of them came home."

She did not dare break into his mood with more questions. She gave him the time to compose himself and to continue at his own pace. All around them the silence breathed like the comforting whisper of an old friend, and she was there, waiting to receive him with support and understanding.

"I was luckier than most," he resumed after a moment. The cigarette had burned to the filter and he absently tossed it into the ashtray, reaching for the pack again. "I was assigned to a medical unit, I was never really in combat...but I saw plenty of it." Again there was silence, and pain tore at his eyes with flickering memories from which he forcefully dragged himself away. Once again he glanced at her for reassurance, and the mixture of uneasiness, remembered horror, and shame there wrenched at her heart. She wanted to put her arms around him and draw his head onto her shoulder and comfort him and tell him it was all right. She knew what he was suffering and she would help....

But he forced a dry, uneven smile suddenly, trying to lighten the mood. "Talk about your typical army inefficiency. This is the kid who damn near passed out at age six when my cat had kittens and spent twenty minutes recovering from the blood tests for the army physical." And he dropped his eyes. "Well, I got over that pretty quick. I never learned to like the sight of blood but I sure got used to it. That and a lot more."

Silence, painful this time and seeming to go on forever as she knew there was nothing she could really do to help, nothing she could do to ease his torment or erase his memories. She watched his fingers absently shred an unlit cigarette into a fine pile of tobacco and slivers of white paper on the table and she thought her heart would break for him.

She said quietly, after a very long time, "My father was career army. He was retired by then, but most of our friends were army people...and most of them were in Vietnam. I saw them change. I heard the stories. I—know." And with those words, honest, plain, and heartfelt, she said very simply all there was to say.

He looked at her and an enormous relief washed over his face. A heavy burden seemed to shift its weight on his bowed shoulders, to become lighter and easier to bear. He suddenly noticed the destruction of the cigarette beneath his fingers and began to scrape its remains into the ashtray. "I had to talk to someone, Kelly," he said with a slow breath. "I haven't before, ever, and—" He glanced at her and some of the uneasiness had disappeared from his eyes, although his smile was still strained and uncertain. "I'm glad it was you."

"I am too," she whispered, and their eyes met in a moment rich with caring and shared emotion. Gratitude swept from him and she felt some of the tension begin to fade. She asked, "Were you there long?"

"A lifetime." He got up and went to empty the ashtray in the trash can beneath the sink. "Eighteen months, actually," he added, not turning. He turned on the faucet and rinsed the ashtray beneath the flow of water. "I came home, went to college on the G.I. Bill, got this house the same way, and tried to forget about it. Sometimes I almost think I have. And then...." He came back over to her and replaced the ashtray on the table. She thought he would resume his seat but he was too tense. There was restlessness in his stance and tightness in his tone, the lines on his face were grim and distressed. He struggled to find the right words. "This delayed stress thing, it's like a time bomb ticking away in your head, or like one of those amoeba you pick up from drinking the water south of the border. It gets in your bloodstream and you can't get rid of it, you just have to sit there and wait for it to strike. It's a nervous breakdown waiting to happen and there's nothing you can do about it." He dragged his fingers through his tightly coiled curls and Kelly's heart clutched at her throat at the sudden glimpse of fear and raw distress she was in his eyes. She had never seen Seth like this before, not ever, and his fear became her own as the ramifications of what he was suggesting struck her.

He took a short breath, turned and walked away from her a few paces, then turned again. "I guess you know the details. It's a psychological sneak attack, guerrilla warfare inside your head, a disease with no cure. No one can predict who it's going to strike, or when, or what it will do when it does. It hit some guys right after they got back, others five years later, and ten. Who knows, maybe twenty or even thirty years down the road it will still be showing up. It's something you just have to live with the rest of your life and sometimes I think the worry alone is enough to drive me crazy."

He turned abruptly and gripped the kitchen counter, shoulders square, neck stiff, staring straight ahead at the blank kitchen window. She heard the soft sound of his indrawn breath and then he continued evenly, "I thought I had adjusted okay. It was rough at first, but eventually the nightmares stopped and I didn't dive for cover every time I heard a door slam or a car backfire. The last five or six years I haven't had any trouble at all. And then, a couple of weeks ago it just seemed like everything started falling apart. No reason for it, no warning...just, suddenly, I was back there. I can't sleep and when I do the dreams are so bad I wish I hadn't. It's in my head all the time, flashbacks, names and faces I haven't thought of in years, the sounds and the smells and the sights, sometimes I can even taste the fear. It just," he concluded softly, tilting his head back a fraction in a stark portrayal of despair, "won't leave me alone."

She ached for him. She bit her lip and felt tears burning in the back of her throat, and there was nothing she could do to help him. She swallowed determinedly on her own helplessness and forced the tremor from her voice as she asked quietly, "Has it happened before?"

He nodded, after a time, slowly. And he answered, "Every time it does I think maybe this is it, the last nightmare, the time I'll go back and never return.... Oh, Kelly," he said tiredly, bowing his head slowly as though against a great weight, "there's nothing worse than living every day of your life afraid you're going to lose your mind."

She pushed back her chair, then got up and crossed the room toward him. She touched his shoulder lightly, and then his arms were around her, crushing her to him in desperation and fierce need. She could feel the tremors in his arms with the straining of his muscles and her face was wet with tears as she slipped her arms around his back, curving them around his bare shoulders, holding him tightly, imparting all the strength she had to give. It was a moment of intensely shared emotions, of needing and giving, a time when all surface attractions were stripped away and their inner selves laid bare, a test of caring. She knew that she would have gladly taken on his burden to give him peace even for one night. Frustration and despair filled her that there was so little she could do to help, and she cried for him. They had shared so many good times in the past—the laughter and the jokes, the quiet times of relaxation, the little intimacies. These were the bad times and they were just as welcome, and even more poignant, because they were shared.

After a very long time the straining muscles of his arms eased their grip somewhat, his warm breath against her neck became steadier. She opened her eyes as the flow of tears gradually stopped and she started to move away. But immediately his arms tightened again on a silent breath of protest, his embrace not quite so painful this time but every bit as urgent. She pressed her fingers against his shoulder reassuringly and relaxed against him, understanding. He simply did not want to be left alone and she did not want to leave him.

She lay against him, her breasts crushed against the steady, powerful thumping of his heart, feeling the heat of his body through her nightclothes and the tingling sensation of the soft mat of chest hair against her nipples. His flesh was like silk beneath her fingers, smooth and warm. She loved holding him and being held by him, she loved the sensation of their bodies pressed close together in the sharing of strength and sorrow... and then, gradually, with the growing awareness of him, it was not enough. The need to comfort and to share subtly grew into another need that was just as strong, just as moving. She did not want it to end here. She did not want his arms to ever leave her. She wanted to kiss him, to feel his lips upon hers, and to be crushed against him in a new desire, to open herself up

to new and more intense levels of sharing and closeness. Beyond that she did not know, she simply wanted
to kiss him and the need was so strong it was like a
suddenly realized hunger within her, the promise of
fulfillment so close she hardly felt the pangs of anticipation. It was simply right, the next step in closeness they
had begun to cement this night. It was simply natural.

His hands moved along her back, cupping handfuls
of her heavy hair, the tension in his arms dissolving
gently into a sort of sensual languor as he explored the
curves of her back and the texture of her hair between
his fingers. His hands moved upward to cup her face.
He looked down at her and in his eyes she saw the
same intent that was in her own. Not a burning passion
or a breathless desire, not a sudden and devastating
awareness of pulsating sexuality. Such emotions would
have been out of place in that moment. It was simply
the natural thing to do, the next step in sharing. His
face was very close to hers; their lips brushed. And
then, at the very last moment, something changed. He
became aware as she became aware; she felt him stiffen
and he changed the kiss to a brief, brotherly caress
upon the side of her mouth, and he smiled.

"You have to go to work," he said somewhat
huskily, smoothing a strand of hair away from her
cheek. "Better get to bed."

She dropped her eyes, accepting with a surprisingly
sharp disappointment the lead he took in the situation.
Without having been aware of it, they had moved a
step away from each other, so that now no part of their
bodies touched except his hands on her face. She
looked up at him uncertainly. "Will you be all right?"

For just a moment there was the need in his eyes, the
question, and the hesitance. His eyes rested briefly
upon her lips before meeting hers again, and then the
longing was replaced with a gentle smile. "Yeah," he
said softly. "I think so. For tonight, anyway. Talking

about it seemed to take the edge off. Maybe that's all I really needed."

She smiled, a little hesitantly, and told him, "Try to get some rest."

He moved his hands from her face and nodded. "I think I can now."

For just another moment she hesitated, waiting for a word or an unspoken signal that he needed her to stay. But he seemed relaxed, more at peace, and, if not exactly anxious to let her go, at least willing. She started for the door.

"Kelly."

She turned anxiously.

"Thanks," he said simply, "for being my friend."

She smiled at him, touched his fingers lightly, and then, in another moment, she left the room.

# Chapter Five

Kelly did not sleep immediately. She waited until she heard the kitchen light go off and Seth cross to his own room, but still she lay awake, thinking about him. Confused impressions of him were tangled in her head, so many of them now just beginning to make sense. In the beginning he had been a source of endless fascination for her, a jokester and a philosopher, a tease and a source of wisdom, a carefree youth with the face of a boy and the eyes of a man. He could be annoying and he could be reassuring, just like a brother. She had alternately resented his interference and been grateful for his protective interest. Trish had once described her relationship with Seth as "closer than a hairdresser, but not quite a brother," and it was a description that was apt, except that somehow, over the years, she and Seth had become more than that. It was nothing in particular, but something just a little special between them that was indefinable and generally accepted. Whenever the other women had a favor to ask of him they always came to Kelly, insisting, "You know you're his favorite; he won't refuse you." There was a special rapport between them, and she had never questioned it or tried to analyze it; it was just there. And as close as she thought she had been to him, it was a little disturbing to realize that she had never known him before tonight.

She drifted off thinking about the trip tomorrow,

glad they were going to get away. Seth really needed it.

When she came home from school the next afternoon she was startled to find Susan lying on the sofa in a bulky terry houserobe, an afghan covering her feet. There was a box of tissues on the floor beside her and the end table was littered with juice glasses and cold remedies. Her face looked swollen and her nose and eyes were red and weepy. Kelly assessed the situation in a glance, dumped her books on the armchair, and said dully, "Oh, no."

"Lousy cold," agreed Susan nasally. "I've felt it coming on all week and last night I thought I'd die. I didn't even go to work today."

"Oh, Susan." Sympathetically Kelly came toward her but Susan waved her back.

"I'm contagious," she said. "Maybe since you're all going to be out of the house this weekend no one else will catch it. You know how it is around this place, we pass colds around like a bread basket and as soon as the last one gets over it the first one has it again." She sneezed violently and blew her nose.

At first Kelly's disappointment was overwhelming that the trip was obviously off. She thought briefly and bitterly that it seemed they just couldn't do anything right lately, everything was falling apart. First David, and then Susan and her legal problems, and Trish with her career problems, and then Seth, and now they couldn't even seem to organize a simple weekend to get their perspective back on life. Mostly she regretted it for Seth's sake, for he had needed the escape badly. But now Susan seemed to assume they would go without her and Kelly felt a brief sense of relief that was quickly replaced by practicality. "Wait a minute," she corrected her, "obviously the trip is off. We can't leave you—"

Susan blew her nose again, glanced quickly over her shoulder to make sure she was not being overheard, and then lowered her voice in confidence. "Listen, Kelly," she said, "I know it's up to you, but I really wish you would go. Get Seth out of the house this weekend. I don't know whether you've noticed or not, but he really needs to get away. I think this strike business is worrying him. And you know how he is when he's got something on his mind." She shuddered dramatically. "Another week and none of us will be able to live with him."

It was true, Kelly knew, Seth did need the trip, much more than any of them—and for reasons only Kelly understood. But she offered reasonably, "Seth's a big boy. If he wants to get out of the house for a while all he has to do is leave. He's done it before."

Susan shook her head. "He won't go without you. He's been such a doll taking care of me all day, but I could tell he was really disappointed about the trip. I tried to talk him into going anyway, but he said it was up to you." Again she glanced over her shoulder. "I don't think he wants to be alone for some reason."

Kelly hesitated. "He won't leave you alone all weekend," she pointed out. "With Trish out of town—"

Susan waved it away. "All settled. My folks were coming into L.A. this weekend anyway, but I told them I wouldn't be able to see them because I was going camping. I've already called them back and asked them to stay here; they'll be here some time tonight." She shrugged. "I can think of better ways to spend the weekend, I guess, but my mother *does* make a chicken soup that works faster than penicillin. And she'll be in seventh heaven having me to fuss over all weekend."

Kelly pretended a reluctance she did not feel. "You don't feel like having company for the weekend," she said.

Again Susan shrugged and blew her nose. "That's the pity of it, you know. I'll probably be feeling a lot better by tomorrow but the last thing you guys need is to be stuck in a tent with me and my germs. Otherwise I'd go, believe me."

"So." Seth sauntered into the room, his hands deep in his pockets, glancing from Susan to Kelly, resting his eyes on her with a slight lift of the brow. "Looks like it's you and me, kid."

She sensed the question there, but she did not consider it for long. She looked once more at Susan, read the command there, and then grinned at Seth. "Sure does," she said. "Give me five minutes to change. Is everything packed?"

He answered in the affirmative as she skipped past, and the happiness in his eyes sent her own spirits soaring.

Kelly was an outdoor girl—another thing the four of them had in common—but she was relatively new to the experience of desert camping. On her second summer in California the four of them had taken their vacations together in the Baja desert and it had been a prospect that at first had had no appeal for Kelly whatsoever. It sounded hot, uncomfortable, and possibly even dangerous. The other girls had convinced her it was an experience simply not to be missed, and trying to be a good sport, she had gone along with them. From that point she was addicted. There was something about the barren wilderness of a desert that simply could not be compared to any other form of camping. Since then they had camped in the mountains, in the ghost towns of Nevada and Arizona, in the national parks of Yosemite and Yellowstone, on the beaches, and in the giant forests, but their favorite spot was along the craggy canyons of the Mojave Desert about a two-hour drive away.

The wind whipped her hair in tickling strands away from its confining braid as the Jeep made its way along the long, empty stretch of highway and seemed at the same time to untangle the cares and worries from her head, leaving her exhilarated and unfettered. She glanced at Seth, saw he was experiencing some of the same sensation, and was glad they had come. He wore dark glasses against the mirrored glare of the sun on the asphalt, hiding the dark circles and lines of fatigue about his eyes. But the tension at the corners of his mouth that had been so noticeable these past few days had completely smoothed out. He drove with ease along the flat, unending desert road, one hand lightly guiding the steering wheel, the other resting on the seat beside him.

Impulsively Kelly took his hand in her own, and he glanced at her with a mischievous grin. "What's this?" he demanded. "Are you making a pass at me already?"

She laughed and tossed his hand away. He immediately retrieved hers and held it casually as he leaned back against the seat, looking tranquil and content. But before that Kelly had not realized this was the first time the two of them had ever been anywhere alone overnight. She considered that with a moment of amusement when she realized as well that this was the first time she had ever been "away for the weekend" with *any* man, imagining the reaction of her parents and some of her less sophisticated friends if they knew, and then she dismissed it.

To Kelly, one piece of desert looked very much like another, and she was impressed with Seth's ability to remember the exact spot at which to turn off the highway and begin the cross-country trek toward their secret spot. At this time of year the desert looked like a Hollywood set for a science fiction movie, a weirdly beautiful alien planet crowded with bristly shaped cacti and sagebrush in shades of gray-green and pale purple, exotic desert flowers, and waves of golden sand glistening in the sun. Strange outcroppings of rock broke the monotony and grew into canyons and rugged steppes as they moved further across the desert, glowing with orange and red and coal-black hues in the fading light. There was something wild and uncivilized about the entire landscape, yet coupled with a natural serenity that made it at once both frightening and soothing. Kelly never crossed the desert that she did not think of the early pioneers, the settlers, the drifters, the renegades, who had lost their lives to its ruthless beauty. And a sort of mystical awe descended over her as she thought how stalwart it had stood through all these centuries, so little changed by human passage. It made her feel very small, insignificant, and reverent.

They set up camp near a bare canyon wall, a small overhanging ledge providing protection from the heat of the sun during the day and the winds at night. And if Seth had remembered the right spot, there was a small natural pool about two hundred yards to the west, one of those unexpected desert miracles, from which they could obtain water for cooking and washing and, in an emergency, drinking, although they were both too wise to drink anything without boiling it first. It also, Kelly remembered delightedly, made a perfect place for bathing off the grime of the day or for a cooling dip in the afternoon. Leaving Seth to pound in the last of the stakes in a purplish twilight, she started off to explore.

"Hold it," Seth said with a warning glance. "Just where do you think you're going?"

She returned, chagrined. It was a hard-and-fast rule that none of them was to leave the camp alone. It was too easy to lose one's bearings in a terrain devoid of landmarks, and horrifying tales had been heard of people dying of exposure within a few hundred yards of their own camp. She had momentarily forgotten that, since there was only the two of them this trip, every adventure and exploration would be made together. It was just as well, for Seth seemed to have a sixth sense about direction and was much more famil-

iar with the desert than Kelly was. She had always felt
safer with him than with either of the women.

They walked in the direction of the spring, gathering
firewood along the way, and discovered that it was, indeed, still there. Kelly paused to rinse her face, hands,
and bare arms in the cool water before they started
back. Of course they had brought a plentiful supply of
bottled water, and there was no need to carry any back
to the camp. They would clean their used dishes with
sand tonight and take them to the pool in the morning
for a more conventional washing.

They cooked over a small charcoal grill because, although the merits of a meal prepared over an open fire
were undoubtedly many, Kelly could not quite get used
to food that was burned to a crisp on the outside and
still cold and raw inside. By the time the steaks and
potatoes were done it was fully dark. Kelly warmed
thick slices of bread and butter on the grill over the
dying coals while Seth built a campfire for warmth and
light. The chill of the night came suddenly to the desert, and they drew camp chairs close to the fire as they
ate, not talking much, simply enjoying the overwhelming stillness and isolation that surrounded them.

Kelly devoured her meal, surprised to find how hungry she really was, and while Seth cleaned the dishes,
she retrieved a box of brownies Trish had lovingly
baked and wrapped before she left. Seth glanced at her
in amusement as she offered him one. "It's beyond me
how you keep your figure, the way you eat. You're going to be fat by the time you're forty."

"No chance," she scoffed. Kelly's figure was firm
and athletic, far from heavy, and weight control had
never been one of her worries. "I'd like to see you do
calesthenics and laps for five hours a day and play two
hours of soccer and/or volleyball and an hour of basketball three times a week and see you worry about
your weight! Besides, everything tastes better out

here." She bit into a rich, chewy brownie. "Umm, these are fantastic. Sour cream frosting. Sure you don't want one?"

He gave her a disparaging look and went into the tent, returning a moment later with a blanket, which he spread on the ground at her feet. He poured himself another cup of coffee from the pot warming over the coals, lit a cigarette, and stretched out on the blanket, leaning back on his elbows.

"You drink too much coffee," Kelly pointed out, taking another brownie. "It's very bad for you."

"Everything tastes better out here," he quoted her, "even coffee and cigarettes." And then he glanced at her. "How did you ever get to be a phys-ed teacher, anyway? I always wondered that. They sure didn't have coaches like you when I was growing up."

"Is that right?" she retorted coquettishly. "What kind of coaches did they have?"

He grinned in the flickering firelight. "Ones with bodies like bulldozers and warts on the ends of their noses."

"I hope that's a compliment," she retorted.

"It is," he assured her.

She shrugged, licking her fingers, and answered his question. "It's something I just sort of fell into. I don't remember ever really making a decision." Like so much of her life, she reflected. She just seemed to wander into situations that charted her destiny—like she had wandered to California and Seth's house, like she wandered in and out of love. She should have been ashamed of having so little control over her life, she supposed, but it was simply the way she was. She was a creature of emotion, not reason, as Seth was all too fond of pointing out to her, and accustomed to following where life led. "I like it," she added, almost defensively. "Except for the pay, of course." She had always been a little self-conscious about the fact that hers was the lowest salary in the household, but it was adequate for her needs and she couldn't really complain, "I can't think of anything I'd rather do."

"Do you know what you remind me of?" he mused, and the tip of his cigarette glowed red in the shadows as he inhaled, looking up at her. "One of those old-fashioned females who sees a job as just a stop-gap between college and marriage, waiting around on the fringes of life for some man to come and take her away from it all."

She was insulted. "That's uncalled for," she returned shortly and snatched up another brownie. "You know perfectly well I'm not any more anxious to be married than you are, and as for being old-fashioned—"

"You are a born wife and mother," he interrupted. "Home and hearth to the core, very old-fashioned—a trait which most men find endearing."

Kelly bit into the brownie, not quite certain whether or not to be mollified. "But you don't."

He tossed the cigarette toward the fire and stretched to take the box of brownies from her. "I never thought about it. Give me one of those before you eat them all."

Seth took one brownie from the box, closed the lid, and put it out of sight. He half sat, one arm looped negligently over his upraised knee, as he ate the brownie and sipped his coffee, and she watched him in thoughtful curiosity. "So," she inquired at last, "when you were looking for housemates, why did you choose women?"

She expected him to give a flip reply, and in fact, he did chuckle. But he answered, "Kelly, I spent eighteen months living with ten guys in a tent not much bigger than the one behind us there. I had about all of that I could stand. I never really liked living alone, but I knew I couldn't live with a bunch of men—that was the first reason. The second is, I just happen to like women better than I do men; they're easier on the eyes first thing in the morning. And third, it seemed to me a couple of women could use the break, money-wise, more than men could, the pay scale being what it is." He glanced at her in amusement. "Do you really mean to tell me you've waited three years to ask me that? Trish and Susan fired it off within three minutes of receiving the offer."

"Maybe I'm just more polite than they are," she answered placidly.

"Or shier." He grinned and grabbed both of her hands, pulling her down on the blanket beside him. "Come here. You're just a silly old-fashioned girl who was too embarrassed to ask me if I was some sort of pervert who got his kicks out of seeing women's lingerie strung up all over his bathroom."

"Maybe I was just afraid of what I'd find out," she retorted, her pulse racing with the unexpectedness of finding herself so close to him on the blanket, his hands on her waist and his eyes laughing into hers.

Seth turned suddenly and stretched out on the blanket, resting his head in her lap. "Now, this," he informed her, "is one very good reason to choose female housemates and camping partners over men. Their laps are much softer."

Kelly laughed, and her fingers could not resist the temptation to play with his curls. He folded his hands over his chest and relaxed, staring up at the brilliant network of stars overhead. "You don't have any close men friends," she observed after a moment.

He hesitated very briefly. "That's a habit I managed to break in Nam," he answered. "Relationships over there were very close but very short-lived and very painful. If you'll notice," he added thoughtfully, almost to himself, "I don't have really close relationships with women, either. A protective device, I suppose. Probably why I'm such a confirmed bachelor."

Kelly thought of Melissa, but really did not want to bring her name into the conversation. She wanted to keep this evening entirely to themselves.

Almost as though reading her mind, he said casually, "Melissa called me today." He glanced up at her, as though wanting to catch her reaction, and she was careful to show none. His eyes wandered back to the stars. "Seems she had gotten the word from her boss that she'd better cool it with nonmanagement-type people until after the strike is settled. So it looks as though we're in an indefinite holding pattern."

The caressing motions of her fingers in his hair stopped. She did not know exactly what her emotions were at that moment, there were so many of them, but one of the most prominent was an unmistakable sympathy for him. "Oh, Seth," she commiserated genuinely. "That's terrible! It's not fair. I'm so sorry." Seth had enough problems without this, and no matter how Kelly felt about Melissa personally—for she really had no right to feel anything about a woman she had never met—she would not have wanted this to happen to her.

He nodded his head against her legs, and whatever his own emotions about the situation were, he kept them well guarded. "It may be worse than you know," he admitted. "You know what they say—nothing is more valuable than what is unobtainable, and absence makes the heart grow fonder. This could be the start of something really dangerous."

Inexplicably she felt her breath tighten in her chest, and she inquired cautiously, "For you or for her?"

"For me, I think," he replied softly, almost on a sigh, and left her to make of that what she would.

After a long time she began stroking his hair again, lightly, absently, twirling her fingers in its tight curls, caressing its springy texture. "Do you love her, Seth?" she asked quietly, not at all certain she wanted to hear the answer.

"I think," he admitted after a time, thoughtfully, "I'm falling in love with her...or maybe I'm afraid that's what's happening. That's why I hate this separation business. Maybe if we didn't have so much against us it would run its course and dissolve into a run-of-the-mill affair, if you know what I mean. This is starting to get a little too serious."

Her breath seemed to be caught somewhere in her throat, but she managed, "I take it she feels the same way."

"She sure acts like she does," he mumbled, and again he seemed to be thinking out loud. Then he turned his eyes to her and grinned. "With women it's hard to tell. I don't suppose you could give me any clues to that one?"

But she simply looked at him. "Would it make any difference?"

He sighed, turning his head more comfortably on her legs. "No, I guess not."

They were silent for a time. The fire crackled and popped, the shadows danced, and stillness lay around them like a rich velvet cloak. And then Seth said, "How's your broken heart?"

Again the absent motions of her fingers stopped. The suddenness of the question startled her, of course, but it was more than that. She realized for the first time that she had not thought of David in almost a week and now, when reminded of him, the emotions that tremored inside her were not at all what she had expected. This was the man she had loved, the man with whom she had actually expected to build a future, and her feelings for him had been the deepest she had ever known, yet how easily she had forgotten about him. When she thought of him now the feelings were not of pain, or even regret for a lost love, but more like disappointment. Disappointment in herself, mostly, because she had expected more from her love—more loyalty, more depth—she didn't know what exactly she did feel.

She answered him uncertainly, "Mending."

When he looked at her, the light caught in his golden eyes and made them look almost transparent; she thought he could see right into the depths of her soul. And his words confirmed it. "That's the catch, isn't it?" he responded softly. "Sometimes falling out of love—or discovering you were never really in it—is the worst part of all. You asked me a minute ago if I loved Melissa," he added very slowly, as though examining his own thoughts on the subject for the first time. "I wonder if any of us really know what that is. I mean, it's easy enough to know about being in and out of love, but loving is quite another thing altogether, isn't it?"

"Maybe," said Kelly softly, "love is just the thing that doesn't go away when the passion dies."

His smile was lazy and vague but deeply understanding. "And maybe," he agreed, "there's hope for you yet, kid."

Of course she realized as he closed his eyes and the silence rested between them again the real trick was in finding that love—and in recognizing it when it did come. On that score there did not seem to be much hope for her at all.

Time was meaningless and it could have been hours or only minutes that she sat, twining her fingers in his hair and listening to the sound of the silence, thinking little if anything at all. But then she became aware that her legs were stiff; she shifted her position a little and Seth blinked and opened his eyes. His eyes were hazy but his smile lazily content. "Sorry, honey," he murmured, "I must have dozed off. Hope I didn't miss anything important." He sat up reluctantly. "You make a great pillow but I think I'd better turn in. You coming?"

She hesitated. It was so peaceful out here, the fire

still provided warmth, and she really wasn't sleepy. She
answered, "In a little while."

"Okay." He started for the tent. "Watch out for coyote."

She waited another minute, trying not to glance
around her too uneasily. Suddenly she felt very vulnerable, sitting there all alone. The desert seemed wild
and tense with crouching shadows and the fire scant
protection. She thought she heard a sound and she
scrambled to her feet, turning toward the tent. Seth was
waiting there for her, grinning, politely holding the flap
open. She made a face at him and went inside.

There was no awkwardness about sharing the tent
with Seth. He had made the ground rules very clear on
that first outing together. He was not about to sacrifice
his own comfort and safety to his female companions'
modesty; the tent was made to sleep four and four it
would sleep. He had no patience with feminine frivolity
and no one changed clothes for bed, thus eliminating
the process of dressing morning and night in shifts.
They placed their sleeping bags on opposite sides of the
tent, and it was really no different from being at home.

Seth was asleep almost as soon as the lantern was
extinguished, but Kelly lay awake a while longer, looking out at the stars through the screened window over
her head, listening to the sound of Seth's steady, relaxed breathing. Her mind wandered aimlessly, easily,
from one topic to another and a pleasant sort of lethargy settled over her that precluded serious cogitation.
She thought about David. She thought about what Seth
had said, about her only waiting for some man to come
along and make her a wife and mother; she wondered if
that could be true. It was funny how Seth was always
making her see herself in different ways, to make discoveries about herself she might never have made
otherwise. He had changed so much about her since
she had known him—her views on human relation-

ships and sexuality, the way she saw herself, even, to some degree, her philosophy on life. It was so much easier to take things as they came and not worry about anything when she knew there was always Seth to go to if she got into trouble. As for his opinion on her station in life, maybe there was some truth in it. Maybe that explained why she was always looking for things in the men she dated that weren't there, and imagining them when she could not find them. But, she thought sleepily, if her destiny in life was to be a wife and mother, she was certainly getting a late start on it. She was twenty-seven years old and no closer to her goal than she might have been at eighteen. But, strangely, that thought did not disturb her as she turned over and drifted very peacefully off to sleep.

It was much later that something woke her. She sat up, her heart thudding with the aftermath of the abrupt awakening, not certain what had disturbed her and seeing frantic visions of wolves and coyote and rattlesnakes race through her head. She glanced immediately at Seth and made out his silhouette in the inky darkness. He too was sitting up and it took her only another moment to recognize the sound of his ragged breathing as what had awakened her. She got out of the sleeping bag and stumbled over to him, whispering his name.

She touched him lightly and felt the trembling in his arm. His hands were covering his face and through them he mumbled dully, "It's okay...it's okay." But his eyes were closed and she did not think he was awake. Her own hands were shaking and her heart sounded like a drum in her ears as alarm pounded alertness through every fiber of her body. She was not certain whether the fear she felt was for him or of him. She had never seen him like this; she was not certain what to do.

She touched his damp forehead, smoothing back the curls, and repeated his own words back to him. "Yes,

it's okay ... go back to sleep. ... " His fingers found her
and gripped them tightly, but slowly, under the soothing tone of her voice, he lay back down. And after a
time the tension began to fade, his breathing became
more regular and natural. He slept.

She sat there, looking down at him, aching inside for
him, feeling helpless, and wishing with all her might
that she could ease his burden. It wasn't fair that he
should suffer so. She would have gladly given any part
of herself to ease his pain just the slightest, but there
was nothing she could do. She brought their entwined
fingers to her lips and kissed them softly, and she
started to move away.

But at her movement she felt the catch of his breath;
his fingers tightened around hers. She hesitated, then,
without releasing his hand, she stretched across the
tent and dragged her own sleeping bag next to his. She
lay down beside him, their clasped hands resting on his
chest, and that way she slept the rest of the night.

## Chapter Six

When she awoke the next morning Seth was already up. She could hear him moving outside, and the enticing aroma of coffee and frying bacon drifted through the open window to her. It was already warm inside the tent and she kicked aside the sleeping bag, quickly changing from the jeans she had worn to bed into a pair of snug denim shorts and a long-sleeved cotton shirt, which she knotted at the waist. She took up her hairbrush and began to unbraid her hair as she went outside, greeting him with, "That smells delicious."

He too had changed from jeans to cut-offs, probably while she slept, and he looked relaxed and well rested for the first time in weeks. He had even shaved—an oddity on camping trips—and the morning sun gleamed off his bare arms and sparkled on the hairs of his muscled legs as he knelt over the pan of bacon on the grill. He glanced at her casually, and then he said quite seriously, "I suppose I owe you a debt of gratitude for the first good night's sleep I've had in weeks."

She busied herself with brushing the tangles from her hair, not looking at him, fighting with embarrassment. She returned nervously, "Oh?"

His grin was devilish as he explained, "You were all over me when I woke up this morning. Just couldn't resist the power of that old animal magnetism, huh?"

She leaned her head forward and brushed her hair

over her face, hiding a blush. It didn't seem quite tactful to inform him that it had been his nightmare that had brought her over, and that when she had tried to leave he had held on to her like a child frightened of the dark. She preferred to take the embarrassment herself and she retorted lightly, "Maybe that was your whole problem all along. You just needed someone to sleep with."

"Maybe I did," he answered in a rather odd tone, and she could feel his eyes upon her. When she parted the veil of her hair and swept it back over her shoulders, he was watching her steadily, a very strange expression in his eyes, although his smile was quiet and relaxed. "Thanks anyway, Kelly," he said simply. "I'm sorry I disturbed you last night. I hope you weren't too frightened."

So he did know. Their eyes met in a moment of quiet understanding and she smiled. Then she said brightly, catching her hair back with a clasp, "How much longer till breakfast? I'm starved. Are there any of those brownies left?"

"You leave those brownies alone," he commanded, turning the bacon. "I happen to like the fit of those shorts just as it is." As she stepped close to him he reached up and grabbed her, grinning, his hands fastened firmly on either side of her hips. "Exactly the width of my hands," he pronounced, eyes twinkling mischievously. "Perfect measurement."

"Your hands," she retorted, removing them, "have no business measuring anything that belongs to me." But her pulses were racing and she felt strangely exhilarated. It was going to be a perfect day.

And it was. They packed a picnic lunch and extra water and left the campsite in search of fossils and rock specimens. They did not find very much, although Kelly did pick up one ugly-looking clump of rock that Seth thought might have a trace of gold in it. But to

Kelly the real pleasure was in watching Seth, looking so healthy and relaxed, teasing her and sparring with her, full of energy and enjoying himself and her company just as he had always done.

They had lunch in the shade of an abandoned mine shaft that had long since caved in, eating sandwiches toasted from the heat, and drinking tepid water from their canteens. Even that was enjoyable. Kelly glanced at him, completely content, and commented, "You're feeling better, aren't you?"

He nodded and his eyes, narrowed against the glare of the sun, were like jewels against the rugged brown of his skin. "There's something about the desert that just seems to swallow your problems. I feel like a different person out here—free, a little uncivilized"—he glanced at her with a mischievous spark—"totally uninhibited, maybe a little wild. As though I don't have to answer to anyone for anything." And to prove his point, as she stretched away from him to replace her canteen in the shade, he pinched her firmly and intimately on the bottom.

She slapped his hand away, pretending outrage but not needing to pretend a blush. "You have to answer to *me*," she promised him indignantly. "Behave yourself!"

His eyes twinkled innocently. "You have," he told her, "the prettiest eyes I've ever seen."

She tingled with pleasure even as she tried to look severe. "Don't try to make up with me!"

"Like lapis lazuli," he said.

"What?"

"Your eyes. They're like lapis lazuli."

She laughed. "That's not the most romantic thing I've ever heard."

"Who cares for romance?" he scoffed, although his smile was strangely gentle, almost caressing, as he looked at her and the mischief had gone out of his eyes.

"You want originality. You don't really fall for those phony lines about your eyes being like sparkling star sapphires or two bottomless pools, do you? Of course not. But when some bright young fellow comes along with a comparison to lapis lazuli...." Affectionately he smoothed a strand of hair behind her ear and his rough fingers tingled against her cheek. "Then," he finished softly, "you want to snatch him up and never let him go, because he's the genuine article."

She dropped her eyes, suddenly shy and very confused. "Well," she said brightly, "a lot of good my lapis lazuli eyes are going to do you. What color are Melissa's eyes?" she changed the subject deftly.

He looked thoughtful for a moment and then laughed. "You know, I never noticed. I guess I was more interested in, er, other parts of her anatomy."

The glance he gave her was wickedly boyish, and she reprimanded him sternly, "You're obscene."

"Yes," he agreed mildly. "Isn't it fun?" Their dancing eyes met for a moment and then they burst into laughter.

They arrived safely back at camp late in the afternoon and went to the pool to wash away some of the dust and stickiness of the day. They ended up splashing and playing in the waist-high water like children until they were thoroughly soaked and then hurried back to camp, shivering against the sudden chill of the setting sun.

Kelly changed into her jeans and a dry shirt inside the tent while Seth did the same outside, and they hung their wet clothes over the camp chairs to dry while Seth made a stew in a heavy iron kettle over the open fire. The savory smell of onions and tomatoes mingling with the scent of woodsmoke on the desert air was wild and intoxicating, bringing to mind again visions of cowboys and desperadoes who had once roamed these same plains. In the orange light of the sunset and the flickering shadows of the fire, Seth looked a bit like one of those rugged old-west characters himself. As Kelly watched him she could not help smiling, vaguely and affectionately, thinking that she had never felt more content and wishing it never had to end.

Once again they spread a blanket on the ground and ate sitting close to the fire, for with the dying light had come a raw cold, much worse than that of last evening and promising an even further drop in temperature before the night was over. Seth lit the Coleman lantern, which, surprisingly, did give off a considerable amount of heat, and then, with a grin, he produced a flask of brandy, which he poured generously into their coffee. "Don't you know alcohol is the worst thing in the world for cold?" Kelly reproved him, shivering as he placed the cup in her hands.

"Sure," he agreed easily, leaning back to sip from his own cup. "You still freeze to death, but you don't mind nearly as much."

The brandied coffee tasted terrible but it did warm her, and a peaceful lethargy settled over her as she relaxed in the glow of the fire and the crystal still night, watching the giant shadows the lantern cast on the canyon wall. "They look like monsters," she pointed out to Seth softly as she reached her arms overhead to begin to unbraid her hair.

When she glanced at him, she was surprised to notice that he had been watching her and there was a relaxed, reflective look on his face, like that of someone who is studying something purely for the pleasure of it, like a fine painting or sculpture or a well-choreographed ballet. That look startled her and then she laughed at her own imagination and ego as he moved his eyes lazily away from her and to the far shadows for just a moment, then back to her again. There was nothing in his eyes now but the familiar, easy companionship.

"Do you want to tell ghost stories?" he suggested.

She shuddered elaborately. "Hardly. And," she warned him as a mischievous spark appeared in his eyes, "don't you dare start putting scary ideas in my head this close to bedtime. I won't sleep a wink."

"You're no fun at all," he told her, sitting up to pour himself another cup of coffee as she started to brush her hair. The larger-than-life shadow of her body on the canyon wall rippled and swayed gracefully with the movements, a profile of a young girl of classic beauty brushing her long hair over her shoulder, and Seth watched the effect in fascination for a time. Then he suggested, turning to her, "All right. You tell me a story. Tell me about yourself."

She laughed a little, gathering her hair into a ponytail at the side and brushing out the ends. "You know all there is to know about me. That would be a boring story."

He set the coffee cup aside and surprised her by taking the brush from her, then, sitting very close to her, he began to draw the brush through her hair with long, gentle strokes. "I know a lot about you," he admitted, "but not all." The motions of the brush through her hair were as sensuous as a caress, and she relaxed with the sensation as irresistibly as a cat responds to stroking. "For example," he continued, "I know that you like walking on the shore at midnight and old Bette Davis movies, champagne cocktails and salted peanuts—"

"Not at the same time," she laughed, leaning her head back toward the gentle tug of the brush beneath his hand.

"Saturday-morning cartoons and roller-skating on the boardwalk...."

"So do you," she murmured, half closing her eyes with the almost mesmerizing pleasure he was creating with the brush.

"You're a fair cook and a tolerably neat housekeeper, a good listener and a horrible chess player, and—" He stopped suddenly, his hands resting on her shoulders as his face moved very close to her from behind. Every nerve ending of her body was alert and waiting and she caught her breath. "You smell terrific," he finished on a deep breath. "How can you smell so good after two days in the desert?"

His warm breath on the back of her neck caused her to shiver. She laughed nervously and took the hairbrush from him. "Trade secret," she retorted lightly.

He noticed her shiver as he moved easily away from her. "Cold?"

She nodded and began to braid her hair with fingers that were suddenly clumsy. "The temperature sure dropped suddenly, didn't it?"

"It does that in the desert," he explained to her patiently, shrugging out of the light Windbreaker he had had the foresight to bring.

She glared at him with pretended annoyance as he draped the jacket over her shoulders. "I know," she said. His fingers brushed against the back of her neck as he lifted her hair to tuck the jacket securely around her and she shivered again.

His hands rested on her shoulders and he looked at her thoughtfully for a moment. He said unexpectedly, "I like being with you, Kelly. I don't know whether I've told you that often enough, but it's true."

She smiled at him, loving the sincerity of the sentiment and grateful for his expression of it. "I wish we didn't have to go back tomorrow," she said softly. "This has been one of the best times I've ever had."

"Me too," he answered, and his forefinger lightly stroked her cheek once in a gesture of tenderness and affection. But there was a look in his eyes she did not quite understand; it made her nervous and she dropped her own gaze.

She hugged his jacket around her shoulders and he

dropped his hands, sitting beside her again easily. She shivered once more, now more from the absence of him than from the outside cold, and was grateful for the warmth of the jacket. But she felt compelled to point out, "Now you'll freeze."

He considered this for a moment. "You're right," he decided, and plucked the jacket from her over her indignant, stuttering protests. "No wonder chivalry is dead," he added with a grin as he got to his feet. "It was based on stupidity."

He laughed at her astonished indignation and grasped both her hands to pull her to her feet. "Come on," he said, giving her a little push toward the tent. "We may as well get into our sleeping bags; it's the only way we're going to stay warm tonight."

He turned down the lantern while she pulled off her shoes and socks and hurried into the sleeping bag, shivering violently now without the warmth of the fire. The lantern light took a long time to die and was still quite bright by the time Seth came in and began to unroll his own sleeping bag on the other side of the tent.

"How are you doing over there?" he inquired after a time.

"F-freezing," she replied from the muffled depths of the sleeping bag, which she had pulled over her cold face. Her teeth chattered and she turned on her side and hugged her arms around her knees, conserving body heat, wondering how much colder it could possibly get.

"Me too," he admitted. She turned down a corner of her sleeping bag to peek at him as he impatiently unzipped his own, bringing it over to hers in the fading light of the lantern. "Get out," he commanded. "This is ridiculous, we'll both freeze by morning."

She hesitated just until he knelt to unzip her sleeping bag, and then she demanded, teeth chattering, "W-what are you going to do?"

"Zip these two together," he explained as she got

up. "They make a double sleeping bag. We'll be a lot warmer that way."

The tent floor was like ice on her bare feet and she danced back and forth, rubbing her arms and trying to warm her feet against the cuffs of her jeans. At that time warmth was all that was important, no matter how it was achieved. "Hurry up," she demanded. "I'm starting to get frostbite."

Seth completed the transformation and stepped back with a flourish, gesturing her to precede him.

The residue of lantern light was all but gone now, and she hurried to the down softness of the sleeping bag. He got in beside her and pulled the top portion of the bag over them, not zipping it. "Better?" he inquired as full darkness fell within the tent.

"Not really," Kelly muttered, still shivering as she drew herself up into a tight little ball, the top of the sleeping bag covering her ears.

"Wait for it," he suggested, and unexpectedly he reached for her, drawing her close to him with one arm around her waist and the other beneath her shoulders. "The idea," he explained to her patiently in the dark, "is to share body heat."

Almost immediately she stopped shivering, more from surprise than anything else. For the first time she realized that they were actually in a bed together, his arms were around her, and their bodies were pressed close to one another. But then she scoffed at her own foolishness. This was Seth, for goodness' sake, and she was being ridiculous.

She relaxed her head cautiously against his shoulder and felt his fingers absently playing with the end of her braid where it fell over her arm. His other arm rested lightly across her chest, just beneath her breasts, and she was beginning to feel warmer already. He said, "Now you know why Noah made reservations for two on that ark."

She giggled and snuggled down deeper into the hollow of his arm; she felt him smile down at her in the darkness. They lay there quietly for a time as warmth gradually spread through her and with it other sensations, not quite so innocent.... The hardness of his muscles beneath her head and the weight of his arm across her ribs, his fingers just inches from her breast. The caressing motions of his fingers on her upper arm, the sound of his breath very close to her face, and an increased tension in her own body, a slight speeding of the pace of her heart. But they were pleasant sensations, not the least bit threatening. She felt comfortable and secure in his arms, and it was all perfectly right.

Yet she became suddenly aware of a tension within him too, a change that might have been nothing more than a slight shift of position or simply the way he suddenly stopped the absent stroking motions of his fingers against her shoulder. His words from the other night flickered across her mind. "I never claimed to be a monk...." She thought perhaps it was not such a good idea after all that they spend the night together like this.

Then he spoke, and whatever vague alarm might have registered was immediately dispersed. "This weekend has meant a lot to me, Kelly," he said quietly. "I don't know how I would have made it without you."

She smiled, looking up at him in the darkness. "That's okay," she responded. "There are a lot of times when I don't know how I would have made it without you, either."

He returned her smile and squeezed her shoulder briefly. "Good night, sweetheart," he said and bent to brush her lips with a kiss.

And then something happened. Kelly would not afterward know whether the change happened within her or within him; it just happened, unexpectedly and uncontrollably, and there was nothing either of them could have done to prevent it. Their lips touched lightly as they had done many times before, an impersonal gesture of affection, and then suddenly they met fully in a kiss that was deep and lingering and took both of them by surprise.

Kelly's breath caught in her throat at the unexpected sensation of his lips clasping hers warmly, moving against hers in a reaction that was as natural as dawn following night, and just as unpreventable. Her response was easy and genuine as her hand moved to caress the back of his neck, for it all seemed perfectly right. This was the kiss they should have shared that night in the kitchen, an expression of caring and compassion, and she accepted and returned it with emotions that were simple and pure.

His lips left hers reluctantly, but only by a fraction of an inch, so that his breath still warmed her face and brushed across her lips, which were parted with uncertainty and still moist from his. She could feel the wonder of him as he looked down at her and until that moment she had not realized how rapidly and unevenly her own breath was coming. The hesitance lasted only a second, perhaps less, just long enough for him to draw a breath, and then, as though by compulsion, his mouth was upon hers again, tasting her, urging her, moving her into an exploration of passion that frightened her even as it thrilled her. And then a sudden jolt of flame shot through her as his tongue slipped through her parted lips to explore the warm, moist recesses of her mouth.

She could not believe this was happening. Her response was helpless as quivering waves of weakness flowed through her, dancing in stars behind her closed eyes with the sensation of his mouth upon hers and his tongue inside her, a part of her, coaxing, teasing, exploring, savoring. No, it wasn't happening. The tight yearning that had begun in her stomach, the sudden pulsing of blood to every part of her body, the tension and the demand she could feel from him.... She could not believe that Seth had let it get this far. She could not believe she had allowed it. But she wanted it. She wanted it to be happening and that frightened her.

A high, startled sound escaped her as his hand moved upward to cup her breast, an automatic movement that was nonetheless unexpected. His lips clasped hers again gently, as though in reassurance, as his fingers moved relentlessly upward to discover the nipple, taut against the straining fabric of her shirt. Every fiber of her body was concentrated on the caressing motions his sensitive fingers made there and the maddening sensations he created that spread like burning wires to the core of her abdomen. His lips left hers throbbing, his breath was hot and quick against her face, and she could feel his eyes rapidly searching her face in the darkness. Yet his own arousal overwhelmed whatever uncertainty or question there might have been there. Her pounding heart shook her entire body as his fingers began to work the buttons of her shirt. No, this couldn't be happening, it really couldn't....

She whispered his name. It was meant to be a protest but it came out as more of a sound of encouragement as her arms traveled around his back, drawing him closer. And then there was nothing else but his mouth upon hers, tasting faintly of brandy and coffee, his hands slipping inside her shirt to clasp her bare back, the scratching sound of the brush of their jeans as he moved on top of her, his strong fingers against her buttocks pressing her into the hardness of his pelvis. It was overwhelming, it was uncontrollable, it was wrong, but it didn't matter.

His lips left hers, moved to her throat, which arched helplessly beneath the burning caress. He lifted himself a little and she thought with a vague relief that was dimmed by the shaft a disappointment that surely he would stop now, one of them had to come to his senses. But he parted the material of her shirt, cupping her breasts firmly in his hands, lifting, pushing them together, gently tightening the pressure of his fingers until she moaned softly with restrained passion, and then she thought nothing else at all as he bent and took one nipple into the moist warmth of his mouth.

Her hands had tugged his shirt free of the waistband of his jeans and were now beneath it, exploring the breadth of his back, smooth warm skin sheathing sinew and bone and taut muscles. And it seemed right that she should be discovering for the first time a body that was familiar yet unknown, just as her own body seemed already to belong to him. But dimly she knew from very far away that it wasn't right, they couldn't be doing this. This was Seth, her confidant and her friend, her protector and her companion, for three years. This was Seth, who was almost a brother to her. This was Seth, whom she loved.

His lips moved away from her breasts and clasped the soft flesh of her abdomen just above her waistband, as his hand restlessly moved over her hips and along the course of her leg, sending startling jolts of electricity through her as it deliberately brushed against the inside of her thigh. A need was building so intensely that it hurt deep inside her, and she knew it would hurt worse because soon they would have to stop. They simply couldn't do this. But it felt so right when their lips met again. She felt the rapid thundering of his heart in counterpoint to her own and she was enveloped in heat and dizzying weakness as his arms tightened around her, drawing her with him as he moved to his side, one leg wrapped around hers and pressing her into his straining muscles. Very dimly she knew they weren't going to do this, they really were not going to do this, but the warning became farther and farther away, and then his hand moved to the catch of her jeans and it was too late for either of them to stop.

His hand spread against the tightening flesh of her abdomen, kneading and caressing. She gasped softly with the sensation and was lost. Nothing mattered beyond the moment as he moved to slip the jeans from her hips and her hands came up impatiently to assist him. She was shaking all over and clumsy, she was hardly aware of breathing, and through the roaring in her ears she heard the sounds of his undressing, the rustle of the sleeping bag, and his soft moan of delight as, at last free of their clothes, he drew her into a naked embrace.

And it was perfectly right. The length of his hard body against hers, her breasts pressed against the warm strength of his chest, the taut muscles and soft hairs of his leg as it moved to cover her thighs. The gentle touch of his fingers beginning intimate explorations, the soothing, wordless whisper of his lips against her face at her first tension, the leisurely encouragement he gave her to discover his body as he did hers as the first urgency passed and a new and more powerful passion began to build. It escalated from wonder and delight to aching need and powerful demand, unpreventable, as natural as life itself, and just as good. The weight of his chest upon hers and the pounding of his heart that echoed the thundering of her own blood in her ears, beneath the unrestrained demand of his kiss. The easing of that weight and the gentleness of his kiss as his hands cupped her face and his thighs slid between hers. The last echoes of that faraway warning as she realized it was happening, it really was. Her arms around him as she welcomed him with joy and a total freedom unlike any she had ever known. It was wordless, natural, intensely loving. It was the final expression of a love that was pure and good, the love that had been there all along, so deep and so unquestioned that she had never thought to notice it before. It was the love she had looked for all her life, and never realized that it had been for the past three years within the reach of an embrace.

Even when physical satisfaction was reached and surpassed they clung together, drowsy with contentment and heavy with love, yet reluctant to part. He drew her into the circle of his legs tightly against him, his fingers entwined with hers against the slow, steady thumping of his heart, their flesh still a part of one another, his light, silent kisses upon her face and her hair speaking of the love they shared and had so late discovered. Within her a steady peace began to build so sweetly it felt like tears, and she drifted away on clouds of happiness, thinking that at last, at last, she had come home.

It was the absence of his warmth that woke her. She stirred and shivered, seeking a warm place within the depths of the sleeping bag, her reaching fingers discovering only soft, cold fabric where he had been. She opened her eyes to the grayish light of the tent and gradually returning consciousness brought a shock of memories, a swift flush of impressions that were sometimes confused, sometimes starkly clear—a sort of girlish embarrassment and wonder that dissolved almost at once into happiness so intense it took her breath away. Seth. Her whole mind, her whole body, reverberated to that note, filling her, wrapping her within its shimmering embrace, sending her soaring into an ecstasy of contentment she had never before dreamed possible. Seth. It had been him all along, and nothing seemed more right, more perfect, more natural.

And then, as the cold once again began to creep over her, it brought with it a vague, uneasy disturbance. He should be here. It was barely light outside and still very cold. Why had he left? The chill air struck her naked body like the abrupt awakening from a pleasant dream as she pushed back the sleeping bag and began to struggle into her clothes. A beautiful secret dwelt and grew inside her, but its warmth could not dispel the signals of dim alarm that something was not right with him.

She pushed open the flap of the tent and stepped outside. His figure was a silhouette in the green twilight of coming dawn as he stood a few yards away from the tent, his back to her, smoking a cigarette. Everything about his stance spoke of tension, and the alarm within her tightened and began to form into an indefinable fear. She approached him cautiously.

"I was cold," she said softly. Her voice seemed to echo in the canyon and over the desert and with the echo was uncertainty, a pleading and an anxiety she had never meant to put into her voice at all. She was happy, she had every reason in the world to be happy. She loved him and he knew it and there was no need for fear.

He glanced at her and his smile was vague, automatic, and strained. He turned quickly away but she caught the glimpse in his eyes and what she saw there sent a chill of horror down her spine. It was the same sort of raw desperation and subdued panic she had surprised in his eyes that night in the kitchen, and it transfixed her with cold dread and disbelief. It was the look of a man who is trapped and terrified.

She tried to speak but could not make a sound. She tried to move toward him but her feet would not work. And then he said abruptly, without looking at her, "Kelly, I've been thinking. Maybe what I really need is to get off by myself for a while. I have a friend who owns a lodge up in Clear Creek, you know, on the Salmon River. It's been a long time since I did any fishing. This strike could go on longer than I thought and there's no point in my hanging around here waiting for a phone call. I can keep in touch from up there just as easily."

She stared at him, her mind working numbly, desperately. What was he trying to say? What was he really trying to say? But she only answered, somewhat tonelessly, "The salmon aren't running this time of year."

She felt rather than heard his tight, indrawn breath. She saw his shoulders square as he tossed the cigarette away, and when he turned, it was in his eyes, exactly what he was trying to say and what she did not want to hear, what she did not think she could bear to hear.

"Kelly," Seth said painfully, "what happened last night—" He paused and there was desperation in his eyes as he scanned hers, as though he were looking for a sign from her to make it easier, as though he were afraid of hurting her but knew the consequences must be faced and wished there were an easier way. She felt ill. "It was...an accident," he said carefully, and the tone of his voice pleaded for her understanding. "I didn't plan it. I wouldn't want you to think that I—"

*An accident.* Kelly gripped her elbows against a sudden racking chill and her knees felt weak. Just a mistake, a misunderstanding.... She had to sit down. She turned and stumbled toward one of the camp chairs near the burned-out fire, sinking to it just before her legs gave way. The pair of shorts and shirt he had worn yesterday were still there, dry now and stiff with cold, and they seemed to belong to another world, someone else's memory that had nothing to do with her. *An accident....*

"It's understandable, I suppose," he continued carefully, watching her, "something we should have been on guard against...the two of us out here alone, you on the rebound from Hampton and me with all this business that's been going on in my head lately, and Melissa...."

Melissa! It struck her in a cold wave of fresh clarity and she felt hysteria rising up inside her. Seth was in love with another woman. Had he been thinking of Melissa while he made love to her? *Had he?*

"We were both caught in a moment of weakness and it was only natural, I suppose." His voice reached her from far away. "But, honey, it was just one night and it doesn't have to change anything between us." There was a note of pleading in his voice now. She felt him take a step toward her. "It was just sex and it didn't mean—"

"Anything," she said numbly. Her voice did not seem to belong to her at all, but to an impersonal stranger who looked down coldly from afar on the woman who was suffering in her body. "It didn't mean anything."

The grip of his fingers on her upper arm startled her for a moment out of her apathy. She looked at him as he knelt beside her and saw sincerity mingled with the pain on his face.

"It *did* mean something," he insisted. "What we shared last night was beautiful. But, Kelly..." Now impatience and frustration crept into his expression and she knew he was asking her to help him, to somehow make it easier. She could not. "Sex," he said carefully, "is just a way of communication. It can express all sorts of things. What we felt for each other last night was real, but it wasn't... permanent. It was just that we let a lot of emotions get mixed up with feeling good about each other, and sex was easy. It was—"

"Convenient," she supplied dully, looking at him with eyes dark with shock, flat with the emptiness and the coldness that had crept into the very network of her soul.

"Natural," he corrected and took her icy fingers between his, looking down at them for a moment before turning his face to her again, pleading for her understanding. "Kelly, don't you see, it was just a physical thing, an accident neither one of us planned or wanted. It can't change anything between us. It's not going to happen again and it can't change anything," he repeated firmly. He dropped her hands on a ragged breath. "Oh, God, Kelly, please don't be hurt. Please try to understand. If I could take it back I would, because I never meant to hurt you. I never thought I could be so stupid."

"Stupid," she parroted tonelessly. The hysterical urge to laugh was fading. She should have felt anger, but even that emotion was beyond her. *Stupid... an accident.* As natural as scratching an itch or taking a drink when you were thirsty and just as meaningless. Just sex.

He took her face in his hands, forcing her to look at him, trying one more time with desperation in his eyes. "Kelly, don't you see?" he pleaded. "This could ruin everything between us. What we have has nothing to do with a relationship between a man and a woman. It's more than that and it's different. But if we start believing, because of last night, that something else is possible, we're going to fail and we'll end up hating each other. I can't let that happen to us. Too many relationships have blown up in my face and none of them has meant as much to me as what I have with you. Can you understand that? Women...sex..." he said, struggling over the words, "are a dime a dozen, but you're my *best friend.* I don't want to lose that."

She looked at him, saw the pain and the despair etched on his face, and far beyond her own agony was the need to ease his. She looked at him and she saw fear beneath the pleading...fear of changes, fear of losing her. She slowly, very slowly, began to understand. Their entire relationship was based on affection without sexuality, on trust, on the ease of companionship without the strains of a relationship. His position in the household revolved around that same principle. Seth, the big brother, the protector, the friend...never the threat. How could she have ever thought there could be anything more between them? Did she really think they could go back to the house and have nothing change except the fact that they slept in one bed instead of two? Had she really thought that one night could change the way he felt about her? For Kelly it had been a night of awesome discovery, the fulfillment of something wonderful that was coming to life inside her, but for him it had been just sex. She was still his baby sister, and he was ashamed.

And he was in love with another woman.

He dropped his hands and looked away from her. He got slowly to his feet. "Kelly," he said heavily, almost in a whisper. "I'm—"

"Don't," she said fiercely, and he looked at her, startled. Her hands were clenched on her knees and her eyes were glittering—but with determination, not tears. "Don't say you're sorry," she repeated lowly. "Because I'm not and I never will be." He would not make her feel cheap or dirty for something neither one of them could help, for something that was right and natural and good. He would not take that memory away from her.

His face softened with cautious hope. "You don't hate me?"

She shook her head wordlessly. How could she hate him? She, who loved not wisely but too well, and who, for the first time in her life, knew what forever meant. Only it was too late.

He took an uncertain step toward her. He knelt beside her again and in his face was nothing but earnesty. "Kelly, we can forget this," he said softly. "It will be as though it never happened. It doesn't have to come between us. We can go on as we were before, can't we? Can we do that, Kelly?"

She looked at him for a long time. Slowly, unsteadily, her hand came out to stroke his hair. "If that's what you want," she whispered.

The relief and the happiness that slowly pushed away

the sorrow in his eyes were her reward. If that was what he wanted, if that was what it took to erase the haunted look from his face, then that was exactly what she would give. She did not know how yet, but she would do it. Because she could not bear to lose him either, and she would sacrifice anything, agree to any terms, as long as she could stay beside him a little longer....

Because, at last, she had found that elusive element that remains steady after the passion dies, and she really no longer had a choice.

# Chapter Seven

Seth was gone for a month. He called once a week to check on things at home and to give them reports on the progress of the strike negotiations, but he never talked to Kelly. Part of the reason was that he always tried to call when he knew she wouldn't be home, and part of it was that Kelly always let one of the other housemates answer the phone. It was wise of him to have left, for she needed the time desperately to try to find some way to live with his terms, to forget.

Of course she could not forget. The details of that night played over and over again in her head, when she closed her eyes at night, at odd moments during class, as she stood washing dishes or preparing a meal, as she walked through a room and spotted something that belonged to Seth. Anything could trigger a signal that would start a chain reaction of memories in her mind. *An accident.* She told herself that over and over again, trying to make herself believe it. It was nothing to be ashamed of, nothing to feel guilty about. Were either of them less than human? Could she deny that there had always been a sexual attraction between them, even if only at a subconscious level? And was it really so horrible that, given the circumstances, they should succumb to it? Surely they were not the first people who had fallen victims to sudden passion and awakened the next morning with regret. It happened all the time.

An accident...perhaps. But an accident with deliberation, with meaning, with purpose, on his part as well as hers. She could not convince herself that it had meant nothing to him, that it was, on his part, nothing more than an accident. Accidents were quick and hot and urgent, mindless and devastating. The remembrance of what it had really been like between them was too clear for her to so easily dismiss it—every motion of his hands and every touch of his lips, the growing wonder, the several times he had hesitated and then gone on, the powerful wanting and the magic it had uncovered. Accidents could be prevented. What had happened between them could not, and though it had meant something different to him than it had to her, still it had meant something.

At first she had not thought she could do it. She did not think it was possible to return to the house they shared and resume living together as though nothing had happened. She did not know how she could possibly keep it from Susan and Trish, how she could pretend around Seth that nothing was changed, how she could look at him or bear to have him look at her without being flooded by memories of their last time together. But it was as though Kelly was pushed over the hurdle of those first few hours, becoming lost in the confusion of their arrival home and his preparation to leave again, hardly having a chance to sort out her anxieties before he was gone, and with him the problem of how she was to hide her turmoil in his presence. And the next few days passed in like manner. The other women were so involved in their own problems neither noticed anything unusual about Kelly. More from habit than deliberation she fell into the role and she began to think it might work after all.

She had the time to come to terms with the situation, to sort out her emotions, to try to find a way to give Seth what he asked and for that she was grateful. She *had* to forget what had happened, she had to go on as before, for the alternatives were all too clear. Seth and she could have no relationship beyond that which they had always had. Theirs was a family structure based on the absence of sexuality; it worked as well as it did because they were all equal partners. Any change in the balance of their collective relationship would destroy the life they had all built together. Seth asked only one thing from her—that she be his friend. That, surely, was something she could do for him. Kelly could put that one night of her life behind her and go on as they had done before, because if she did not, they could not go on at all. That one thing, at least, was clear, and she knew now that was what Seth had been trying to tell her on that last nightmarish morning in the desert.

He could not live with her under any circumstances other than those to which they were accustomed. He would not destroy his relationship with the other housemates by showing a sexual preference for one of them; he would not jeopardize the code of morality all of them had come to trust. He would not become a victim to those sexual tensions himself. Home was the place where each of them came to leave behind the game-playing and the uncertainties and the strains of outside relationships. If he began to sense demands from her, a strain in the atmosphere, or a change in any of the easy companionship they had shared, it would be intolerable for both of them. He would have to ask her to leave and she would have to go. It was that simple.

Besides, what had she really expected of him? What had she expected to change with one night of intimacy? Did she really imagine that they could continue a sexual relationship simply because the door had been opened, that they could share a bed as easily as they

shared a meal, or use each other to satisfy sexual needs
in the same convenient manner they used one another
as escorts on a last-minute basis? The very thought was
abhorrent. It would be to him as much as it was to her,
but the harsh reality of it was that was all there could
ever be between them. Kelly had discovered in that
one night something deep and pure and permanent,
but to Seth it had been no more than a sexual encounter—one that embarrassed and disturbed him. She
could not distress him further with declarations of undying love, nor increase his guilt by begging of him
what he could not give. She would never, ever do that
to him.

And how could she ask him to believe that what she
felt for him was the true and abiding emotion she had
searched for all her life? How could she expect him to
believe that it was not just a pathological justification to
erase the guilt of what had happened between them, or
another one of her flighty tumbles into headlong romance? It was only a few weeks ago that she had sworn
to him her love for David was the real thing. He had
seen her through dozens of such emotional crises, and
he knew her too well. Seth would look at her with embarrassment and pity in his eyes and Kelly simply could
not do that to herself, or to him.

At first she even tried to convince herself that he was
right. After all, she was just getting over David and perhaps she had transferred some of her fantasies about an
unfulfilled love onto Seth. And it was true, she had
never been very wise where emotional matters were
concerned. How could she be certain her feelings were
not just as misplaced as all the other loves she had
known? But deep down inside she knew this was nothing like any other love. It was not heady and dizzying
and ecstatic, not another emotional whirlwind that took
her in one moment from heights of euphoria to the
depths of despair. It was something quiet and deep that

grew from the core of her, and try as she might she could not escape it or deny it. It had no definable beginning and no end, it was as much a natural part of her as her own thoughts or her mirror image. It just would not go away.

But she could not tell Seth that; he did not want to hear it. She would not make him a victim of something she could not control, or fling her love in his face like an accusation. Because, once again, he had been right about her—when she had at last found her love she discovered that she wanted it forever, she wanted marriage and children and her man beside her always, and those were things in which Seth had made it abundantly clear he had no interest. All else aside, their relationship was limited by the difference in their needs and their goals in life.

And, most importantly of all nothing could change the fact that Seth was still in love with Melissa Hollander.

So her choice was painfully clear. She would either live with him on his terms or lose him forever. She would find the courage to disguise her longing and the strength to hide her needs. She would give him her friendship, her companionship, her support, just as she had always done, for those things were his by right. And she would love him quietly, secretly, steadily, never threatening him or embarrassing him with the depths of her feelings. That was what he wanted, and that, because she loved him, was what she would give.

The strike ended two weeks before Seth actually returned. He called them and told them that, since he had already scheduled vacation time, he was spending two more weeks in the mountains and would see them at the end of the month. That was when Kelly began to get scared.

Perhaps it was because now she actually had a deadline within which she must completely resolve her conflicting emotions and present a calm and unchanged front to Seth. Perhaps it was because he seemed reluctant to return, and she was afraid of what she would see in his face when he did come back. He too had had plenty of time to think, and perhaps he had decided that it simply wouldn't work out no matter what she promised him or how she behaved. Perhaps he was simply dreading coming home and telling her she must leave. Perhaps he would come home and she would not recognize him. He might have changed. He might resent her for what had happened, he might be uncomfortable in her presence by being reminded of it every time they saw one another; the beautiful rapport they had always shared might have completely disappeared. Her self-confidence began to fade. She might not be able to control what was written in her eyes when she saw him, she might not be able to keep her resolution about maintaining a sisterly relationship, he might sense it and hate her for it. The knot in her stomach grew tighter with every day that brought his return closer.

The last few weeks of school were always hard, but the combined anxiety was making her physically ill. She could hardly drag herself through the day and when she came home she was too exhausted to eat dinner. Often she collapsed on her bed as soon as she walked in the door and slept straight through until the next morning. One day at lunch a sudden black despair overwhelmed her; she excused herself and ran to the restroom where she locked herself in one of the stalls and wept, helplessly and uncontrollably, for almost half an hour. When the bell rang for the next period, she tried to repair her face and go to class, but she couldn't stop the tears. She hadn't felt this lost, this alone and hopeless, since she was a child. And the worst part was, of course, that for the first time in recent memory Seth was not there to help her.

She heard his voice in the hallway on a Friday afternoon as she lay in a stuporous lethargy on her bed,
trying to gather her strength to join Susan and Trish
for dinner and somehow get through another evening.
He was two days early, and she was unprepared. She
wondered if there was any way she could have readied
herself for what the sound of his voice did to her—the
sudden jolting of her senses, the racing of her heart
and the dryness of her throat, the sweeping happiness
and the wonderful relief—the simple joy of having
him near her again. And then the dread. The nervousness that crawled in her stomach like the beginning of
nausea, the dampness of her palms, the unevenness
of her breath. This was the moment of truth. She
would go out there and face the man she loved and
see either rejection or contentment in his eyes. She
would stand before him and try to convince him with
an easy smile, a light word, that nothing had changed.
She would look at his hands and try not to remember
the way they had caressed her body, his lips and try to
forget the way they had felt against hers.... She
would welcome him home like a sister fondly greeting
a returning brother and hope that she could feel it, or
at least make him believe it, not at all certain she
could.

Kelly got up somewhat shakily and went to the mirror to smooth her hair. She looked pale, drawn, and
there were dark circles under her eyes despite the almost constant sleep she had been getting. She tried to
pinch some color into her cheeks, knowing Seth would
notice if she put on makeup, which she rarely wore to
school, and think it odd. She heard his laughter over
the clamoring, teasing voices of Susan and Trish, and
then, quite clearly, heard him say, "Where is Kelly?"
She could not delay any longer.

She stepped out into the hall, answering brightly,
"Right here. Welcome home!"

He had made it as far as the foyer before being way-laid by his housemates. One arm was around Susan, his hand was being tugged by Trish as they both talked at once, his duffel bag and backpack were stacked at his feet. In a glance that was swifter than a heartbeat she took in all of him at once with the urgency and relief with which a diver surfaces to gulp air—the way the faded jeans stretched tight across his abdomen and his thighs, the fit of his T-shirt and the open red plaid shirt he wore over it cuffed to the elbows, lean brown arms and the silvery hairs at his wrist, the column of his throat and the way his eyes crinkled and sparkled in the deeply tanned face, and then, as he looked at her, the way that laughter faded just a fraction and was replaced with a leap of welcome and then, very vaguely, a hint of uncertainty.

And, like a diver, she restored herself with that one glimpse of him and strengthened herself to plunge again. She was surprised at how easy it was as she came over to him. "You look gorgeous," she said, smiling. "Where'd you get that tan?"

He was even browner than before, and his hair and his eyebrows and lashes so sun-bleached they were al-most white. He looked rumpled and a little tired from the drive, but otherwise healthy and relaxed, and if there was wariness now behind his smiling demeanor, it was something only Kelly noticed. "Northern California has sun too," he retorted, and because the others would have been surprised if he hadn't, because it was the natural thing to do, he leaned forward and brushed her cheek with a kiss.

She steeled herself against the tingling jolt that im-personal caress sent through her, she tried to keep her smile from fading. It was easier because he did not meet her eyes, and he turned brightly back to Susan and Trish, demanding, "Which one of you ladies is re-sponsible for fixing my dinner? I'm starved."

Susan remembered the casserole she had left in the oven and hurried to check on it, calling over her shoulder, "It's nothing fancy! We expected," she added with a wink, "you to take us all out on your first night home!"

With a gasp Trish remembered the bath she had left running, and then Kelly was left alone with Seth, trying to act natural, frantically casting about for something to say, trying not to notice the way his eyes searched hers and the sudden tension that seemed to have crept over him. There was reserve in his stance, caution in his face, and uncertainty in his eyes. She felt as though those eyes were picking apart every detail of her life for the past four weeks, looking for something with which to accuse or reject her, and anxiety was tightening like icy fingers in her stomach.

But he only said casually, "Well, I guess I have time to take a shower. I'd better get out of these clothes before they start growing on me."

She smiled, faintly, but he did not move. He kept looking at her, probing her, and at last she couldn't take it any longer; she dropped her eyes. He said quietly, "If you don't mind my saying so, lady, you look like hell."

She glanced at him briefly. "I've had a stomach virus the last couple of days," she admitted, and it was not entirely a lie. There was no point in denying that she had been ill, but she must not let him know that the cause had been emotional, not physical. "As a matter of fact," she added, forcefully unclasping her hands and starting to turn away, "I still feel kind of queasy, so I guess I'd better pass on dinner tonight. I think I'll go to bed early."

"What?" There seemed to be a note of challenge behind the lightness of his tone. "And miss my welcome-home dinner?"

She hesitated. No, of course she couldn't do that.

She wouldn't have done it in ordinary circumstances and she could not let him think she was afraid to face him, that she could not even pretend sufficiently for one meal across a common table. She smiled, rather weakly. "Well," she agreed, "I'll sit with you, but don't expect me to eat anything. After all," she added, and the brightness she forced into her expression was rewarded with a cautious relaxation of his, "I've got to hear all about those two-hundred-pound salmon you corralled."

The conversation at dinner was bright, constant, and chaotic, and Kelly relaxed beneath the familiar boardinghouse atmosphere, losing herself beneath the chatter. Trish and Susan competed for his attention, for they had a month of catching up to do, and nothing was required of Kelly. Vaguely she listened to their lists of chores that had been saved for him and his returned banter, the amusing anecdotes he shared about life in the wilds, and her girl friends' rather reluctant answers to his increasingly probing questions about their personal and career lives.

Some rather amusing developments had occurred in both Trish's and Susan's lives since last he had seen them, and under other circumstances Kelly would have enjoyed sharing the retelling, laughing at his changing expression and his dry observations. Trish had returned from that fateful trip to San Francisco with her archenemy strangely subdued and secretive, and under Susan's relentless questions had admitted only that Mr. Peter Devers had turned out to be "not such a bad guy"—and she blushed when she said it. During the following weeks she had seemed not to mind so much working late, and it was impossible not to notice that she took extra care with her apparel and makeup. Several times she went to a "business dinner" and returned home after midnight looking flushed and starry-eyed, which of course earned her

Susan's ruthless teasing, until the tables were turned on Susan.

Under Seth's clever questioning and Trish's amused encouragement, Susan admitted reluctantly that, having finally met Senator Apling, he had turned out not to be quite the ogre she had imagined. He was young and, Seth dragged out of her, quite nice-looking. It seemed he really wasn't investigating or accusing their agency of anything at all, but merely researching a widespread practice in preparation for drafting legislation at some far future date. Seth suggested blandly that it was unusual for a senator to do that sort of research personally, as he had a staff of underlings employed just for that purpose, and Susan admitted, blushing, that perhaps it was, but they seemed to get along so well that he appeared to enjoy working with her personally. Of course that confession precipitated a burst of laughter and a fire of good-natured teasing that left Susan scarlet with embarrassment.

Recovering herself, Susan retaliated mildly, "Have you seen Melissa since you've been gone?"

The sharp knife-twist of pain in the center of Kelly's chest was totally unexpected, and it dulled to an aching throb as Seth replied casually, "No, but I talked to her on the phone almost every day." He grinned. "Hell of a long-distance bill, but nobody could make any rules about management and labor fraternizing over the phone. We're going out tomorrow night."

The voices faded around her and Kelly felt herself sinking into a totally irrational numb despair. The few bites she had taken of Susan's tuna casserole sat like an iron fist on her stomach and she wondered if she would be able to keep it down. Her reaction was totally uncalled for. Seth had never made a secret of his feelings for Melissa, nor was there any reason to expect him to forget about her just because he had lain with Kelly in one night of passion too soon regretted and determinedly forgotten. It was only natural that he should seek out Melissa. "It's all sex." Wasn't that what Susan had said in reference to their various problems on that long-ago day when they had been no more than four close friends facing individual crises? Sexual discrimination, sexual intimidation, sexual confusion...and Kelly had felt so lucky because her problems in that area had been mild compared to theirs. Now she felt a hysterical urge to laugh.

"Kelly?"

Seth's voice and three pairs of eyes on her dragged her out of her misery. Obviously he had just addressed a question to her, and the look on his face was oddly reserved, cautiously speculative. She was just too tired to pretend any longer. "I'm sorry," she managed with a wan smile. "I have a splitting headache. I think I'd really better go to bed."

"You've been working much too hard," commented Trish wisely. "You really shouldn't have gone to work today feeling as bad as you did. You're going to spread the flu all over campus."

"Serves them right," answered Kelly, trying to sound more like her usual bantering self, "after the rough time they've given me the past couple of weeks. I hope every one of the little monsters spends his first week of summer vacation in bed."

But as she stood a wave of prickling dizziness swept her; she had to grip the table for support. "Whoa, girl." Seth's voice reached her from far away, his hand touched her elbow lightly in support. She realized she must have actually swayed on her feet as his face cleared before her and she saw the concern there, and he demanded, "You're not going to faint, are you?"

"Don't be silly," she scoffed, and the weakness passed as swiftly as it had come. "I've never fainted in my life."

She could feel his eyes upon her as she turned away

from the table, and in a moment heard him push back his chair. "You don't look too steady," he decided, closing his fingers gently about her upper arm. "Maybe I'd better walk with you."

She laughed, weakly and nervously, as they left the room. "Totally unnecessary," she assured him.

"I know that," he answered quietly and pushed open the door of her bedroom. "I wanted to talk to you."

She swallowed convulsively on a sudden biliousness in her throat and made her way without his assistance to the bed, where she sank onto its cool softness gratefully, gripping the bedpost. This was it, then, the moment she had dreaded.

"Seth," she said a little desperately as he sat beside her, "I really am sick."

The lines about his mouth were grim as he brushed his fingers tightly across her clammy forehead. "That I can tell," he answered. "And I don't suppose the shock of seeing me again helped any."

She tried to laugh. "Shock? Why should I be shocked? You live here, after all."

"And that's the real problem, isn't it?" he answered evenly. And then the expression on his face dissolved into frustration and helplessness as he shook his head once, curtly, as though to clear his thoughts. "I never said it was going to be easy," he told her briefly, "for you or me. I know what you must have been going through these last few weeks—"

"No," she said quickly, almost desperately. "It's okay, really."

The look on his face was of impatience mingled with mild disgust, and she did not know whether that disgust was directed at her or at himself. Either way it frightened her. "Don't lie to me, Kelly. I know you too well to try to fool myself into thinking you could get over this thing as quickly as—" She thought he was going to say "as quickly as I have," but he changed it to, "Some other women might. You feel hurt and used, mixed up and betrayed. Don't you think I know how your emotions work?" Now his expression softened. "Kelly, don't try to hide it from me. Don't start pretending and lying to me. I can take anything but that."

She dropped her eyes, suddenly weary with relief. She should have known, nothing had really changed between them, not basically. Seth was here to share her problems just as he had always done and the heavy weight of the past weeks began to gradually disperse. He understood. He would not reject her. "No," she said softly. "I don't feel hurt or used or any of those things. I think," she told him, meeting his eyes honestly, "that I've about got it straightened out in my head, and I can live with it." And for the first time she realized that was true. She could accept it; she even thought she could go on just as they had before, because now that he was here nothing else mattered. Just being with him was all she could ask, just having him near was enough.

He smiled, faintly and tenderly, as he lightly pushed back a strand of hair from her forehead. "Then why," he questioned gently, "did you look like a condemned criminal facing the executioner when you saw me this afternoon?"

She swallowed hard and dropped her eyes. She had thought she had pretended so well. "I was afraid," she answered hesitantly, "that you were going to ask me to leave."

He stared at her in astonishment, which gradually became mixed with dismay and patent incredulity. "Ask you to— good God, Kelly don't you know that's the one thing I could never do?" His hand suddenly tightened fiercely around her wrist. "All these weeks I've been scared to death I would come home and you wouldn't be here. I made myself stay away because I knew it was a decision you had to make for yourself. Oh, Kelly, no.'' His eyes were dark with intensity. ''I don't want you to leave. Not ever.''

A wonderful relief trembled through her, a cautious happiness. That was all she wanted, just to be with him, just to love him in her own quiet way...forever. As their eyes met they shared a moment rich with emotion and pulsing with a quiet need, and as they sat there so close together on the bed his eyes slowly left hers, as though on a reluctant compulsion, and traveled downward to her lips; then his fingers came up to lightly touch her face, brushing across her lips in a delicate, lingering caress as tender as the kiss she knew would soon follow. His face moved closer to hers and her heart tightened in her throat, for it was no use, the need was too strong and she did not want to fight it any more than he did.

Then they were both startled by a heavy weight bouncing on the bed as Fleetwood pushed himself between them. Seth dropped his hand with a rueful smile and straightened up; whatever had been in his eyes a moment ago was now completely gone. He said, ''You don't have a fever, maybe you just picked up a touch of food poisoning.''

Her laugh, so natural and easy, surprised her. ''Don't tell Susan that!''

He grimaced as he stood. ''Don't worry. I'd like to live a little while longer.'' He paused, once again the big brother and the protector. ''Have you taken anything? Do you want me to go to the drugstore?''

She shook her head, but grateful for his concern. ''No, I think the worst of it's over now.''

''How about a cola or ginger ale or something?''

Again she shook her head, settling back onto the pillows, stroking Fleetwood, feeling secure and protected and...loved. ''Just sleep.''

He smiled gently. ''Okay, babe. Get some rest.'' He

came over to her and suddenly bent and brushed her cheek with a kiss. "Feel better," he said softly and he left her.

For a long time after he was gone, her fingers rested against her cheek where his lips had touched it. Sweet, gentle, impersonal...and for her, at that moment, it was enough. It had to be.

# Chapter Eight

"Do you have a date for the party tonight?"

It was eleven o'clock on a Saturday morning, and Kelly and Seth were washing windows, he on the outside, she on the inside of the kitchen. She answered absently, jumping down from the counter to refill her bucket of soapy water, "What party?"

He looked at her through the cloudy window in exasperation. "The beach party, scatterbrain. The one we've been talking about all week?"

Kelly poured liquid cleanser into the bucket and turned the taps on full force to produce a thick froth of bubbles. Vaguely she did remember something about a party, but that was the last thing in the world in which she was interested. These last two weeks of school had been the hardest she had ever completed; she had never been so glad to say good-bye to a class in all her life as she had been this one. And now that the school year was finally over she had one week and one week only before she started her full-time summer job at the health salon; she intended to spend every moment of that vacation sleeping.

She answered Seth, turning off the water, "No. I'm not going."

She carried the heavy bucket of water back to the window with both hands, straining to lift it on to the counter. She wished she was still in bed.

She missed the odd, speculative look Seth gave her as she concentrated all her energy on wringing out the sponge. Then he said, stepping down from the ladder, "This is hot work. How about a break?"

She breathed a sigh of agreement and let the sponge plop back in the water as he came inside. He had been working in the direct force of the morning sun, and his curls were dark with perspiration, his face, arms, and bare chest gleaming. She sat down at the kitchen table and watched him as he poured himself a glass of milk, shaking her head when he offered her some.

Somehow it was working between them. Perhaps it was because, with Seth back at work and Kelly so busy at school, it was habit that ruled their spare hours, and it was easy to fall into the old routine of a relationship that had been formed with three years of living together on an impersonal basis. Perhaps it was because Kelly was usually so tired at the end of each day that they actually saw very little of one another, for when she did manage to stay up past nine o'clock he was generally out with Melissa. It was not that she could forget about it. He haunted her dreams almost constantly, and she would sometimes awake from those dreams so lonely and aching for him that it brought tears to her eyes. Then she would lie there and think of his bedroom only two doors down the hall and think how easy it would be to just slip out of her bed and into his, how wonderful it would be to put her arms around him and to have him hold her, for that was all she wanted, just to be held by him. Yes, those late-night times were the worst...those, and times like this, when her eyes were drawn irresistibly to his strong brown chest and slender waist, to the muscled thighs below the cut of his white tennis shorts. It was so hard to forget the way that body had felt next to hers, to pretend her fingers had never made the discoveries about him that should be among the most treasured secrets between a man and a woman.... She really didn't want to forget.

He sat across from her and inquired mildly, "Why not?"

"Why not what?"

"Why aren't you going?"

Kelly shrugged and leaned back in her chair. "Not interested."

"Everyone else is going."

"Susan's not," she pointed out.

He grinned, lighting a cigarette. "Susy's gotten too high-class for us since she started hanging out with that Sacramento crowd. But," he added, shaking out the match, "she does have a date tonight, so that means you'll be sitting around here all alone."

"So what?" she responded irritably, waving away a cloud of smoke that had drifted her way. "I'm a big girl."

He leaned back, one arm crossed over his bare chest, smoking thoughtfully, not saying anything. His reflective gaze made her nervous, and the smell of the cigarette smoke was thick, pungent, and unpleasant. She let her eyes wander away from his and her fingers restlessly played with the narrow row of lace edging the vee-line of her halter top. When she happened to glance his way again, his eyes had followed the course of her fingers and were resting on her breasts. It was only a second, but in that second searing memories burst within her—the feel of his fingers and his mouth there and the devastating sensations he had created, the need for him and the intimacy they had shared—and in that second before he jerked his eyes away uncomfortably, she knew that he was thinking the same thing.

Despair filled her, and then frustration and anger. It wouldn't be easy. No, it would never be easy, and she did not want to live the rest of her life with memories of what would never be hers again. She did not want to be plummeted by sensations of yearning and denial whenever their bodies accidentally brushed or she felt his eyes upon her, she did not want to see that embarrassment and guilt in Seth's face every time he was reminded of what had been so precious to her. Helplessness settled like nausea in the pit of her stomach and she had to break the sudden awkward silence that had grown between them. "For God's sake, Seth," she complained, waving at the cloud of smoke drifting toward the window, "put out that filthy cigarette, will you?"

He looked surprised. "It's never bothered you before."

"Well, it bothers me now," she snapped irritably, scowling. "Will you just put it out?"

"Don't use that tone of voice with me, lady," he warned mildly, but his eyes told her he meant it. It was very unlike Kelly to pick a fight with anyone, and she was clearly overreacting. Because it wasn't the first time she had come close to losing her temper over the past few weeks, she knew she was in for a lecture.

She dropped her eyes and reached for his half-finished glass of milk as he crushed the cigarette in an ashtray. She took a sip and in a moment said, "I'm sorry. I guess I've been barking at everyone lately." She looked at him apologetically and saw that he was not about to offer her an argument on that score. "It's just this has been a terrible year at school and I'm so worn out, and I'm wishing I didn't have to work this summer."

"So don't," he suggested sensibly.

She gave a little laugh and took another sip of milk. "It's necessary," she informed him dryly, "in order to maintain the standard of living"—she gestured about her—"to which I've become accustomed."

"It wouldn't kill you to take one summer off," he

answered. "Your salary pays your rent and living expenses; you don't need the extra money."

"Speaks the big financier," she retorted. "Sure, I could do without the extra money, if I'm prepared to do without a few other little things, like gasoline for my car, and clothes—"

"Stay home and go naked," he suggested blandly, and she laughed, glad to see the awkwardness between them fade so easily.

But as soon as her laughter had died, his eyes became serious again, and he said, "You haven't had a date since I came back. Any particular reason?"

Kelly could have given him a dozen reasons, and not one of them would have erased the very faint suspicion she could sense within him that the reason she was keeping herself from other men was because of him. She could only tell him the truth...or as close to the truth as she was allowed to reveal to him on this subject. "I'm just not interested in that scene anymore," she answered simply, not afraid to look at him. "I've thought about it a lot, and it's like— Well, it's redundant to go out looking for good times when I have everything I want here. I'm not lonely, I like my own company and," she added honestly, "yours and Trish's and Susan's. I'm never bored. It's not as though I'm looking to get married and have my own little house and all the frills. It's like you said before—I've got all the conveniences of marriage without the problems. And so I figure why go through all the hassle and heartbreak of shopping around when I'm not looking to buy?"

He looked cautiously impressed. "Good Lord," he said softly, "you've grown up. You sound as though you really mean that."

She finished off his glass of milk, not certain whether to be pleased or insulted at his reference to her having grown up. When she ventured a glance at him, she saw by his reflective look that he had meant it as a compliment.

"I guess you're lucky, then," he added thoughtfully, "if you really are satisfied with what you've got."

She lifted her shoulders lightly. "Who wouldn't be?"

"A lot of people," he answered seriously. "Hardly anyone is completely satisfied with the status quo, seems as though we're always looking for something. I mean, that's what single life is all about, isn't it? No matter how much we tell ourselves we're not interested in anything permanent, that we like our lives the way they are, it seems we're all condemned to keep searching for that soulmate everyone is always talking about and no one seems to have." He shrugged. "The human condition."

She knew, in a moment of wrenching sorrow, that he was talking about himself. He would keep on looking, though he would deny to himself that was what he was doing, for the one person who could make him complete, the one person who could belong completely and irrevocably to him, a part of him. Kelly had already found that person, and that was why she needed no one and nothing else. It was so very simple, so easy, so clear. All the time love had been standing right before her and she had waited too long to recognize it. A relationship had been formed that could not be changed, and though her love could never run its natural course, at least she was luckier than most for she *had* found it. But Seth would keep on looking.

And then he said, "Anyway, no one's saying you have to go in for anything heavy right now, but you need to go to that party tonight." There was a decisiveness in his voice that would tolerate no argument. "You haven't been outside all summer and you're starting to look like a washed-out old schoolmarm." She bristled at that insult, which was, of course, exactly what he wanted her to do. "School's over," he challenged her. "Celebrate. You're going."

"I told you, I don't have a date and—"

"So come with me."

"You're taking Melissa," she pointed out uncomfortably.

He hesitated just a moment. "She won't mind," he decided.

"Oh, for goodness' sake!" She could tell there was no point in arguing with him. "I'll go with Trish," she agreed finally, very disgruntled. "The last I heard, Peter couldn't make it. At least with her I won't have to worry about being a fifth wheel."

He looked at her mildly, satisfied. "You'll meet some new people," he assured her, "let your hair down, have fun. It'll be good for you."

But of course Kelly knew from the beginning that that was the last thing it would be.

Trish chattered about Peter Devers all the way to the beach, and Kelly tried to look interested. She really did not want to hear about Trish's happiness when her own mood was somewhere between apathy and abject misery and the only thing she was really interested in at that time was the cool sheets of her own bed.

The gathering was at Malibu, where the host owned an expensive beach house on a cliff overlooking the festivities. As they arrived at five o'clock, food and drink had already been carried down to the beach and the party was in full swing. Turning to take their beach bags out of the backseat, Trish was surprised by a pair of hands about her eyes, and Kelly managed a weak smile as she knew Trish's date had been able to make it after all. Peter Devers was very nice, obviously adored Trish, and Kelly tried to be enthusiastic as introductions were made and radiance glowed fom her friend's face. What she was really wondering was how she was going to get home without feeling, once again, like a fifth wheel.

There were many people she knew at the party, so she couldn't possibly have felt left out or unwelcome. There were also several unattached males wandering around to whom her well-meaning friends made immediate introductions. And why not? Kelly thought with a rather bleak sigh as she took their good intentions in the spirit they were meant. She was living in a world in which sex was the only marketable commodity, where naked women in ice cubes sold booze and everything was made for two. There was something mildly offensive about anyone being alone, it was impossible to believe that such an occurrence was deliberate.

Kelly tried to have a good time. The sunset over the Pacific was magnificent, the powerful roar and crash of the waves provided a moving background rhythm for the thunderous stereo cassette players that created dance music, and the food was extraordinary. There were steaming pots of lobster and clams, a dozen different hot and cold salads, and an endless array of creative desserts and wines to match. Kelly had even, through no fault of her own, acquired an escort who went out of his way to be charming and entertaining. He was tall and blond, but rather shallow, and although his attentions were flattering, Kelly thought she would have made a much better attempt at enjoying herself had she not had him to contend with. She did not like the way he watched her when she slipped off the pair of shorts she had worn over her one-piece bathing suit to go swimming, and when they were in the water he pulled her under the breakers and tried to kiss her. She did not like that at all—aside from the fact that his attentions were unwelcome, there had been a moment when she had experienced a very real fear of drowning—and she told him so in no uncertain terms. He was apologetic, patient, and undeterred. She did not go swimming again.

All things considered, however, the outing was not turning into quite the disaster she had imagined, and she was even beginning to relax and enjoy herself. Then she saw Seth and Melissa. Even before he spotted her, it struck Kelly with a sinking feeling of dismay that they made a beautiful couple. Seth, in tight white jeans and a brown velour top zipped to midchest, looking so tanned and casual, with his arm around the bare waist of a small auburn-haired girl in a bikini top and matching floral sarong skirt. They looked as though they belonged together, happy and relaxed. And when Seth brought Melissa over and made the introductions, Kelly hated herself because she could not really dislike the woman. Melissa was friendly, witty, and unpretentious. She wasn't particularly gorgeous, although she did wear that bikini the way few other women could have. She wore her thick auburn hair in a bushy ponytail, and her hazel eyes sparkled a lot, and she had freckles on her chest and shoulders. How could anyone dislike a woman with freckles?

So, she thought bleakly when they were gone, Seth had good judgment. Did she ever really doubt it? Hadn't she really known all along that it would have to be someone very special to matter as much to Seth as Melissa obviously did. But after that it was much harder to pretend to enjoy herself.

The beer, wine, and mixed drinks went rapidly, and the romance of the moon on the midnight-blue water, the thundering crash of the breakers, and the flickering light of dying bonfires had the predictable effect on people. The music grew slower and more romantic, and couples with their arms twined tightly about each other wandered off toward the house or the shelter of the dunes in search of privacy. Other couples stretched out on beach blankets or cuddled in the shadows and made their own privacy. Trish, Kelly noticed in some amusement, was one of those who wandered away with her true love, looking rapturous and secretive—and then that amusement changed to alarm as Kelly wondered how she was going to get home. She supposed rather bleakly she would have to ask the young man who had established himself as her date to take her. She was not looking forward to that at all.

Kelly's date tried to put his arm around her. She let him, mostly because she was cold. He tried to nibble at her neck and she brushed him away like an annoying insect. He desisted for a while, although she did not like the way his fingers caressed her waist and moved along her ribs, nor the way his arm seemed to be incessantly tightening around her, drawing her ever closer to his overly warm body. As she always did in such situations, she looked around for Seth. She found him, and she wished she hadn't.

He was lying on a blanket with Melissa, their arms were around each other, they were kissing. She watched the way his hand moved to her scantily clad hip and the way her hands tangled in his hair and she thought, she couldn't help but think, how it had been between them, how Seth had touched her and coaxed her and loved her.... She felt ill. She had to look away.

She felt a hot hand on her knee, and she shivered. Misinterpreting her reaction, the hand became bolder, sliding up her thigh. She tried to push it away, but without much real interest. Her eyes were drawn irresistibly back to Seth. Seth's hands were on Melissa's waist now, gently holding her, his leg moved across her ankles in a posture of lovemaking. His lips moved away from hers; he was whispering something in her ear. It was no different from anything a dozen other couples were doing, but to Kelly it seemed obscene. A pain knotted in her stomach and she felt breathless. She made herself look away again.

She shivered violently as the hot, clammy hand moved farther up her thigh, fingers feathering inside the cuff of her shorts. She pushed it away forcefully, but his arms came around her, drawing her against him. He murmured huskily, "Ah, come on, baby," and tried to put his mouth on hers.

She struggled briefly and violently. "Stop that!" she hissed, pushing at his face with her sharp nails. Her head was aching and it was hard to breathe; cold perspiration was beginning to gather around her eyes. "I said *stop it*!" She got to her feet, leaving an astonished would-be lover gaping at her and swearing softly. But she hardly saw him. A wave of weakness flooded her; her teeth were chattering and her head was pounding. She turned blindly and stumbled away from him.

The noises and the lights receded as wave after wave of cold sickness swept her and she pushed herself farther away from the party, half running and half stumbling, until at last she collapsed against a barrier of rocks and dunes and was violently ill.

An immeasurable time later she felt a hand on her shoulder, and Seth's face swam into view. "Oh, go away!" she gasped weakly. "Don't look at me! Please!"

"Don't be silly," he returned curtly. "I've seen you in worse shape."

Her humiliation was complete, but there was nothing she could do about it as, too weak to fight it, she gave in helplessly to another wave of uncontrollable retching. He held back her hair and steadied her head until the last awful spasm had passed, and then she was too miserable to do anything other than sob weakly into her hands.

"All right, that's enough of that." His voice was stern but his touch gentle as he pried her hands away from her face and placed a clean handkerchief in one of them. "When are you going to learn," he added on a faint note of amusement mixed with exasperation, "that you don't have the stomach to drink like a sailor? Are you better now? Can you walk?"

She was too exhausted, too miserable, and too sick to even cry any longer. She couldn't seem to stop shaking. She managed weakly through chattering teeth, "I—I'm not d-drunk." She hardly thought half a paper cup of beer qualified her for that category, and she did not want Seth to think that her condition now was the result of overindulgence. She was wretched enough as it was.

But his grin was cheerful and slightly mocking as he agreed, "Not anymore, you're not."

He started to lead her away with an arm lightly around her shoulders, but her knees felt like water and her head was still swimming in awful, strobing waves of green and yellow. She stumbled and almost went to her knees, but he caught her quickly and firmly. When next she looked at him she was sitting on the sand against the shelter of a rock, her hands were held tightly in both of his, and the amusement on his face had been replaced by grim concern. "Your hands are like ice," he said briefly. "I'd better get you home."

Another violent shiver racked her, and the effort to speak was almost too much. "You—you can't," she whispered. "M-Melissa..."

He hesitated, and then touched her damp hair lightly. "I'll get a friend to drive her home. Will you be all right here by yourself for a few minutes?"

She did not even have the strength to nod. She just wanted to lie down on the sand and die.

It seemed only a matter of seconds had passed before he was beside her again, wrapping a blanket around her shoulders and urging her to her feet. She did not know how she would walk all the way up the cliff to the car. She was so cold, colder than she had ever been in her life, and the blanket hardly helped at all.

And then she was in his car. Without her having to request it, he had turned the heater on full blast, and she snuggled down into the folds of the blanket as the shaking gradually subsided.

After a time he inquired, "Do you think you're going to live?"

"Oh, Seth," she replied miserably, "I'm sorry you had to leave."

He shrugged it off. "Next time," he answered dryly, "I'll listen to you when you say you don't want to go somewhere. Can we do without the heater now? It's got to be eighty degrees outside."

She nodded and tried to sit up a little straighter. The effort made her head swim, and she leaned back against the seat weakly, closing her eyes. After a time he inquired, "Present difficulties aside, of course, how did you like the party? Who was that fellow you were with? You seemed to be getting along pretty well."

If there was anything other than polite curiosity in his voice, she was too weak to analyze it. She replied tiredly, "A creep. All hands and no mind."

There was a brief silence, and then he said with no expression in his tone whatsoever, "That's too bad, babe." Was he relieved or disappointed? It occurred to her in a transient moment of clarity that perhaps Seth had hoped she would meet someone tonight, that he would never have her completely off his conscience until she was as involved with someone else as he was with Melissa. But she was simply too tired to pursue that line of thought, or even to be depressed over it.

Inside the house he advised her, "You go ahead and get into bed. I'll bring you a cup of tea."

She hesitated, looking at him. "Aren't you going back to the party?"

To her bleary eyes his smile seemed perfectly innocuous. "And leave you alone in your hour of need? Don't be absurd. Now, go on."

The short walk to her bedroom seemed to restore her strength a little, but it seemed to take an extraordinary long time to complete the simple routine of dressing for bed. She paused many times to rest, and she was just sinking back against the pillows when Seth came in with the promised cup of tea.

Weakly she fumbled to pull the sheet over her legs; he assisted her and then propped the pillows behind her shoulders, insisting that she drink the tea. He sat beside her and gave her an encouraging smile, and she felt secure and warm and protected, and she loved him with a quiet certainty that was as much a part of her as the beat of her own heart.

After a few sips of the tea she did feel stronger, and he commented, "Your color's better anyway. I don't mind telling you, you had me scared for a minute there."

She managed a smile, but in her eyes was real chagrin. "You would have stayed with Melissa tonight," she suggested, "if it hadn't been for me."

He shrugged, but his eyes crinkled with a smile that was mostly relief at having her address him in a normal tone of voice, a sign that she was feeling better. "Probably."

"Was she very mad?"

"She wasn't exactly thrilled," he admitted, but if there was a flicker of regret in his eyes he hid it well. "But let's not talk about Melissa," he insisted, smiling. "After all"—he took her hand—"*she* has never stayed up half the night listening to me talk out my problems or held my hand when I had nightmares."

The reminder of shared closeness was so sweet, so poignant, and so loving, that Kelly felt herself sinking into the soft waves of emotion sweeping over her. She had to break the moment. "Or loaned you money," she suggested.

"You've never loaned me money," he retorted, but he was smiling as he tossed her hand away playfully.

She looked at him, feeling her strength return be-

neath the warming influence of the tea and the soothing certainty of his presence. He looked so relaxed and
at ease sitting beside her; it felt so perfectly natural
when they were together. There was no more of that
perpetual anxiety in his eyes; the haunted look she had
come to recognize recently was completely gone. Since
his return from the lodge he had looked healthier and
more fit than ever, and, despite the few moments of
occasional awkwardness that now appeared between
them, Kelly had never known him more relaxed or
sure of himself. She could not help wondering how
much of that was due to her . . . and how much was due
to Melissa. She said softly, "You're feeling better,
aren't you?"

He knew immediately to what she referred. "It
comes and goes," he admitted, "in phases. I'm sleeping at night again and I think the worst is over—thanks
to you." She looked surprised, and he insisted, "It's
true. You wouldn't believe what a difference it made,
sharing it with someone." He dropped his eyes, examining the yellow-and-bronze pattern of her floral-
printed sheet. "Those first few weeks after I left . . .
were pure hell. I didn't think I'd make it for a while. I
kept turning to say something to you, and you weren't
there. I'd wake up in the middle of the night and for
just a minute everything would be all right because I
would think you were just around the corner, but of
course—" And he broke off suddenly, remembering
why he had left and the circumstances that kept him
away. Their eyes met in a brief moment of sorrow and
yearning on her part, regret and embarrassment on his.
And then he changed the subject abruptly.

"Did I tell you I met Trish's boyfriend?"

He leaned back, resting his weight on one hand, and
the expression on his face was carefully schooled casualness. She quickly dropped her eyes to her half-
finished cup of tea and took a sip. "Do you mean at the

party tonight?'' she answered, matching his conversational tone.

"No, before that. It occurred to me,'' he explained, relaxing as the topic became well-established on neutral ground and Kelly finished her tea in an attitude of interested listening that was no different from that she always displayed with him, ''that she was seeing a great deal of this fellow, but had never brought him to this house. Well, you know what that means—she was either trying to hide me from him, or him from me.''

Kelly giggled. It was an unspoken rule that none of the housemates should see the same man more than two or three times without making the introductions to Seth. Besides demanding the right of approval over any man they dated seriously, Seth felt that it saved awkwardness in the long run to have the details of their living arrangement exposed at the beginning of a relationship, and many a prospective suitor's character had been tested by his reaction to his girl friend's housemate. It was probably a very worthy philosophy, but it could also be rather difficult to handle, and Kelly could understand Trish's reluctance.

"So,'' he continued, "I decided to take matters in my own hands and stopped by the office one afternoon last week on the pretense of offering her a ride home. Trish was in a meeting, but Devers wasn't too hard to find.'' Again Kelly giggled, imagining Trish's embarrassment, for Seth could be positively obstreperous when he got an idea in his head, as impossible to manage as a bulldog who had formed an attachment to a bone. She was certain he had treated poor Mr. Devers like a hostile witness in a felony charge, and she supposed the very fact that he had shown up at the party tonight had to say something for his courage—if not his wisdom.

But Seth surprised her. "He turned out to be a pretty nice fellow. Crazy about Trish. I introduced myself, of course, and he said Trish had told him about me, about all of us. I think," he concluded wisely, "this could be the start of something big."

Kelly agreed silently. If she had not already gotten the signals from Trish, the fact that she had already told Peter about her living arrangement would have confirmed Kelly's opinion of how the relationship was going. None of them wanted to go into a discussion of their male housemate—risking rejection and possible aspersions on their moral characters—unless something really serious was at stake.

She set her cup on the night table and inquired, not looking at him, "What did Melissa think of your living with three women when you told her?"

"It took a little explaining," he admitted ruefully. "But I think she finally got the picture." And then he looked at her, trying to mask the eagerness in his tone with the nonchalance in his eyes. "What did you think of her, anyway?"

Kelly hesitated, and then managed a small, coquettish smile. "She's not good enough for you."

He grinned and touched her nose lightly. "One woman's opinion." And then he sobered as he looked at her, his fingers lightly brushing over her face and resting in a moment on the soft material of her nightgown on her shoulder. "Kelly," he said seriously, "I want you to see a doctor. You've never really gotten over that virus thing you had last month, and it's starting to worry me."

She sighed, flickering her eyes away from him uncomfortably. She really did not want to be reminded of what a fool she had made of herself tonight. "I have an appointment next week for a physical before I start work at the salon. I'll probably be completely well by then."

He nodded approvingly. "It doesn't hurt to check. After all, there could be something really wrong with you, like anemia...." Then a playful light came into his eyes as he suggested, "Or some dread social disease, or something nice and contagious, like hepatitis."

She laughed, relaxing under his teasing. "I think," she informed him, "if I had hepatitis, you would know it. Aren't my eyes supposed to turn yellow or something?"

He assumed sobriety as he pretended to examine her eyes. "Clear as a bell," he announced at last. "Still"—his expression softened as he stroked one eyelid tenderly—"like lapis lazuli."

And as her eyes met his she saw the gentling there, the darkening of intent, and she made no move to stop it as his face moved a fraction closer to hers. Her lips parted on a wondering breath and it was unpreventable; the spell that had fallen over them held them each completely helpless as she felt his fingers lightly on her face, near her mouth, and then his lips clasping hers. Sweet, warm, gentle, escalating into joy and a deeper desire.... Her hand moved without volition to clasp his neck and she felt the weight of his chest brushing her breasts as he moved over her, the tightening of passion within him, which was reflected by the painful thumping of her heart and the tingling rush of sensation spreading from her face to her fingertips and weakening her legs. The surprise, the wonder, the wanting, the helpless joy of being in his arms again...loving him, needing him. His lips began to part hers gently with an increasing demand, and his hand slipped beneath the sheet to clasp her waist. She gasped with the sensation of warm fingers separated from her flesh by only the thin layer of nylon which was her nightgown, and he tightened his hold, kneading, caressing, exploring... just as he had done with Melissa.

A sudden surge of horror wrenched at her and she twisted her face away violently. "No!" she gasped, shock and disgust turning the fire within her to a pain-

ful flood and the rhythm of her heart to an angry
sledgehammer. Her eyes were glittering and her
cheeks stained as she pushed him away, her mind
hardly registering the surprise on his face. "I won't
have Melissa's leftovers!" she spat.

For just another moment their eyes met, and Kelly
would never forget the shock and the slow agony that
crossed his face. For a second he looked as though he
might speak, but then he compressed his lips tightly
and left the room abruptly.

Kelly bit her lip and turned her face to the pillow,
steeling herself against the racking shivers. She determined she would not cry herself to sleep.

As a matter of fact, she did not sleep at all.

Three days later Kelly was sitting on the examining
table, wrapped in a sheet, discreetly checking her watch
while the doctor made his presumably routine nota-
tions on her chart. She had arranged to meet Trish and
Susan for lunch, for it was a rare occasion that they
were all in the same area of town at the same time, and
she thought she would just about make it . . . if the doctor would hurry up and tell her she could get dressed.

At last he glanced up, putting the pen in the pocket
of his white lab coat. Apparently he had a habit of re-
placing the pen uncapped, for the pocket was stained
with tiny blue and black marks. He said, "Well, I imagine you've already guessed my diagnosis, and now all
you want to know are the details."

"Details?" For just a moment a tiny shaft of alarm
tightened within her. She had not really expected a diagnosis of any sort. According to the doctor's scales she
had lost a little weight, but that was surely nothing to be
concerned about. She looked at him anxiously. "What
details?"

He consulted her chart again. "About eight weeks, I
should say."

She tightened the sheet around her and shifted her weight uncomfortably on the table. "Is that when you want me to make an appointment?"

"Hmm? No." He glanced at her absently. "No, I want to see you again in a month." And at her blank look of confusion he explained, "Pregnant. You're about eight weeks pregnant."

# Chapter Nine

Kelly's first reaction was, of course, disbelief. She thought, *No. Not me. This can't be happening to me, there's been a mistake. It simply can't be.* And far back in her mind, like a bubble of wild laughter ready to burst, a voice mocked her. How many thousands of women hear those words every year, that dread anathema of single womanhood—"You're pregnant." *And now you're one of the statistics. You, Kelly Mitchell, another foolish girl fallen by the wayside....* She thought she would either laugh or throw up, so she struggled hard against doing either.

The doctor, noticing her stunned look, registered some surprise of his own. "Now surely, Kelly, this can't come as a complete shock to you. You must have suspected—"

She shook her head slowly, just once. "I've ... never been very regular," she managed numbly. But she knew the signs had been there, she had just chosen to ignore them. She was not so ignorant she had not noticed the changes in her own body, but if the suspicion had ever been there, it had been smothered far back in her mind because such a thing simply couldn't happen to her ... it simply couldn't.

The doctor flipped back through her chart as though to confirm her observation. "Hmm," he said at last, "that's so. Still, it's good you came in when you did.

Early prenatal care is very important. Why don't you go ahead and get dressed and we'll discuss this further in my office?''

Through the whirling vortex of half thoughts and bursting brain impulses courage was born, a fierce denial, the instinct for self-preservation. "No," she cried. "No, wait! You don't understand! There must be some mistake, this is impossible...." The doctor looked at her patiently. "There was only one time," she pleaded desperately. "No one gets pregnant from just one time!"

The doctor smiled faintly as he turned to go. "Famous last words," he said.

The nurse came in to assist her, and Kelly hardly remembered dressing or making her way to the doctor's private office. *Pregnant.* She kept repeating that word over and over again as though it were in itself some horrific charm. *You're pregnant.* As though it were an incurable disease. It couldn't happen to her but it had most undeniably happened. She was pregnant.

Like most women, Kelly did not have a family doctor, but used her gynecologist for all routine physical concerns. Gynecologist-*obstetrician*, she remembered suddenly, and the scores of pregnant women she had encountered in his waiting room on each of her visits took on a whole new meaning to her. And because he was an obstetrician, he approached the matter of her condition routinely and competently, for he must have delivered this same speech a dozen times a day. Somehow there was reassurance in his calm tone and matter-of-fact approach. At least, as Kelly sat stiffly in the leather chair before his desk and wound the straps of her purse compulsively around her fingers, she no longer felt quite so much like being sick.

"I don't see any real problem with the delivery," he told her at the conclusion of a medical outline of the findings of his examination. "But you shouldn't lose any more weight. Are you having a lot of nausea? Tension will make that worse. You should find some hints to relieve your discomfort in the literature I'm going to give you, but if the weight loss persists, I'll have to put you on medication. Your blood pressure is a little high, but that could have been just because you were nervous today. We'll want to watch that too. I'm going to write you a prescription for an iron supplement and prenatal vitamins." Kelly stared in fascination at the little ink-dots on his pocket as he took out his pen. She did not think anything, she did not feel anything, she just stared.

He passed the prescriptions to her and she reached for them automatically. She was just going to murmur something inane and totally inappropriate like "thank you" when he leaned back in his squeaky green leather chair, hands folded across his chest, and fixed her with a perceptive, compassionate look. After a time he said, "Unless our records need updating, I don't believe you're married."

"No," she whispered and dropped her eyes. Then she cleared her throat, lifted her eyes, and faced him squarely. "No," she repeated more firmly, "I'm not." There was no use denying it, she had to start accepting it, right now. Somehow she had to accept it....

He nodded, his expression unchanging. "Is that going to be a problem?"

She could not keep the incredulity out of her eyes. A problem? Since when had being an unwed mother been anything else? Again she felt that insane urge to laugh.

"A lot of unmarried women are choosing to keep their babies these days," he explained, "and raise them alone. However," he leaned forward and once again began to scribble on the pad, "as you probably know, we do perform abortions here. The only thing I insist upon is a one-week waiting period and that you get some counseling in the meantime. This"—he pushed the paper toward the end of the desk—"is the name of the counseling service I use. Don't wait too long, though," he advised. "You should make your decision within a month. After that, it won't be safe."

Kelly stared at the slip of paper on the desk with an instinctual recoiling. Abortion. Even the word sounded ugly. Kelly was living in a modern world and thought she had acquired all the sophisticated values, but she had been raised with her parents' sense of morals and she did not think she could break away from that code now.

Abortion. It would solve all her problems. In a few swift minutes her world had been turned upside down; in just a few more minutes it could be righted again. It would be as though it had never happened. It would be better for everyone. She had no life to offer a baby, she had nothing to give it, she was not even sure she could manage raising a child and providing a home for it and working to support the two of them. What kind of life would that be, for either of them? It wasn't fair, this shouldn't have happened to her.

But it wasn't the baby's fault that its mother had made a mistake and gotten the both of them in this mess. Mother. The word had an odd, frightening, yet strangely reassuring sound. It meant strength, responsibility. She was responsible for this child, for protecting it and nourishing it.

It would be so easy to just sweep it away.

"No," she said quietly. For the first time her voice sounded calm, even to her own ears. "I won't need that."

She thought she saw a faint flicker of approval in her doctor's eyes. He stood, and she did the same. "All right, then, make an appointment for a month from now. And, Kelly," he added kindly, "I know this is not going to be easy for you. But try to remember how important it is to avoid stress. Rest as much as you can, follow the diet, take the vitamins—and don't let yourself get upset or worried, because that won't do any good for your health or the baby's.'' And he smiled at her. "You're going to do just fine," he reassured Kelly again as she left his office and headed for her car.

*You're pregnant. You're going to be fine.* The words echoed hollowly through her mind like a lone ball on an empty court. *You're pregnant.* Perhaps if she said it often enough she would begin to believe it. How could this have happened to her? Her life was so secure, well-organized, protected. Nowhere in her dreams or goals for herself was there room for an unplanned pregnancy. *This couldn't be happening to her.*

She was scared. That much she could admit to herself. She was as frightened as a sixteen-year-old girl who had just learned that the facts of life were not always pleasant. But she wasn't a sixteen-year-old girl, she was a twenty-seven-year-old woman who should have known better, and unlike the sixteen-year-old, she did not have the option to run away and hide from her problems. No one was going to help her out of this one, to smooth it over and make it better. This was something she was going to have to face on her own and work out by herself. Still, she suddenly felt lost and small and helpless, and she wanted her mother.

Her mother. Instant horror recoiled within her as she thought about telling her parents. How could she tell her parents? How could she *not* tell them? She imagined her father's reaction as she was getting out of her car in front of the restaurant at which she had arranged to meet Trish and Susan, and she felt herself go pale. She actually experienced a moment of dizziness. Her father would use this as an instrument of mental flagellation for the rest of her life. And after he had finished torturing her and preaching to her and making her feel like the lowest creature who had ever drawn breath, she was not even certain he would recognize her as his daughter again, or the baby as his grandchild. He might reject her completely, turn her away to fend on her own and keep her mother from contacting her too. Kelly did not know if she could bear that. But she would have to tell them sometime.

Not today. She simply couldn't bear it today.

The restaurant inside was cool and dark. The sounds of clinking silverware and the quiet murmur of conversation were reassuring, for in the midst of so much normal humanity she did not feel quite so isolated anymore; it was easier to convince herself that the world had not really ended less than half an hour ago. Here were people laughing and talking and eating, going on with business as usual, and no one knew or cared that one female's life had suddenly been turned upside down and would never be the same again. When she saw Trish and Susan at a corner booth, relief instilled courage and she went over to them. They looked so normal, sitting there. And somehow seeing them made Kelly believe she could pretend everything was normal. Just a nice, normal chatty lunch with friends.

She smiled and murmured something about being late, but Susan brushed it away. "The drinks haven't even come yet. We ordered for you, and if you don't mind my saying so, you look like you could use it. Did you have to wait very long? Sometimes an hour can seem like a day when you're sitting in a doctor's office. Here's your menu."

"Oh, let's order something extravagant," suggested Trish, not giving Kelly a chance to respond to any of Susan's questions. "I feel like splurging. We can put it on our credit cards and not have to worry about it until next month. Look at this—roast duck!" She giggled. "Can you imagine what Seth would say if we told him we had roast duck for lunch?"

Seth. The name struck her consciousness and sank like a lead weight to the pit of her stomach. What would Seth say?

The drinks arrived, and Kelly reached for hers automatically, gratefully. Was she supposed to drink? The doctor hadn't said. It didn't matter, because today, just to get her through this day, she was going to.

"Do you remember that time," Susan was saying, "that Seth laid into you for ordering champagne cocktails at lunch? He said—"

Seth. She had to tell Seth. How could she tell Seth? But she wanted to; more than anything in the world she wanted to run to Seth with her problem. Seth would know what to do, what to say; he would somehow make it all better just for having shared it.

And it crept through her slowly, the icy fingers of reality...this was not just her problem. It was Seth's problem too. What would this do to his life? Seth, who shrank from marriage and openly admitted he did not like children. There was no more room for this accident in his life than there was in hers. How would he feel, how would he react, when that one night of passion of which he was so ashamed came back to haunt him— forever? How could she do that to him?

She couldn't do that to him. It wasn't his fault, he hadn't planned it, he hadn't wanted it, and he shared even less responsibility than Kelly did. He regretted the entire incident and wanted only to forget it. It was only an accident...but accidents had an unfortunate way of changing people's lives—permanently.

Kelly did not remember what she ordered. It was something Trish suggested, which had a foreign-sounding name and a heavy wine sauce. She tried to eat it but it smelled horrible, and at any rate her heart was pounding so dryly in her throat she could hardly swallow. What was she going to do, how could she tell him? How could she not tell him? Did she dare try to keep it from him, and if so, for how long? He would have to know eventually, it was only fair. It was his child too, a part of him.

What could she say? Insane little vignettes ran through her head. Seth, I know this is going to come as a surprise to you... or, Seth, try not to be too upset.... Or maybe the roundabout approach: Seth, do you remember that night in the desert...? Or perhaps the time-honored classic, Seth I have something to tell you....

Suddenly it all struck her as funny. Here she was, a woman closer to thirty than twenty, caught in a situation that was only appropriate to teen-age girls and just as panicky.... And there was poor Seth, blissfully unaware one moment of indiscretion had already led to repercussions beyond his scope.... She began to giggle. Really, it was ridiculous, things like this just weren't supposed to happen in real life. Soap operas, yes, melodramas, quite often, but not in the life of plain, unimaginative Kelly Mitchell. *And I was raised to be such a* good *girl*, she thought helplessly and gave in to the uncontrollable laughter that was bubbling inside her. She simply folded her hands in her lap, stared at her plate, and laughed.

"Kelly?" There was concern in Trish's voice, alarm in her eyes.

Susan, always ready to share a good joke, looked more amenable, though slightly confused. "What is it?" she inquired, leaning toward her.

Kelly said simply, "I'm pregnant." And she began to laugh again, only this time somehow the laughter turned to sobs, tears smeared across her lashes and wet her cheeks and she couldn't stop it, any more than she could stop the sudden wave of cold nausea that swept her. She pressed her hands to her face in horror, willing control, but it was no use, everything was a senseless blur and she knew she was going to be sick. She pushed away from the table and ran, blindly and heedlessly, toward the ladies' room.

When she came out, a long time later, Trish and Susan were waiting for her by the lavatories. On each of their faces was stamped their individual reactions to horror, as though they had just seen a particularly gory film or had a near-brush with a traffic accident. Kelly made her way over to the sink, turned on the tap, and splashed her face with cold water. Physically she felt weak and drained, but somehow stronger inside. A combination of numbness and resignation had taken over within her and the core of determination had begun to grow. She *would* be fine. Accepting it had been the hardest part, now she would learn to deal with it.

At last Trish said sympathetically, "Oh, Kelly."

And Susan echoed in quiet distress, "Oh, God."

Kelly blotted her face with a paper towel, staring apathetically at her reflection in the mirror. Her eyes were two dark smears in a washed-out face, features melting into a white blur surrounded by a tight frame of dark hair. She looked like the last survivor of a war—and in a way, that's exactly what she was.

Susan came forward and put her hands on Kelly's shoulders awkwardly, giving her a brief, reassuring squeeze. Kelly managed a wan smile in the mirror. Trish said, "Maybe you'd better sit down. You look awful."

"I feel awful," answered Kelly tonelessly, and she sank into one of the low vinyl chairs lining the entranceway. Kelly and her friends were the only ones in the room, and it was very quiet. Trish sat beside her and Susan pulled up one of the light plastic contour chairs to sit across from her, so close their knees were almost touching, and their supportive silence and the concern and understanding on their faces gave Kelly courage. It was better now that she had told someone. Just knowing how easy it was to say made a difference, and seeing the total lack of condemnation in her friends' eyes erased her own deeply rooted shame. But of course telling them had been the easy part. There were still her parents to be faced, and Seth.

Trish said quietly after a long time, "What are you going to do?"

An eminently practical question, and one Kelly had to face with first priority. Once more and for the last time the thought of abortion flickered across her mind. Simple, quick, and final. No one need ever know. Not Seth, not her parents... and all her problems would be wiped away as though they had never been. But she could not destroy Seth's child. She had clung to the memory of the love they had shared that night, had treasured and preserved it, and this was the living proof—a part of the man she loved, forever and all time. It was precious to her, she realized slowly. Deep down inside it was precious to her. He might regret a moment of weakness or be ashamed of the emotions that had prompted it, he might want to take back the night they had shared, but he had given to her the gift of his own immortality, and nothing could take that away from her.

She said simply, "I can't have an abortion."

There was quiet approval in Trish's eyes, unqualified relief in Susan's. "Oh, Kelly, I'm so glad," Susan said sincerely. "It would be the wrong thing for you. Other women might, but you could never be happy with a decision like that."

Trish agreed, "That's the hardest part—making a decision. At least now you know where you're going." And then she paused, looking slightly uneasy. "The, er, father... does he know?"

It occurred to Kelly for the first time that Trish and Susan could have no idea who the father really was, and it struck her with a sort of muted horror that they must never know. How would they react, what would they think of Seth, of Kelly? The foundation of trust on which Seth had so carefully built his relationship with all the women would come tumbling down, he would lose their respect and their confidence, and Kelly could not do that to him. She knew more clearly than ever that this secret must remain hers forever.

She answered Trish, "No."

Susan inquired hesitantly, "Are you going to tell him?"

Again the answer was simple and firm. "No."

There was a moment of confusion and protest of Trish's face, but Susan did not give her a chance to voice an opinion. "I know how you feel," she agreed with Kelly. "When I think of some of the creeps I've—" She broke off with a hint of embarrassment, but then rushed on, "Anyway, Kelly, these things happen. We've all made mistakes, and there's no reason to tie yourself to a man you don't love anymore just because of an accident of nature. You'll do just fine on your own. After all," she said, smiling encouragingly, "you've got all of us to help you, haven't you?"

Kelly said quickly, "I don't want Seth to know. Promise me you won't tell him."

Now both the girls looked confused. "Well, of course," Trish offered after a moment, " *we* won't tell him. But why—"

Once again Susan came to the rescue, almost doing Kelly's thinking for her, and Kelly was silently grateful. "Maybe she's got a point, Trish," she agreed slowly. "I mean, you know how Seth is, so protective and old-fashioned. Good Lord, he's liable to go out and punch the guy in the nose and Kelly doesn't need that kind of worry right now."

Kelly could not help smiling at that image even as she felt a wrench of guilt for Susan's innocent misinterpretation of the situation.

"I suppose," Trish admitted, though her brow was

still creased with concern and puzzlement. "But," she pointed out, "how long do you think you can keep it from him?"

"I don't know," Kelly sighed. "Long enough for me to get a few things straightened out in my own head. To make some plans." She had so many plans to make, so many things to straighten out. The rest of her life seemed like just one giant tangle of problems and insurmountable obstacles from where she sat right now.

Susan squeezed her hand bracingly. "You just remember that we're behind you, whatever you decide to do."

"One hundred percent," agreed Trish with a smile. "You don't have to go through this alone."

Those were the best words Kelly had ever heard in her entire life.

They stretched their lunch hour out as long as they possibly could, but eventually Susan and Trish had to go back to work. They left Kelly reluctantly, but actually in much better spirits than when they had met her. The secret to surviving this thing, Kelly began to realize, was to face one problem at a time. It was all happening too fast. It was impossible for her to assimilate and organize everything in her mind at once. If she tried she would smother under the avalanche. And it was undeniably clear to her that one of the first things she must deal with was her prospective employer for the summer. And she had best get it over with today, while she still had a tenuous hold on her courage.

Each year the salon requested a simple physical form to be filled out by her physician, and it was for that reason that Kelly had made the appointment in the first place. This year, in addition to the required medical data, in the space reserved for "Disabilities and other Physical Limitations" was the notation: "Pregnancy, eight weeks advanced." Kelly watched the changing expressions on the salon manager's face with dread knotting in her stomach and her heart thudding in her throat as she read the paper.

But in the end all the woman did was look up, smile faintly, and say, "Congratulations."

In a quick moment of insight Kelly knew the indecision that was going on in her employer's mind. She was wondering whether or not she could be mistaken about Kelly's marital status, and if she was not, what to do about it. She was afraid to make a rash decision because of the possibility of being accused of discrimination. She was on uncertain legal ground, but she had an affection for Kelly through the three summers they had worked together and she knew Kelly was one of her best instructors. Kelly knew she had to strike now, to make the woman commit herself to employing her before she had a chance to get all these questions sorted out in her mind.

Kelly said, surprising even herself with the courage in her voice, "Of course I want to work as long as I can." She needed this job, even more desperately than before. "There shouldn't be any problem this summer, as I won't—won't start to show for some time yet, and as you can see, I'm in perfectly good health." That wasn't strictly true, but the white lie would do for the moment. She needed this job. She needed the money and if she had nothing to do this summer but sit around the house and brood about her problems she would surely go mad.

Her boss still appeared uncertain. "This is very strenuous work," she pointed out. "Are you sure you'll be able—"

"Quite certain," Kelly replied with a bright, very false smile. She gathered up her purse and stood with an air of brisk authority she was very far from feeling. "There'll be no problems at all, I promise you. I'll report for work Monday morning as planned." And she left without giving the woman a chance to deny or detain her.

*See,* she told herself once outside the building, *wasn't that easy? Everything is going to be so much easier than you thought.* But she was shaking as she got into her car and prepared for the long drive home.

But she could not go home immediately. She had a lot of adjusting to do, a lot of rearranging of thoughts and attitudes, before she could walk back into that house and feel as though she belonged there. She drove slowly along the back streets and into residential areas, and everything looked different to her. The space of two hours separated the life she had once lived from the one she was leading now, and she felt as though she had been transported to another world. She could hardly remember the time when she had been plain Kelly Mitchell, whose life was simple, secure, and uncomplicated. Now she was special, different. She was no longer one person but two, and her life would never be the same again.

She parked in front of a playground and simply sat there for a long time, watching the children. And, after a time, she began to find a somewhat uncertain reconciliation within herself. It was true, this was not the way she had planned it. She supposed, somewhere deep inside, she had always envisioned herself as a wife and mother, just as Seth had said. She had included in that remote daydream some unknown figure of a man she loved, a beautiful, well-kept home, and, inevitably, children. She had found the man she loved—only he did not love her in return. She had had the home—until today. She was not a wife, but she was soon to be a mother. Somewhere within that list of assets and deficits there had to be a compromise for happiness.

But at least she had her job. Somehow she would manage financially. She would have to check her insurance policy regarding maternity coverage. So many things to do, plans to make, questions to answer. They all came tumbling down on her at once and she knew she couldn't handle it, not yet. One thing at a time, she told herself with a bracing breath. And the most important test right now was to go home and face Seth and pretend as though nothing unusual had occurred today.

It was late by the time she arrived home, and all three cars were in the driveway. She was starving, for she had had a very light breakfast and missed lunch completely, and hunger was making her a little light-headed. She quickly checked her reflection in the rear-view mirror—a little pale, but that was nothing unusual lately. Seth would probably not even notice.

The moment she stepped into the house she was overwhelmed with the aroma of garlic, tomato sauce, and cheese, and it tightened around her stomach like a clammy claw. Repulsion mixed with the weakness of hunger and made her ill. *Get used to it,* she thought vaguely, *for the next seven months....* She braced herself and went into the dining room.

"You're late," Seth announced, beginning to serve their plates. Seth made a homemade pizza that could not be outdone this side of Italy, and it was usually the highlight of the month when it was his turn to cook. Any other time Kelly would have gorged herself, but tonight she could hardly bear the odor.

"I'm on vacation," she returned lightly, and took her place at the table. "I'm not on a schedule." She was aware of the anxious looks that flitted her way from Trish and Susan, but she did not return them. She needed every ounce of her energy to somehow get through this meal.

Seth placed a thick, gooey slice of pizza on her plate and Kelly swallowed hard, trying to mask her revulsion. Susan and Trish were making enthusiastic, appreciative sounds, but there was no way Kelly could eat that, even the sight of it turned her stomach. She was not even certain she could sit at the same table with it. And of course Seth noticed.

"What's the matter with you, Kelly?" he demanded. "Don't tell me you've lost your taste for pizza."

"No," Kelly returned weakly, "it's not that, exactly."

"What then?" he insisted, pouring glasses of very aromatic Chianti. And, with sharpening perception, "You look awful. Are you still—"

Kelly's obvious discomfort was apparently too much for Susan to bear, and she felt compelled to rescue her. "Leave her alone, Seth," she said sharply. "Kelly's had some bad news and she doesn't need—"

Kelly's eyes flew to Susan's in a moment of warning too late, she saw the quick regret in her friend's eyes and the sudden alertness in Seth's as he said, "Bad news? Didn't you have a doctor's appointment today?"

The moment of horror between the three girls was electric, and Kelly could think of absolutely nothing to say. Not like this, she pleaded silently in a panic of misery and despair. She simply couldn't tell him like this.

And then Trish volunteered on a sudden inspiration, "Weight. She's five pounds overweight."

Kelly was so grateful it almost brought tears to her eyes.

Seth removed the pizza and left her salad. "Don't say I didn't warn you," he commented mildly, and it was as simple as that.

Susan quickly changed the subject and Kelly tried to relax. Of course it was impossible. Seth's presence radiated around the table and filled the room. The corners of her eyes registered details about him: the tight jeans and sandaled feet, the muscles of his forearms beneath the short-sleeved knit shirt, the way the light struck his curls, and the crinkled lines about his eyes when he laughed—casual, relaxed, completely at ease with all of them. She ached for him. She wanted to feel his arms around her and lay her head against his chest and sob out her problems and have him understand. She wanted to share with him the miracle of what their love had created inside her and she wanted him to think it was a miracle too. But he would never welcome that, and despair filled her throat and tasted bitter.

The conversation went on around her, and she knew Trish and Susan were outdoing themselves to keep Seth's attention away from Kelly. Kelly tried to show her gratitude by keeping her attention away from Seth and concentrating on her meal. How could she concentrate on anything when all she wanted to do was to tell Seth? Tell Seth, as though the telling in itself would be a magical cure, as though it could somehow lift the burden threatening to crush her. It would of course do nothing of the sort, it could only compound the problem and pass to Seth a responsibility and a guilt with which she had no right to inflict him. She couldn't do that to him. But how could she live the rest of her life without telling him? How could she even get through this night?

She tried to eat her salad, but it was topped with bleu cheese dressing and it smelled horrible. She always had bleu cheese on her salad and Seth would think it was odd if she complained, but she knew if she did not eat something she would probably faint. She said, standing abruptly, "Don't we get any crackers with our salad?"

"So take it out of my tip," returned Seth, and Kelly found the crackers in the cabinet, resting a moment before making her way back to the table.

After a few of the crackers and half a glass of water, the queasy feeling abated, but the inner despair did not. Never in the past three years had she had to solve a problem or bear a burden all on her own. There had always been Seth's shoulder to cry on, Seth who was ready with wise suggestions or quippish remarks to tease her out of her self-pity. Seth to share, and to care, to simply be by her side when she needed him .... She had never, ever, kept a secret from him. And now the most important thing in either of their lives must be the most desperate secret she had ever kept. She was not at all certain she could do it.

Even the sound of his voice filled her with yearning. This was the man she loved, the only man she had ever loved, and it was right and natural that she should be carrying his child. It was not right that there should be so much misery attached, so much secrecy and deception.

Suddenly the sound of that voice was directed at her, disapproving and impatient. "Crackers and water for dinner?" he demanded. "Don't you think that's carrying a diet a little too far?"

Once again Trish rescued her, and once again Kelly was so grateful she could have cried. "Peter has asked me to go to Las Vegas with him next weekend," she said, dropping her news like a well-timed bombshell whose reverberations spread slowly around the table.

Seth turned to her, his attention effectively diverted from Kelly. One eyebrow quirked and his tone was dry as he commented, "To meet his parents, I presume?"

"No," replied Trish evenly. "To have fun."

"I think it's marvelous," volunteered Susan excitedly. "You'll have a great time! Where are you going to stay? What are you going to take with you?"

"Come on, Trish," Seth interrupted impatiently, "I thought you were serious about this guy!"

"There's something wrong with going away for the weekend with a man you're serious about?" Trish challenged him.

Seth's scowl was disapproving, his tone contemptuous. "To Las Vegas? I thought he had more class than that—I thought you did!"

"I've lived on the west coast for six years," defended Trish, "and I've never been to Las Vegas. I don't see anything wrong with—"

Kelly murmured, "Excuse me," and took her dishes to the sink. No one noticed as she slipped quietly out onto the deck and slid the door closed behind her.

It was cool outside, and the air was fresh and clean. She took a deep breath and sank onto the chaise longue, swinging her feet up and leaning her head back. In the darkness she could have been isolated on a high mountain, only the vague shapes of bushes and trees below indicating the floor of the canyon. Combative voices from inside the house reached her vaguely, but she did not trouble to interpret the words. After a time the tones became calmer, and soon abated altogether, leaving only the sounds of Seth moving around in the kitchen, doing the dishes. Kelly closed her eyes and felt the cool breeze on her cheek and tried to think nothing. But behind those closed eyes she could not blot out the face of a child, a child with bright topaz eyes and curly blond hair. The picture filled her with a strange sort of contentment, the first real peace she had found all day. It was a feeling very much like love.

The sound of the door opening brought her back to the present, and with it a certain amount of tension returned as Seth came out onto the deck and lit a cigarette. He walked over to the rail a few feet away from her and leaned on it. His profile was just a darker shadow among shadows as he looked out over the canyon, and the tip of his cigarette glowed like a small red beacon. At last he said impatiently, "How about that Trish? Las Vegas!"

Kelly could not help smiling at his paternal disapproval. It was all part of what she loved about him. "Sin City," she agreed. "Center of vice, corruption, and quickie marriages."

"Fat chance," he retorted, drawing again deeply on the cigarette.

She laughed softly. "Hypocrite," she accused gently. "It's not the city that bothers you and you know it. It's the fact that Trish is actually going away for the weekend with a man. But how many women have *you* taken away for the weekend who didn't have big brothers to advise them otherwise?''

"That's different," he returned shortly.

"Oh, yeah? How?" It was easy talking to him, just as it had always been, easy to talk about other people's problems and to momentarily forget her own. Seth had always been able to make her forget.

"I didn't love any of them," he answered her directly. "Trish is really in love with this fellow. I mean, she's seeing orange blossoms and white lace and I really thought he felt the same way. But you don't ask a girl you really love to go to Las Vegas for the weekend, and Trish should know that. I don't know which makes me madder, the way he's treating her or the way she's letting him."

She shook her head helplessly. Dear Seth, so protective, so caring. How had any of them ever gotten along without him? "That's just your opinion," she pointed out. "Maybe *you* wouldn't take the lady you loved to Las Vegas for the weekend, but for Trish and Peter it may be just the thing. Who's to say?"

He tossed the half-smoked cigarette over the rail and came over to her. "Would you do it?" he demanded.

She looked at him for a long time. She almost could not answer. "If the man I loved asked me," she said at last, very quietly, "I would go anywhere in the world with him."

He knelt beside her. She felt his hand lightly on top of her head, stroking her hair. There seemed to be a change in the atmosphere between them, one that made her breath quicken and her heart suddenly speed, and she could not read his face in the darkness. He said softly, "Any man worthy of loving you would never ask you." And then he smiled very faintly. "Trish doesn't even understand how I feel. But you and I are two of a kind, you know that? Romantics at heart, idealists, waiting for that one and only true love to come along, and willing to settle for nothing less."

Only Kelly was not waiting any longer; she had found hers long ago, before that night in the desert, perhaps on the first day she had walked into this house. He had been there all along, waiting for her, just as true love always is, in the place she least expected.

She could feel his eyes on her, very dark, very intense. His finger now stroked her earlobe and she suppressed a sudden warm shiver. She was no longer thinking about her secret. She was not thinking about the events of the day at all, but in her mind was a jumble of bittersweet images—she and Seth walking hand in hand on the beach, Seth taking her picture while she posed with Mickey Mouse at Disneyland, Seth reaching to her for comfort one night in an empty kitchen, the starlight in the desert, and the last time they had been alone together when he had given her the kiss that was meant for Melissa and she had rejected him so violently. She would have welcomed that kiss now, she would have taken the love that belonged to another woman and suffered any humiliation for one moment in his arms, to feel his heart beat against hers and his strength flow into her. But dark despair crept over her again as she knew even that was not her right, and she heard her own voice inquiring evenly, "Have you found yours—your one and only true love?"

His fingers left her hair to gently trace the curve of her jaw, he was so close beside her that she could feel the warmth of his breath on her cheek. She was confused, and a cautious anticipation tightened within her as he said softly, "I don't know." Was there a meaning there she was afraid to read, or was her desperate imagination only searching for an opening, a sign that he was letting down the barriers that had stood so stalwartly between them and one night of love. If only he would take her in his arms. If only he would hold her, no more, and give her some sign that he remembered, that it was possible for him to care for her again as he had that once, then she might be able to tell him and, in telling him, share her love.

But then he removed his hand, almost as though being suddenly brought back from a pleasant daydream, and he said in a more normal tone of voice. "You mean Melissa." He sat easily on the deck beside her, his arms looped around his knees. "You notice," he answered with a shrug, "I haven't asked her to go to Las Vegas with me."

She released a breath that was slightly unsteady and stilled the quivering of her pulses. Melissa. Always Melissa. She was the one Seth wanted, and if he wanted her, then he should have her. That was only one more reason she could never tell him her secret. *There is someone for everyone,* she thought, bleakly, *and if Melissa is the someone for you— if you love her only one half as much as I love you— then nothing must come between you. Not me, not our baby, not anything. A person gets only one chance at happiness in this life, and if I can't have mine then Seth must surely have his.* That one resolution, coming from the very depths of her as she sat with him in the night, gave her a courage she had never before known she possessed. This was one crisis she would see to its completion completely on her own, not for herself, but for him.

And then, as though reading her thoughts, he said quietly into the darkness, "I don't know, Kelly. This is very serious business, love. If there is only one person for everyone, you're always afraid you've chosen the wrong one. I mean, will it *really* survive after the passion dies? I don't understand," he concluded softly, "how Trish can be so sure."

"Maybe," suggested Kelly with an effort, "because she has really found the one and only."

He looked at her for a long moment, and she thought that gaze could surely read everything that was written in her soul. He searched for her hand and clasped it lightly, and in the end all he said was, "I think you and I are just two old-fashioned characters in a fast-paced world. We don't really belong here."

They sat there in the dark for a long time, holding hands, saying nothing.

The rest of the week was easier to get through than she had imagined. The occasional sickness she had felt in the mornings grew worse, but she managed to keep it from the others by staying in bed until they all had gone, squeezing her eyes shut against the daylight and trying to smother with a pillow the nauseating odors of perking coffee and frying bacon. She knew the doctor was right, tension was only making it worse, but tension was one thing she could not seem to avoid. She awoke with it every morning and took it to bed with her every night. She had to think of something to do. She had to find a way to guard her secret from Seth, and it was obvious her time was limited. Already he had begun to watch her peculiarly, several times in private he had started to speak to her and only the timely interruption of Susan or Trish had saved her.

She would have to leave, of course. That was the one painful truth she tried desperately to avoid with her conscious mind, but it haunted her constantly. Two, or three months at the most, and she would no longer be able to hide her condition from anyone. She did not know where she would go. She did not know what she would tell Seth. She did not know what excuse, if any, he would accept for the sudden severing of a friendship they had both acknowledged to be among the most treasured of their lives. For once she left, she must never see him again. She must make certain that their paths never accidentally crossed and that he could not find her even if he wished. It was too much. Too much for her to think about and to sort out right now. She thought she had until the end of the summer. Surely by then something would have occurred to her. And in the meantime she tried to think about it as little as possible, for thinking only made her ill.

She had grown used to sleeping late in the mornings and taking long naps in the afternoon while everyone else was at work—pregnant women required more sleep, she had learned from the pamphlet the doctor had given her—and on her first day of work at the salon she did not think she would make it through. She knew that exercise was not only permitted, but recommended in pregnancy, so she was not concerned for the baby's sake, but she just didn't seem to have enough energy anymore. And because she knew the manager was watching her carefully, she worked extra hard to assure her there was no cause to regret hiring Kelly. After three days Kelly no longer even tried to pretend for the sake of her housemates at the end of each day. Hardly speaking, rarely even glancing up, she forced herself to eat what she could, tried not to fall asleep in the bath, and collapsed for the night shortly after seven thirty.

On Saturday she slept most of the day, and no one disturbed her. Trish, ignoring Seth's disapproving warnings, had gone to Las Vegas with Peter the night before. On Saturday afternoon Seth took Susan to a movie and Saturday evening they both had dates, Susan with her young senator and Seth with Melissa. Seth was home early, but Kelly, half drowsing, did not get out of bed to inquire why. She heard him moving around in the house, but it was a comforting sound. In her half-asleep state she heard him start down the hall toward his room, and with sudden alertness she thought she heard his footsteps pause by her door. She waited, anticipation flooding her senses with adrenaline, but nothing happened. After a time she heard him close the door to his own room, and she thought she must have imagined the entire episode. It was a long time after that before she slept fully, but when she did she dreamed he was lying in bed beside her, holding her, loving her. The ceiling was a canopy of stars and beside their bed was a cradle. She did not want to wake up from that dream because Seth was looking into the cradle and smiling.

But of course, it was only a dream.

Sunday was one of the hottest days of the year thus far, and even the usual canyon breeze failed them. Seth spent the morning trimming shrubbery with the electric hedge clippers while Susan priced swimming pools in the Sunday paper and Kelly took him glasses of iced tea and advised him that such chores were really better performed in the cool of the evening. But he seemed to have a need to use up excess energy, and he accepted the tea but not the advice.

Aside from the heat, Kelly felt much better than she had all week and was grateful for the rest, which had restored her energy. Susan confided when Seth was out of hearing that she had been worried about her, but Kelly assured her the constant fatigue was nothing to be concerned about and would soon pass—her body just had to adjust to its new circumstances, that was all. Secretly she hoped the adjustment would not take too much longer. Susan, sensitive to Kelly's need for privacy, did not press further, although Kelly knew she was curious about what plans, if any, Kelly had made and how she was coping with prospective parenthood. Susan simply let her know that she was there if Kelly ever needed to talk, and that was the most generous thing one friend could do for another. Kelly was grateful.

Seth completed the shrubs about lunchtime, and both women came out to admire his handiwork. Susan volunteered to go to the local delicatessen for sandwiches, and Seth offered to pay for them. Kelly felt the least she could do was help him gather up the trimmings and stuff them into the lawn bags.

In only a few minutes the heat began to affect her, and she wondered how Seth had stood it. He was working shirtless, and perspiration oiled his back and arms and beaded on the hairs of his chest. His face gleamed and his curls were damp, but he worked with the same effortless energy with which he had started. Kelly had only been out a few minutes and already her shirt was damp and her head was throbbing. "I wish we had air conditioning," she complained.

"Now, don't start that again." He tied up one of the filled bags and tossed it aside. "I told you, it wouldn't be worth it. We would only use it a few days a year." He changed the subject. "What are you doing this afternoon?"

Kelly slowly and laboriously stuffed another handful of twigs into a bag, scratching her arms on their prickly leaves. Her breath was coming with difficulty and her hair felt like a tin helmet magnifying the sun's rays. "Nothing," she answered, trying to gather another handful without standing up. Standing up made her dizzy.

"How about taking a ride up the coast?"

She sat back on her heels, lifting her shirt away from her sticky breasts, and squinted up at him. She was suddenly very hungry, and hunger was making her weak. She wished Susan would hurry up. "What happened to Melissa?" she inquired.

He shrugged. "We had a fight."

"What about?"

He grinned, tying off another bag. "Sex, what else?" And then, carrying the bag over to the others, he added seriously, "No, I'm just kidding. I really don't know what it was about." He looked at her, his eyes bright and clear in a deeply browned face, and he told her,

"You know something else? Right now I really don't care. That kind of bothers me," he added seriously. "People shouldn't fight."

With a great effort Kelly managed a smile. She felt hot and damp all over, and she was so hungry her stomach hurt. "They say it's good for a relationship."

"'They say' a lot of things," he replied, bending to scoop up another pile of shavings. His muscles rippled in the sunlight, like a desert mirage. "I guess I'm just expecting too much. My standards are too high. So what do you say?" He looked at her, and there was seriousness in his tone and his expression, almost a plea. "Will you come with me this afternoon? We'll talk like we used to, maybe stop for dinner some place, would you like that? We haven't talked much lately," he added meaningfully, "and I think there are some things we need to talk about."

Anxiety clutched at her stomach with that, anxiety and guilt. What could he mean? She had never been afraid to talk to Seth before, but she had never tried to deceive him before either. She had never dreamed in the beginning what a truly painful process it would be. She got quickly to her feet and said, "I'm going to get a drink of water."

He said something; she did not hear it. His voice faded into a thin, high ringing in her ears and a prickling cold wave spread from her fingertips to her face. His features were a white blur between pinpoints of dancing shadows and she felt the ground tilt beneath her feet as slowly, very slowly, the curtain of gray descended.

## Chapter Ten

When Kelly opened her eyes she was lying on Seth's bed. She opened her eyes just long enough to see the enormous round bedpost directly in her line of vision and the wide expanse of wine-print coverlet beneath her fingers, and then she closed them weakly again as everything started to swirl into a sickening blur. She felt drained, beaten, and every muscle of her body ached. She wondered vaguely what she was doing here, on Seth's huge soft king-size bed, but she did not think about it very hard. She just wanted to rest.

Then she felt something lightly touch her face, and with a very great effort she opened her eyes again. Seth's face filled her vision, something remotely resembling a dry smile on his face, and he said, "So much for the woman who's never fainted in her life."

She swallowed dryly, remembering. She had fainted, and Seth had taken her to his room because it was the closest....

She felt his arm beneath her shoulders, lifting her to a sitting position, and a glass pressed to her lips. She thought with distant humor, *Just like in the movies,* as he commanded curtly, "Drink." But the liquid that passed her lips was not alcohol, only refreshing and immensely welcome ice water. She had not realized she was so thirsty, and she drank half of it before sinking back against the pillows, still weak, but now fully alert.

She watched Seth cautiously as he placed the glass on the lampstand beside the bed and stood, his back to her as he crossed the room.

"Well," he said at last, and there was a tension to his stance that belied his casual tone. "I guess you think I'm a pretty big fool. I mean, you'd think I would become suspicious when a woman who's never been sick a day in her life suddenly takes to her bed five days out of six, has mysterious doctor's appointments, and experiences a complete personality change." Kelly's heart was pounding painfully in her chest and her hands were clenched into instinctual fists of fear. "Of course," he went on, without looking at her, "the swooning into my arms was a classic piece of indisputable evidence. Nice touch. Maybe I can be forgiven for being a little slow; you see"—he turned, and his eyes were like ice—"I haven't had much experience with pregnant women."

The moment between them was frozen forever in a classic vignette of melodrama. The controlled fury of his posture and the challenge in his eyes that almost commanded her to deny it; the helpless misery that would not let her look away from him; the admission that was written starkly on her face; the sudden incredulity and horror that swept him; and then the icy control that demanded, "How long did you think you could keep it from me?"

How long, how long...? Oh, God, she should have known she never had a chance. All her defenses crumbled and her noble plans lay shattered at her feet, for there was nothing for her now but to face with him the mess she had made of both their lives, to somehow seek his understanding and plead for his support. "I'm...sorry," she managed, but she wasn't sorry and surely he could see it in her eyes. She wasn't sorry to have conceived his child in love or to carry within her a part of him. Couldn't he see that? Couldn't he see that because she loved him she was not ashamed or sorry, that she would proudly commit the rest of her life to this child because it was his? And wouldn't he surely, as soon as he recovered from the shock, come to share even a small part of that emotion with her? If only he wouldn't look so angry, so distressed....

"Sorry!" The one word burst on her senses like a thunderbolt, so short and so vicious that she actually shrank back. His face darkened and his fury lashed at her like a whip, and when he took a step toward her, she actually put out her hand in self-defense, certain, in one cold moment of shock and confusion, that he was going to strike her. But he stopped short, rage churning in his eyes, and he demanded fiercely, "My God, Kelly, how could you be such an idiot?"

His anger was incomprehensible, for it was more than anger, it was barely controlled violence, and she had never expected this from him. Shock, distress, anxiety, but not anger. She had never seen him like this; she was not aware that Seth could possess such a temper much less that he would direct it toward her, and an awful pain of disappointment and rejection churned in her stomach. She had never expected this, not from Seth. She whispered, searching his face with wide and frightened eyes, "I...don't understand—"

"That's obvious!" he bit back, and his lips curled in a contemptuous sneer. "What did you do, skip Elementary Sex Education? Don't you know how babies are made?"

She gasped in humiliation and pain, and tears stung her eyes as she struck back, "You have no right to talk to me like that! You—"

"The only thing wrong with what I'm saying to you now," he spat back in disgust, "is that it's coming a little too late! I said I was a fool, Kelly, not a complete imbecile! What was this, some sort of old-fashioned marriage trap? You get pregnant and—"

"No!" she cried. She felt as though she were drowning in a whirlpool of horror and outrage and bitter disappointment, and confusion was the undertow. "Stop it! It wasn't like that at all, it was an accident—"

"Accident, hell!" He took one more furiously controlled step toward her, but she was too hurt now to be frightened. She could not believe he was doing this to her, she could not believe the hatred and disgust she saw in his eyes was directed at her or that it belonged to the man she loved and knew as well as she did her own mind. "Grow up, baby," he spat. "This is the twentieth century and no woman gets pregnant unless she wants to!"

Could he really believe that? Could he really believe that she, Kelly, would try to trap him or deliberately hurt him? Somehow it was that breach of trust that cut through all the hurt and surfaced into righteous indignation. She defended in a high, furiously shaking voice, "It wasn't like that, you know it wasn't! I wasn't expecting—"

"Sure, now tell me another one!" His voice was ugly with sarcasm. "A good woman is always prepared."

She gasped out loud with horror and rage and suddenly she wanted to hit him. "You bastard!" Her voice was shaking and so was her arm as she lifted it weakly to strike out at him. Tears were flowing down her face but they were tears of fury and shock; he had taken something precious and beautiful and turned it into a dirty joke and she wanted to kill him. "You have no right...you have *no right*—"

He caught her flailing arm in a vicious grip and flung her back onto the bed. "By God, if I don't have the right, I'd like to know who does!" His fingers were digging into her wrist, hurting, and his face was a dark mask of fury. He gave her arm a shake and the bed bounced beneath the force of it; she did not have the strength to fight him as her own anger melted into despair. "How the hell do you think it makes me feel," he hissed into her face, "to know that while you were making love with me you were carrying another man's child?"

Silence. It echoed with the pulse of blood in her ears and the stream of his breath on her face. It seemed for an immeasurable time nothing moved, not a muscle or a current of air, not a thought wave or a molecule in the atmosphere around them. And then, as though a portrait had been painted for her, she was taken back two months into the past and she saw it all very clearly. He thought it was David's child. David Hampton, that long-ago ghost of her past, whom she had claimed to love and whose lover Seth thought she had been. He didn't know. Oh God, he did not know....

Her mouth opened on a silent cry, although Kelly wasn't sure whether it was of protest or relief. She brought her fist to her mouth to smother it and she tasted tears. Her face turned into the pillow for she could not look at him, she had to think. She was too tired to think, she was aching and confused and Seth did not know. "Please," she whispered thickly, almost on a sob, "I can't take any more now...please." The last was hardly audible, and the pillow beneath her face grew hot and damp.

Slowly the pressure on her arm eased. He stood. From very far away she heard the sound of his breathing. She could not look at him. "Stay here," he said curtly. "Don't get out of bed. I'm going for a walk."

His footsteps crossed the room, paused, and she thought he turned back. She was beyond caring. Then the door closed with a firm click and she was alone.

After a long time she turned over heavily and focused her eyes on the ceiling. Within her were conflicting feelings of numb acceptance and hysterical amusement. Seth thought it was *David's* child. All this time she had been so concerned about protecting him from the responsibility of fatherhood and it had not even occurred to him that *he* might truly be responsible. After all, no one got pregnant from just one time. That was when she almost laughed.

But then she found her mind working clearly and calmly, and she felt a determined strength return as she rationally looked at her options. Seth had every reason to believe the child belonged to David. After all, only weeks before, she had sworn to Seth an undying love for the actor, and she had given him every reason to believe they had been active lovers. If she tried to tell Seth differently now, he would not believe her, but of course she wouldn't tell him. This was his escape, a heaven-sent chance, the one way that he could survive knowing of her pregnancy without being harmed by it. And if he hated her for it, then hate her he must. It would be far better than spending the rest of his life under a weight of guilt and moral responsibility for an accident that was not his fault. Yes, it would be much better this way.

Susan opened the door cautiously and peeked in. "Are you all right? Seth practically ran me down at the front door and said I was to make sure you stayed in bed. Oh, my God." She came into the room and the concern on her face deepened to alarm as she took in Kelly's ravaged, tearstained face and stunned expression. "What happened? Seth looked like he'd seen a ghost and you— He found out, didn't he?" she concluded softly.

Kelly nodded and swung her feet over the side of the bed, taking a steadying breath as she braced herself for the dizziness to pass.

"He was upset?"

Again Kelly nodded and even managed a wry smile. "You could say that." She got to her feet somewhat shakily.

"Wait a minute." Susan came toward her. "Seth said—"

Kelly waved her away. "I'm all right. Just hungry."

"Maybe," Susan insisted, "I should bring you a tray in here. Seth didn't want you to get out of bed." Everyone was so used to taking Seth's word as law.

Kelly moved past her toward the kitchen.

"What did he say?" Susan asked quietly over roast beef sandwiches and ginger ale at the kitchen table.

Kelly had eaten most of her sandwich and was now feeding the remainder by carefully shredded bites to Fleetwood, who rested his paws on her lap and yowled impatiently when she dawdled. She shrugged and sipped her soda. "He was shocked" was all she could answer. She hated to lie and she was not very good at it, she always tried to stick as closely to the truth as possible so she would not forget what she had said. Did she really imagine she could embark with any success on this, the biggest deception of her life against the man she loved, who knew her better than any other person living?

Did she really have a choice?

"I take it," ventured Susan, "he wasn't very understanding."

Of course Susan could not know the real reason for his reaction, but even knowing the facts, Kelly had to defend him. "He's never dealt with anything like this before. It's a little outside his field."

"He takes everything so personally," agreed Susan with a sigh, and Kelly almost smiled.

Trish came in while they were clearing away lunch, and for a moment both of them started because they thought it might be Seth. They tried to hide their relief and disappointment as Trish launched into an ecstatic account of her weekend, how glamorous the city was, how wonderful Peter was, how she had won fifty dollars on a slot machine and had champagne for breakfast and how terrific Peter was; how they had had front-table seats for two spectacular shows and had hardly slept four hours between them in the past three days, and how fabulous Peter was.... Eventually she paused for breath, apparently sensing she was getting less than the full attention her exploits deserved from her audience, and she demanded, "Okay, what's wrong?"

In simple, concise sentences Susan explained what had transpired within the past few hours, and concluded, "Seth is giving Kelly a hard time."

Trish looked thoughtful for a moment, almost uncertain, and then she slipped her arm around Kelly's waist as they walked out of the kitchen. "This may not be the best time to tell you and I'm not sure whether you'll think it's good news or bad," she said, "but Peter and I are talking about—well, about living together."

Kelly stopped and looked at her, and Susan echoed her astonished exclamation. "You?" For a moment Kelly's own troubles receded in delight and amazement over her friend's announcement. "Why, that's wonderful, but, Trish! You were always so—so straitlaced and sensible. I never thought you'd be the one to go off and live with a man!"

Trish made a rather rueful face, and Kelly was suddenly reminded that the same could apply to her. Of the three of them Kelly would have certainly been voted Least Likely to Get Pregnant. *The things we do for love,* she thought, and for some reason the entire situation looked a little brighter. Trish was prepared to break the rules just as Kelly had done and it had brought her happiness. Perhaps there was hope for Kelly too.

Susan was teasing Trish and making jokes, but her excitement was as evident as Trish's. *How odd,* Kelly thought, as they all sat together on the sofa and the voices receded about her, *our lives are changing completely in ways we would have never thought about a few months ago ... and it all boils down to sex. Or does it?*

"Anyway," Trish was saying to Kelly, "this is all still in the talking stage, you understand. I'm going to be very careful about making a commitment like that and Peter is incredibly patient. But the thing is, Kelly, if it does work out—and I think it will"—her smile was secretive and content—"then my bedroom will be empty." When Kelly looked blank, she explained, "For the baby. You'll need the extra room, you know, and in case you were worried about that, this could be a solution."

Kelly was struck by two things. First, incredulity that in her secret worries and anxieties, bedroom space had never been one of her concerns. She had simply not let herself think that far ahead, that one day there would be an extra person beside her and that long before that day came she would have to find some place for the two of them to live. And secondly, there was an overwhelming gratitude and wonder that Trish had assumed she would stay here even after the baby's birth, that this was her *home*, and she wondered if, by any far stretch of the imagination, Seth could feel the same.

But she also knew something else. "Thanks, Trish," she said quietly, squeezing her hand, "but that won't help. You see—"

And just then Seth came in.

He must have walked for miles. He looked tired, and the denim shirt he had hastily pulled on over his jeans was crumpled and stained with perspiration, shirttail out, buttoned only to midchest. Still, only the fine edge of his anger seemed to have worn itself off, and the effort he was making to appear calm was painfully visible. His eyes were distracted and the lines around his mouth grim as he greeted Trish casually and inquired about her trip. His gaze kept flitting to Kelly and his posture was of tightly controlled energy, tense restlessness.

Trish summed up her weekend in three short sentences, which no one, least of all Seth, heard. By the time she had finished, all eyes were on Kelly, anxious and waiting, but Kelly's eyes were only upon Seth. Beyond the tension and the facade of control there she thought she saw something else. Was it sorrow, or hurt, or perhaps only a simple apology? She could not be sure, and every fiber of her being tightened in response to him, ready to capture any signal of unspoken communication, no matter how vague. Hoping desperately for some sign that he did not hate her, that he had forgiven her.

But he was very reserved as he said simply, "I think we have a conversation to finish." His glance flickered to Trish and Susan. "Would you rather do it privately?"

Kelly sensed, rather than saw, her friends tense for her defense, and she loved them for it. It was three women against a man, and their protective instincts bristled. They would not leave unless Kelly requested it. "No," she said with a faint smile. "There are no secrets in this house." She did not realize until after she had said it what a poor choice of words she had made.

"All right." Seth sat in the chair across from them, but he directed himself only to Kelly, and there might have been no one in the room but the two of them. His voice was very controlled, very emotionless. And so was his face. "First of all, I acted like a complete fool a while ago and I apologize. You don't need that kind of hassle, especially from me."

Kelly said nothing, and he went on mildly, "Now, I guess there are a couple of things I need to know. When is the baby due?"

She hesitated. If she told him that, he might be able to count back to the date of its conception and realize that David had been in England two weeks by then, but no, she was being overly dramatic. Two weeks was only two weeks and no one would ever know the difference, even if he did care to count. That was one more stroke of fortune to keep her secret safe. She answered, "January."

He nodded impersonally. "How's your health? What did the doctor say?"

"He said I'm fine," Kelly hedged.

A look of impatience crossed Seth's face, and he stood and crossed the room to the telephone. She twisted in her seat to watch him as he flipped through the address book and took the phone off the hook. "What are you doing?" she demanded.

"Getting a straight answer," he replied. "If not from you, then from your doctor."

"All right!" she admitted in exasperation, nervousness heightening her own impatience. "He said I shouldn't lose any more weight and that tension only makes the nausea worse and that my blood pressure is a little high. That's all."

He nodded, still completely expressionless, as he resumed his seat. Trish and Susan were like wary spectators at a mystery-thriller that had gotten bad reviews, reserving judgment but definitely prejudiced, waiting for the final act to save the show.

Seth said, "All right, it's obvious one of the first things you have to do is quit your job." Over her breath of protest he continued imperviously, "It's too strenuous and you're in no shape for it. Don't try to tell me it hasn't about killed you this past week. If you're going to do this thing, do it right."

"I'll manage," she returned curtly. "I need the money, and that's the only job I have."

He decided to leave that argument for a later date and move on to more important matters. "Knowing you," he continued coolly, "you haven't bothered to inform Hampton of this latest development. That's the first thing you're going to do tomorrow morning."

Susan could not sit still for this any longer. "Now,

you wait just a minute!'' she insisted angrily. "You can't just go around giving her orders like she was some kind of programmed robot! Quit your job, tell David," she mimicked. "It's her life!"

"That's right," Kelly managed somewhat more evenly, though her heart was racing and her breathing was rapid as she tried to think of some excuse, some way to put him off or get around this one. "I've decided not to tell David." God, what a smooth liar she was! If only her heart would stop pounding so painfully. "It's over between us, and this has nothing to do with him." At last a grain of truth! "My feelings are different now, and I—"

"I don't give a damn what your feelings are." His eyes were like ice. "You loved the man once enough to let him father your child, you can damn well find enough of that 'feeling' left over to marry him."

Trish gasped, "That's absurd! You can't ask her to marry a man she doesn't love when she is willing and wanting to raise this child on her own—"

"But she's not going to." Seth's eyes never left her face, and the hard shield there was so much like hatred that she wanted to cover her face and hide from it. "That man has a responsibility, moral and practical, and if you're not going to see that he faces it," Seth told her with deadly cold warning, "then I will."

Susan's and Trish's outraged defense of her rights blurred in Kelly's ear. She knew Seth meant it and he would certainly take matters into his own hands if she proved to be uncooperative. She was also aware that he was much too upset right now to try to reason with, much too determined and angry. Her mind was working in a cold panic as she realized she could not prevent him from calling David unless she admitted that the child was not his, and she needed time, time to try to find a way out of this mess of lies in which she had entangled herself.

"No, it's all right." Kelly's tired voice cut through the heated defense of women's rights and Seth's cool rebuttal. Kelly met his eyes as steadily as she could manage. "Seth is probably right," she said. "I'll do as he says."

Trish and Susan fell back, stunned and deflated, but not even a flicker of satisfaction crossed Seth's face. He looked suddenly worn and aged, and he dropped his eyes. "That's good," he said, and his voice was low, with an odd tone she could not quite decipher. It sounded very much like grief. "It's the best thing," he added, and as he stood abruptly to go into the kitchen Kelly was suddenly struck by the realization that he was trying to assure himself more than her.

A slow agony of despair filled her. Oh, God, how could this have happened to her? She loved him, but he was hurting and she could not comfort him. She loved him, and she was the cause of his pain; she needed him, and he was turning away from her. She loved him with all her heart and soul, but that wasn't helping either of them now.

Why couldn't it be simple? Why couldn't he sense how she felt? He had always been so easily able to read her mind, but to this, the most important matter of her entire life, he seemed to be completely blind. It was perhaps because he did not want to know. Because on a long ago, nightmarish morning in the desert he had made the rules very clear: He wanted her friendship, just as it had always been, and nothing more. Yet she had betrayed even that. And should she go to him now and say to him, "You are the man I love, the only one, and by the strangest coincidence, I am also going to have your baby"? No, she thought bleakly, it really was better this way.

For the next three days a sort of pall hung over the house, as Seth stayed strictly out of her way—or perhaps it was the other way around. She did not want another confrontation with him in which he would demand to know what she had done about contacting David, at least until he had cooled down somewhat. She needed time to decide what to tell him when he did ask, to find the courage for more lies or perhaps the simple truth—that she had no intention of marrying David Hampton now or ever. Either way, one thing was clear, as it had been from the beginning: She could not stay here much longer. She could not face that haunted, bitterly disappointed look in Seth's eyes every time he looked at her, and she certainly could not expect him to welcome a baby into the house. The boundaries of friendship would be extended just so far. And quite simply she did not know how much longer she could go on lying to him.

On Wednesday afternoon Kelly was the first one home. She was gradually adjusting to the demands being placed upon her body by her job, but still at the end of each day she was exhausted. On that one point she could not argue with Seth: She did need to find a less strenuous form of work, but it was too late in the season to start looking for one now. She could surely hold out for two more months, and according to all she had read upon the subject, the sickness should pass after the third month of pregnancy. After that it wouldn't be so bad.

She changed into a loose caftan, and she smiled at her reflection in the mirror. By fall she would be filling out the folds of this dress, which now clung to the curves of her still-slim figure, emphasizing the new fullness of her breasts and the amazingly flat plane of her abdomen. She found herself impatient for that event. She knew she was pregnant, she felt pregnant, and she was secretly eager for the changes in her body to begin advertising her condition to the world. Why should she be ashamed of a child who was conceived in love and whom she would welcome into the world with the same deep, abiding emotion she felt for his father? Surely when there was love no problem was insurmountable.

She poured herself a glass of milk and took it out onto the deck where, with Fleetwood purring contentedly in her lap, she lay back in the chaise longue and watched the sun turn the distant treetops a glowing chartreuse. The breeze fanned her cheek and ruffled the hem of the dark print dress about her bare ankles, and the stillness of the canyon settled over her like a benediction. In these moments of privacy she could forget the harsh truths of the real world and find deep within herself a peace, a contentment, to be alive and to be carrying Seth's child.

Kelly heard a sound inside the house, and she turned as Seth opened the sliding glass door and came out onto the deck. On his face were emotions only Kelly could read, for behind the thin veneer of casualness there was wariness, a grim determination, a vague hint of distress mingled with uncertainty, and, so far beneath the other emotions that she could not be certain she interpreted it correctly at all, there was a glint of excitement in his eyes. She tensed, because she knew this was the confrontation she had dreaded and because, if she had read his mood correctly, she knew it was going to be a volatile one.

He looked for a moment as though he might say something, but instead he glanced at the open magazine he held in his hand, and then, as though that item could do his talking for him, he tossed it into her lap. Fleetwood gave him a startled glare before jumping to the floor with an air of great injury. Kelly winced and rubbed her thigh where cat's claws had registered his indignation before departing, and then she took up the magazine.

It was a popular publication of the movie industry,

opened to the middle section. Kelly saw immediately the item to which Seth had meant to draw her attention. It was a picture of David Hampton with a pretty young woman, and the caption read: "David Hampton with bride." She scanned the first line of the paragraph underneath, "David Hampton, star of..." And no more. She stared at it, waiting for emotions that did not come.

She should have been hurt. Perhaps for Seth's sake, she should have feigned hurt. But in fact she felt nothing—except, perhaps, a vague sense of goodwill toward a man against whom she bore no grudge and who deserved to find happiness. David Hampton belonged to another life, there was no room for even the shadow of him to touch her present one.

She returned the magazine to Seth, her face completely expressionless, and she suddenly understood the meaning behind those tangled emotions she had read on his face. This was the answer to her most immediate crisis, and the relief that swept through her was very close to euphoria. She would not have to lie to Seth or fight with him about David's responsibility. How could he expect her to marry a man who was already married? It was as though the gods had swooped down to save her, and she uttered a silent, generally directed prayer of gratitude. As long as Seth was resigned to the fact of her single motherhood, perhaps they need not fight about anything at all, perhaps she could even count once again on his support and his help, and perhaps they could even part friends, although from the dark, tense expression in his eyes that possibility seemed at the moment extremely remote.

He said shortly, "You don't seem to be exactly torn up about it."

"I told you," she replied evenly, "It's over between us."

"Not exactly," he returned dryly, and his eyes swept

her figure in a meaningful way that made her suppress a shudder of repulsion and dread. And then suddenly he burst out in an explosion of frustration and impatience, "Good God, woman, I don't understand you! It wasn't even three months ago that you sat right here and cried your heart out about Hampton being the only man you would ever love and now you feel *nothing*? You're carrying his child, for God's sake, and you feel *nothing* for him? Don't you see what he has done to your life? Don't you care?"

She was battered by the sharp pellets of truth and untruth and she shrank beneath them. Even if she dared try, she could never make Seth believe that she had not really loved David after all, and that the child was not his. It hurt her to have Seth think she was so fickle and coldhearted, but she had no choice. The despite she saw in his eyes wounded her as effectively as any sharp instrument could have done, twisting in her chest and bringing stinging tears to her eyes, but she determined to rally against it. Her voice was heavy with a sarcasm she did not feel as she returned, "What would you have me do then—insist that he make an honest woman of me? It's a little bit late for that, isn't it?" She gestured sharply to the magazine in his hand and then jerked her head away so that he could not see her blink back the tears and misinterpret the reason for them.

"No, dammit, I just want you to look at this thing realistically!" He tossed the magazine toward a chair and missed, and it skidded along the deck and landed against the rail, where the wind riffled its pages with an impatient, lonely sound.

She swallowed hard and felt tension settle into her shoulders and neck as she turned to face him. "Look, Seth," she said as calmly as she could manage, "I tried to tell you before—I'm going to have this baby on my own, there's no law that says I have to be married to do it. Thousands of women manage every year. It's not completely unheard of, you know. I have a career that pays enough for two if I'm careful and it has the extra advantage of giving me summers off so that I can be with the baby more than most mothers. Of course there will have to be baby-sitters at first, but after he starts school it will really be an ideal situation."

She was puzzled by the slow bitterness that crossed his face, by the way he lowered himself with utmost care to the chair next to her and by the deadly calm in his tone as he said, "Well, now, you have it all figured out, don't you? Just like in a fairy tale. Little Miss Liberation meets her just end through hard work, determination, and guts. I think it's time someone acquainted you with a few not-so-pleasant facts." She hated it when he spoke to her like that, and she flickered her eyes away uncomfortably. He went on in the same patient, exhaustively reasonable voice one might use when explaining a difficult concept to a not-so-bright child. "So you think you have job security, do you? Let's just really consider that for a minute. Even you have to admit you can't keep up this pace much longer, not unless you want to end up in the hospital several months too soon. And what about when you start to lose your figure? You won't exactly be a walking advertisement for the benefits of your salon then, will you?"

"That's just for a couple of months," she interrupted uncomfortably. "I'll be fine for the rest of the summer, and then I'll go back to school."

"Will you?" His smile was very cold. "Check your contract, lady, especially the fine print. I wouldn't be a bit surprised if you found a morals clause tucked away in there somewhere. This is the public school system, after all, and do we really want unwed mothers keeping our kids out of trouble when the teen-age pregnancy rate is at an all-time high? Be serious!"

She stared at him, feeling her color drain into a cold

wash of emptiness. How could she have been so stupid? How *could* she? She hadn't even thought of that. And California was one of the most liberal states, if that were true here what chance did she have getting a job anywhere else? Her mind was racing, desperately ticking off options. Parochial schools wouldn't even consider her, and the chances of finding a position with a modern, independently governed private school were almost nil, even if she did have three or four years to wait for an opening. And what else was she qualified for? Oh, God, she thought numbly, *Oh, God!*

For the first time expression flickered in his eyes as he saw her reaction, but he went on ruthlessly, "Moral aspects aside, remember your specialty. You have one of the few professions in the world for which a woman has to be physically qualified, and you don't see too many pregnant coaches walking around. Face it, kid, you're out of work."

*No,* she thought dully. *I'm pregnant, unmarried,* and *out of work. There's a difference.* Oh, God, Seth was right, she had been living in a dream world, she had been deceiving herself into thinking she could make it on her own, and what was she going to do? "What am I going to do?"

She was unaware that she had whispered it out loud until her eyes focused on Seth, and she saw him staring at her thoughtfully. She could not read what was in his face and her mind was too filled with desperate, despairing, and dead-end thoughts to even try. Yet she lifted her chin defiantly and she told him, "I'm not going to have an abortion."

Swift surprise crossed his face, and then harsh anger, which was subdued in the deceptively mild tone of his voice. "You're damn right you're not. You just remember this was your mistake and there is no easy way out. You've gone this far and you're damn well going to see it through because there's another life at stake besides

your own, now, and I don't want to hear any more talk
about abortion.''

Mistake, easy way out! That was all it was to him, an
unfortunate event, an accident, a complication, and he
could no more understand her feelings about the child
that was growing inside her than a boulder in the field,
nor even try. Swift angry tears stung her eyes once
again and she said sharply, ''I didn't ask for your opinion!''

''Well, you're going to get it.'' He got up and walked
over to the rail, his back to her. It was a long time before he spoke, and when he did, it was very quietly,
very firmly. ''It seems to me you only have one option,'' he said distinctly without turning. ''And that's to
marry me.''

For a moment even her heart stopped beating. For a
moment all she heard were the words, not the tone in
which they were said or the circumstances under which
the offer was made. For a moment she imagined it
could be real, and a fleeting ecstasy whipped through
her with the response, Yes! Oh, yes! Above all things
that was what she wanted, to be with him, to be loved
by him.

But she could only stammer, ''M-marry you?''

''Why not?'' He turned, and his face was harsh.
''I'm going to be accused of it anyway.''

And that was when the foundation of her entire
world seemed to be pulled out from under her feet. She
stared at him. ''You—that's all you care about isn't it?''
she said weakly. ''It's a matter of pride.'' His pride, not
hers. That was why he had been so upset from the beginning, because, living in the situation they did, it
would be only natural for outsiders to assume that he
was responsible for the pregnancy of the woman who
shared his roof—and not only outsiders, but even close
acquaintances who had never been quite convinced
that Seth could share rent with three women and not

also share their beds. That rankled him. He had always been so careful to protect them, to preserve their reputations. "All you're worried about is your reputation!" she said dully, but there was a far note of rising hysteria deep in her voice.

"*My* reputation!" he shot back. "It's yours that needs worrying about! What do you think people are going to say when they find out? Your friends, your students, the people you work with? Your parents? Doesn't that bother you at all?"

It bothered her, more than she wanted to admit, but now that was the least of her problems. She shook her head in carefully restrained incredulity. "And marrying you is supposed to solve that? For God's sake, Seth—" Here her voice almost broke with the nugget of quivering rage and pain that had begun inside her. "Be serious!"

"I am serious," he told her, and there was nothing in his face to deny it. "It would solve your financial problems, your social problems, and it would give your baby a name. It's the only sensible thing to do."

Sensible. *Sensible.* She had to stand, to move around, to somehow give vent to the incredulity and despair that was bubbling like molten lava within her. She paced tightly back and forth, twisting her hands together, restraining hasty words. And still, somewhere far in the back of her mind, was the need to find some way to make it work. This was the one thing that she wanted more than anything else, her one chance for happiness, tainted because of the spirit in which it was offered. She loved him, she was carrying his child, he had asked her to marry him—what could be simpler? She wanted to marry him, but not like this. Dear God, not like this.

At last she turned to him, unclasped her hands with a forceful effort, and in a tone almost matching his for its reasonableness, demanded, "What about Melissa?"

He looked momentarily startled, as though that were one contingency he had overlooked. There was a moment of hesitance almost too brief to be noticed, and then he decided, facing her squarely, "We're not necessarily talking about a lifetime commitment here. If you like, we'll agree to stay married only until after the baby is born and then divorce. I'll pay you support, of course," he added. "I can afford it, and it's the only legal way."

Support! Legal! This conversation was straight out of a nightmare, she could not believe they were having it. She thought she knew him so well, but he was a stranger, talking about sensible solutions and divorce and child support and legality. Her heart was thudding coldly in her ears and it seemed to shake her entire body, but her voice was clear and her expression unflinching as she pursued, "And in the meantime? While we're married?"

Again only a second of hesitance, and then he squared his shoulders deliberately and told her, "I won't see anyone else in the meantime, if that's what you want."

She could not take it anymore. Something within her just seemed to crack and spill forth all the venomous hurt that had festered within her from the wounds he had inflicted. "How very generous of you!" she cried. She was shaking and her voice had a high note of hysteria in it. "I can't tell you how much I appreciate your offer, *Mr.* Mason, but I won't have you throwing yourself in front of any speeding trains for my sake! I don't need your pity or your noble gestures of self-sacrifice."

"Dammit, it's not a sacrifice!" He caught her arm and whirled her around, and his eyes were blazing. "You're the one who's determined to play the martyr in this thing, and I'm not going to let you!"

"Let me go!" she screamed at him and gave her arm

a vicious jerk. The last thing she saw was the fury in his eyes before his face came down on hers.

She was crushed against him in one swift move, she lost her breath beneath the cruel force of his mouth. For a moment she was rigid, her fingers digging into his arms, and their bodies were locked together with the hard stance of combatants—but it was only for a moment. Because suddenly there was urgency in the way his lips moved against hers, and desperation in the tightening of his arms around her. Her lips parted helplessly on a cry, but one of welcome, not of protest, and her arms slipped around him, holding him, just holding him. In the depths of his kiss she discovered all she had ever wanted from him—a need for her that was as great as hers for him, a tenderness, a fierce protection, a possessiveness—or perhaps it was only that she was discovering simply what she wanted to find.

The heat from his face flamed in hers and the desperate hunger with which he took her lips was dizzying. And she welcomed him, clinging to him, letting herself for a moment be blinded by the ecstatic happiness that soared within her, imagining it was true. She loved him, she wanted to be with him like this forever, and to give to him forever; she loved him and she wanted to believe, for just that moment, that he could really be hers. Her hands were against the back of his neck, hot and unsteady, feeling the texture of coarse skin and hard muscles beneath her fingers, tugging at silky curls. She remembered every inch of him with a powerful yearning that made her weak. His hands grew restless as his kiss gentled, becoming more leisurely and exploratory, tantalizing her with his tongue and his breath; his fingers exploring the curves of her buttocks intimately, possessively, definitely sexual now, and she knew vaguely and from far away she should stop it, for both their sakes, but she did not want to. Just like before, she did not want to.

And then his hand moved upward, along the curve of her waist and the delicate indentation of her ribs, seeking her breast, and the entire world was shaking with the reverberations of her heart. She felt his soft gasp as the fullness of her breast met his palm, the instinctive cupping pressure, the urgent demand of his mouth upon hers. It was right and it was good, for she belonged to him, body and soul, just as she always had.

And then abruptly, he dragged his mouth away, leaving a searing path of breath across her face and a shocked emptiness in the core of her stomach as he whispered viciously against her neck, "Good God, what am I doing?"

His hands gripped her waist, pushing her away, and she could feel the trembling in the muscles of his arms even above the shuddering of her own body. His face looked haggard, his breathing was ragged, and his eyes were filled with self-contempt. She felt sick. He repeated with low violence, bunching his hands into impotent fists against his thighs, "What the *hell* do I think I'm doing?"

And then there was a sound from inside, a call and a movement. Seth flung himself away from her and crossed abruptly to the other side of the deck as the door opened and Susan came out.

## Chapter Eleven

It was one thirty in the morning. Kelly was sitting on the sofa, her knees drawn up to her chin, her long pink plissé nightgown pulled down over her legs. Her hair was loose and gleaming, covering her shoulders and her bare arms like a heavy shawl, emphasizing the delicacy and the whiteness of her face. The television set was on before her, but she was not watching it. Her dark brows were drawn together in concentration, her eyes troubled and foggy with thoughtfulness. She was thinking about Seth.

He had hardly said a word all evening. Over dinner he was tense and preoccupied, and directly afterward he went to his room to read, emerging only once to bid them all a general good-night shortly after ten o'clock. Several times during dinner his eyes had met Kelly's and what she saw there was an uneasiness, a regret or an apology, and Kelly had always immediately shifted her gaze.

She tried to understand his behavior since he had found out about the baby, and once she tried, it really wasn't very hard. He felt threatened. The secure lifestyle he had built for them all was in an upheaval because of Kelly's situation. For the first time in their acquaintance something was coming between them, and in believing that the child she carried belonged to an old lover, he had lost respect for her. If she had felt as though he had become a stranger in these last few days, what must he think of her? He could not understand how she could be so heartless regarding the father of her child because he did not really know who the father was. He had never known her to be a woman of loose morals and had never expected it of her, but now, because of the circumstances and her desperate need to protect him, she was being forced to act like one. This baby, and her feelings for it, made her separate from him for the first time since they had known one another, he could sense she was building a new life for herself and it was one in which he could not share. He felt betrayed, not knowing how much a part of her new life he truly was and would always be.

And this afternoon. She could not forget the disgust in his face when he had realized that he wanted to make love to a woman who was pregnant with another man's child. He had wanted to make love to her, but still he was ashamed of it. He had offered her marriage in a noble gesture of misplaced loyalty and he would never know how much that hurt. And she had wanted to accept even as she had hated him for turning her secret dreams into a travesty. God, how could it be so complicated? How could she love him so much and understand him so well and still have made such a mess of their lives?

But he was right. She had big problems to face and very little time in which to find a solution. Like a cat chasing its tail, it ran around and around in her mind in a sort of dry panic. Money. A job. A place to live. All desperate necessities with no glimmer of salvation in sight. Why couldn't it be simple? Why couldn't she just live with him and love him and let him parent the child he had biologically fathered? Why couldn't she ignore the fact that he did not love her in return and forget the shame she saw in his eyes every time he recalled their one night of passion? Why must she put his own needs, for freedom, for exoneration from guilt, and even for another woman, above her own? Because she loved him, that was all. She loved him, and his needs would always come before hers. It was that simple.

Yet he had volunteered to take legal and financial responsibility for a child he sincerely believed was not his own. A gesture of friendship, of protection, of guilt—or a last-ditch attempt to salvage his own reputation and piece together the fabric of morality and trust under which they had all lived these past years? Perhaps no more than a chivalrous instinct that had no place in a world that had outgrown chivalry. She did not know. She was so very tired, and she could not see any way out. She only knew she could not accept Seth's offer, even if it had been meant with only the kindest intentions. Her love had been dragged through so much rejection, humiliation, and pain already. She simply could not face a marriage of convenience to the man she loved, a marriage that would end in seven months so that he could pursue his own happiness.

But she didn't know what she was going to do. She simply didn't know.

"What are you watching?"

She started at Seth's voice behind her, then quickly regained her control. She should have expected this. *"Dark Victory,"* she answered, lowering her legs and curling them beneath her, pulling the thin fabric of her nightgown over her bare feet.

He came around the sofa to sit beside her, and he looked calm, genuinely relaxed for the first time in almost a week. He had been to bed, for he was wearing nothing but a short brown robe that did not cover his bare knees and was open to midchest, and his hair was rumpled. But he had not slept. There was no sign of fogginess in his eyes; they were slightly bloodshot and strained, and faint shadows stretched toward his cheekbones. She wondered for the first time whether he had slept at all since discovering her news, and a sudden ache tightened within her to think she had been the cause of his distress.

He glanced at the television and, in a moment, back to her. "You're not crying," he commented.

For a moment she was confused. "What? Oh, it hasn't gotten to the sad part yet."

His smile was gentle as he pointed out, "It gets to the sad part right after the first commercial." He leaned forward and switched off the set. When he turned back to her, his expression was serious, she could see the resolution building in his eyes, and she tensed herself for the conflict. "Kelly," he said quietly, "I know I made a mess of things this afternoon...." For just a moment his eyes shifted away, the familiar sign of shame and regret. "But maybe now we can talk about this thing more reasonably."

She could not take any more of his reason, his sensibility. Not when her heart was breaking and her mind was aching with monolithic problems and undiscovered solutions. She said swiftly, calmly, and with the determination born of a resolution formed deep within the core of her, "I won't marry you, Seth. I'm not going to do that to your life or—or to mine. I'm not going to make a mockery of—of an institution I was raised to respect." As soon as she said it she knew she was leaving herself wide open for biting sarcasm, but she rushed on, not giving him a chance, "That's no solution at all, it's just another problem. The baby would be better off with just one parent than two in a pseudomarriage, playing house and marking time until a legal divorce came through." She added with a proud lift of her chin, "And you know me better than to think I would ever accept money from you, no matter what the courts said, so if that was the only reason—"

Sharp impatience crossed his face and he shook his head in exasperation, as though completely unable to comprehend her naivete. "Kelly, don't you see money is just part of it? Will you for God's sake just stop a minute and think of what you're doing to your life, to the baby's? That child doesn't deserve what you're condemning him to—the stigma, the name-calling, the insecurity, always feeling like a freak, second-rate. If you think you can protect it from that, you're burying your head in the sand. There's no amount of mother love in the world that can make up for knowing that your father didn't even care enough about you to marry your mother."

She stared at him. He spoke so violently, so intensely, that she was completely taken aback. But she defended, "It doesn't have to be that way. No one ever has to know—"

"That's a great way to start a relationship with your kid," he shot back, "by lying to it! And I'll tell you something else—those kinds of lies never work. They're always found out."

For a moment she floundered. "Then—then, I'll prepare him for it somehow. I know children can be cruel, but he doesn't have to be hurt if he's prepared. When he's old enough to understand—"

"You're never old enough to understand," he said shortly.

She was growing frustrated herself. He was trying to back her into a corner again, throwing problems at her to which there were no solutions. "You can't guarantee that it's going to be that bad!" she insisted. "This child will be growing up in a whole new world, people change and prejudices die. You can't know—"

He looked at her. His eyes were hard and his face was grim. "I know," he said quietly, "because I've lived through it." She caught her breath with a jolt of cold shock at the brief, remembered pain that flickered across his features, and he went on, "My parents were never married. The story I eventually got was that my father was in the navy and he was killed before they could get married." He shrugged. "Who knows? My mother did her best, she tried to keep me with her for a few years, but it was too much for her. I went to live with my grandmother. For a while I saw my mother off and on, or got letters from her... but then even those stopped." He stood suddenly and began to pace the room, his hands thrust deep into the pockets of his robe. "I started school, and you're right, kids can be cruel. You learn to fight real quick when you're a bastard brat that nobody wants. Illegitimate. Not legal. Outcast. Unwanted. Sometimes not even real. You learn to fight and you learn to lie and you spend half your life daydreaming about the parents you never knew and the other half trying to be the fastest, the smartest, the strongest, the best at everything to prove to everyone, especially to yourself, that you're *somebody,* not just an accident." And then he turned to look at her, and the pain in his face tore at her like a living thing, a pain she could feel as surely as if it had been her own. "Do you really think I'm going to stand by and let that happen to your kid? *Do you*?"

The agony she shared with him shone like tears in her eyes. For the first time she understood—really understood—why her pregnancy had affected him so deeply, what torturous memories must have prompted his irrational behavior. She wanted to run to him and put her arms around him and promise him that nothing would ever hurt him again. But she said brokenly, "I...can't, Seth. I can't marry you for that reason. I—I don't regret the baby and I don't think it's a mistake for it to be born, but if I married you, it would be a mistake. I—I can't live"—she dropped her eyes, and her voice was barely more than a whisper—"in a marriage without love."

The silence around them was very thick. She could feel his eyes upon her, scrutinizing her, she could sense the workings of his mind as he considered and rejected various arguments and assessed her determination. And then at last he expelled a long, tense breath and he laced his fingers together into one tight fist of subdued frustration and brought it slowly to his chin. His eyes upon her were like instruments of torture, accusing and condemning and boring right into her soul. "Then what," he demanded, "are you going to do?"

And this was the hardest part. To face with him, and for the first time to herself, the inevitable. "I suppose," she managed in a voice so soft it was barely audible, a reflection of her own intense rejection of the only possible solution, "I'll have to go home to my parents."

The hiss of his breath was angry; he took one short step away from her and then whirled suddenly. She prepared herself for the unleashing of a full-blown tirade, but somehow, after a long time and with a great effort, he controlled himself. He came back to sit beside her, so close that his bare knees brushed hers, and though the contact sent a shiver through her, he hardly seemed to notice. His expression was grim, determined, tensely controlled. "Look," he said tightly, "I don't know your father but what I know about him I don't like. If he's anything like the colonels I served under, I can pretty damn well predict his reaction when he discovers a pregnant daughter on his doorstep. If he made a federal case out of your moving in here, what do you think he'll do with this little piece of news? You can't be thinking at all, Kelly! He'll make your life pure hell—if he doesn't marry you off to the first male under sixty he can get to stand still at gunpoint. And even after he tortures you with sermons and lectures and every kind of mental cruelty known to man there's no guarantee at all that he'll help you out—in fact I'd be very surprised if he did. Kelly, you've got enough to deal with and your health isn't all that fantastic as it is, you are not going to put yourself through that. I won't let you, by God, if I have to put a padlock on your door and feed you through a crack in the wall for the next seven months you are *not* going home to that!''

She shook her head, tears of exhaustion and helplessness burning her eyes because she knew he was right. "I don't have any choice!" she cried. "Do you think I want to? But what else can I do?''

"You'll stay here," he said calmly.

She leaned her head back and closed her eyes against despair. One tear crept onto her temple but she swallowed determinedly, reaching for courage as a drowning man grasps at bobbing flotsam. "I can't afford to stay here," she said distinctly, and the sound of her own voice, so steady and sure, strengthened her. She opened her eyes. "You were right this afternoon—I haven't been looking at things realistically. The money I have saved won't even cover the medical bills and no one is going to hire a pregnant woman. Until after the baby is born I won't be able to work and I—"

"You'll stay here," he repeated. "I told you, I have money, I can afford—''

"No!" she cried, and once again tears burned her eyes. "I told you I don't want your pity and I won't have your charity! Will you please just—''

"Kelly, for God's sake!" His hands gripped her balled-up fists with a sudden ferocity; there was insistence in his eyes and pain, and a deeply subdued pleading. "Don't you know what this is doing to me, seeing you like this? Why won't you let me help?'' She shook her head numbly, and his hands tightened on hers with such a force that her nails dug into her palms and she felt surely her fingers would be crushed. "You are not going to leave me!" he said lowly. Frustration and a vaguely defined need warred in his eyes. "I haven't gone through all this hell these past months ever since we—just so that you could walk out on me—" He broke off, but the pressure on her hands only increased, and she caught her breath in cautious wonder as he dropped his eyes. When he looked at her again, a veneer of calm had replaced whatever raw emotion she had glimpsed so briefly in his eyes. "I care about you," he said simply. "You're not leaving."

She looked at him, sudden overwhelmed by wonder and the desperate need for him. Far back in her mind a voice whispered, *Tell him. Tell him.* All her defenses and all those eminently practical reasons for her secret were wiped away and she simply wanted him to know. I love you, Seth, she thought. I loved you before I ever knew what physical love was, before our child was conceived. I love you and we share the life that's growing inside of me. It isn't a stranger to you but a part of you and it can't come between us because it is a part of *us*. What would he say? What would he feel? *Tell him, tell him.* She whispered, "Seth, I—" And she could go no further.

His eyes sharpened with sudden intensity, searching her face. "Yes?" he insisted softly. "What is it?"

*Tell him.*

"I—" She dropped her eyes. "It's nothing," she said, and she quickly pulled her hands away and left the room.

On Sunday morning, Trish made the announcement: The decision was final and she was moving in with Peter that very afternoon.

Seth gave her a skeptical look that was more teasing than disapproving. "What's the rush? Afraid you might change your mind?"

And Susan protested, "No, no, you can't just run off like that without even giving us a chance for a good-bye party! That's not fair!"

Seth looked thoughtful for a moment, and then decided, "So since when do we need notice to throw a party? Call your fellows, ladies, and have them meet us at the beach in an hour. And, Susy," he told her with a wink, "since your date is the richest, he's bringing the champagne."

Something had changed about Seth over the past few days. Since that midnight conversation with Kelly in which so many emotions had been bared, he seemed calmer, more relaxed, almost resigned. There was no more sign of the distress that had lurked just below the surface, no more pressure or demands. It was as though a decision had been made, a solution resolved, and a peace found—and Kelly was afraid he had simply resigned himself to losing her, as a housemate and a friend.

In many ways he was just like his old self, and the turmoil that had split the house over the past weeks evaporated as though it had never been. They spent more time together, in the evenings over Monopoly or cards or simply sitting around watching television together, as though they all sensed the breakdown of the family structure they had shared for so long and were determined to take advantage of what they still had for as long as possible. Seth even stayed home with Kelly on Friday and Saturday nights while Trish and Susan had dates, and never once tried to lead her into a personal conversation or another confrontation of her problems. It was just like old times, only in some ways better. He referred to her pregnancy casually and without reticence, and there was no longer accusation in his eyes when he looked at her. In ways so subtle they were almost instinctual in nature, he made his concern for her and his support of her known, gently insisting that she eat balanced meals and rest before dinner, effortlessly engaging her in light conversation when the moods of thoughtfulness and anxiety threatened to turn into depression. Once when he was cleaning out his jacket pockets she happened to notice he tossed away an almost new package of cigarettes, and when she commented he replied casually, "I read somewhere that second-hand cigarette smoke is bad for an unborn baby's health." And then he grinned. "I just needed a good excuse to quit." She felt warm, sheltered, and cared for—all the things she had always wanted from him, only it was too late. She knew she could not stay.

Often she would feel his eyes upon her and turn suddenly to discover an expression there she had never seen before—deeper than tenderness, intensely thoughtful, more sincere than simple concern—and she always turned away quickly from the pain that look caused her. She simply couldn't stay. She knew now she could never keep her secret from him, loving him so deeply, needing him so desperately. She would not have him tied to her by a sense of moral obligation, she simply could not accept him on those terms and she could not do that to his life. She wanted to treasure all the good things of their relationship and remember it just the way it was now.

An impromptu party was no chore to them. They simply packed food, drinks, charcoal grill, and beach blankets into the Jeep and departed. Susan's senator was spending almost every weekend in town now, and he was delighted to be included. Peter did not object to postponing the chore of moving in favor of a celebration, but Kelly had to inquire of Seth, "Where's Melissa?"

He gave her a rather odd look and replied, "You're my date for the day, okay?"

It occurred to her that Seth had not seen Melissa since the day he had found out about Kelly's pregnancy. She wondered in a cold dread if Seth had told Melissa about his housemate's condition, and she had leaped to the wrong conclusion, and Kelly knew she would never forgive herself if she had been the cause of Seth's losing the woman he loved. Yet far away an irrational little voice, perhaps prompted by jealousy, assured her that if Melissa had been that narrow-minded and distrustful she really didn't deserve Seth at all.

The beach was crowded on Sunday afternoon, but it was a pleasant cacophony of bright swimsuits and noisy volleyball games and splashing children, the smell of suntan oil and lighter fluid blending pungently with the salt air. Under a blinding blue sky the sea sparkled and rolled, and for the first time in weeks, perhaps months, Kelly felt the burden of anxiety lift from her and she felt free, unfettered, and perfectly happy. On a day like this no one had any business borrowing trouble from the future.

The men carried down the coolers and hampers of food, and then, at Seth's insistence, the other two couples went for a swim while he and Kelly set up the grill. They laughed and joked together just as they had always done, he teased her with sand crabs and lobster pincers and she threatened to throw sand in his face, and they generally enjoyed themselves and each other's company with as much enthusiasm and as little inhibition as the group of preschoolers who raced around their mother's blanket in the spot next to them. And then Seth sat back on his heels, his eyes sparkling with the golden light of the reflected sun, and he said simply, "You look gorgeous."

Kelly laughed and tingled with pleasure. Over peach-colored shorts she wore a collarless long-sleeved white muslin shirt. Its clinging material, close to transparency, outlined her figure and met the cuffs of her shorts. She wore her hair tied loosely at the nape of her neck and the constant breeze kept it in disarray, tickling her face and fluttering around her shoulders. She felt the sun on her face and the sea in her eyes and she felt beautiful, with the kind of deep happiness that comes from the inside. She wished this day never had to end.

"I've heard pregnancy does that to women," Seth added thoughtfully. "I never believed it before."

She shrugged and looked away shyly toward the hot orange flames of the blazing grill. "Not necessarily pregnancy," she said. "I'm just happy, to be here with you."

As she glanced at him there was a sudden quickening in his eyes, a preparation for saying something very important, but just then the other four joined them, laughing and dripping water, and she was never to know what it was.

Kelly had never met Susan's senator, whose first name was Carl, before, and she was impressed with him. It was obvious, however, that he and Seth had already met, probably at some length, and Kelly wondered in amusement whether Carl had passed Seth's inspection as easily as Peter had. And then she decided he must have or he would not have been here today. He was a rather studious young man who was contrarily very easygoing and possessed of a quiet, gentle humor, the perfect contrast to Susan's effervescent nature. And from the first moment she saw the two of them together Kelly knew that they were quite deeply in love. It was in nothing they said or did, but in the aura they exuded—tranquillity and adoration, a sort of exclusive interpersonal communication—something that could not be defined, and was perhaps recognizable only to someone who had known it herself. They were perfect for each other; Susan seemed to know the exact words to say to make him smile and he was the only person Kelly had ever known who could actually exert a calming influence over Susan. She was happy for them.

While Susan was busily advising Seth on the proper way to make hamburgers, an argument which had been going on between them for as long as Kelly could remember, and Peter and Trish were quietly engaged in making plans of their own, Kelly found herself momentarily alone with Carl Apling. His affectionate glance went from Susan to Seth, and then he smiled at Kelly. "How long have you two been married?" he inquired.

Kelly was startled. "You mean Seth? We're not married."

He looked uncomfortable and apologetic. "I'm sorry, I just assumed—Susan never said, and just watching the two of you together it looked as though you had been married for a long time. Not just lovers, you know, but— I'm sorry," he apologized again. "It's none of my business."

But that was how she felt, Kelly realized slowly, when she was with Seth. It was how it had always been. As though they had been together forever, and she tried to push away the cloud of sorrow that reminded her it must soon come to an end.

And then Carl said, "You're Susan's best friend, aren't you?"

Kelly smiled a little sadly. "We're all best friends."

"I was wondering...." He seemed to be working up his courage for something. "How do you think Susan would feel about moving to Sacramento?"

Kelly could not hide her surprise, but she was also amused by his earnesty. "Why, Senator," she teased, "what are your intentions?"

He relaxed into a smile. "Strictly honorable," he assured her. "In fact, they couldn't be more so. You see, what I had in mind was marriage."

Kelly's eyes fell on Susan, who was still berating Seth spiritedly as he lifted his hands in helpless surrender and walked away. She was happy for her friend, and excited, and she knew it was the right thing. "Ask her," she encouraged.

"I intend to," he replied, and he glanced around ruefully at the chaotic activity upon the beach, "as soon as we have a little more privacy."

Seth grasped Kelly's hands and pulled her to her feet. "Come on, honey, help me get some exercise. We'll leave the cooking"—he cast a derisive look over his shoulder toward Susan—"to the expert."

"Seth," Kelly said, glancing back to see Carl get to his feet and start toward Susan, "he's going to ask Susan to marry him! Can you imagine that? Our Susan, the wife of a politician!"

"I can imagine it," he agreed idly. "I've been expecting it for some time."

She stared at him. "I had no idea!"

"You've had other things on your mind," he reminded her.

First Trish, now Susan.... And through the happiness she felt for her friends a slow sorrow began to creep. The day of bright colors and reverberating promise seemed suddenly to be a time for mourning, a time of good-byes and changes, and there was grief for all the times they had shared and would never share again, for the life they had known which had outgrown its time. "Oh, Seth," she said sadly, "it's all falling apart, isn't it? We're breaking up."

He closed his hand lightly and warmly around hers. "We're finding our own lives," he agreed. "It's not a bad thing, Kelly."

But it was. The others were going off to the promise of happiness and love; she was leaving her only love behind. And, just as she carried a living part of him within her, she would leave with him the only part of her that had ever lived—her heart. Oh, she had wanted so badly to keep this day perfect and unspoiled, to remember, out of the horror of the past weeks, one moment that was shining and pure and encapsulated all the good times they had known together. But she couldn't avoid the inevitable; it dogged her like a persistent shadow, and she must somehow make him see that she must leave without hurting him too much.

And, surprisingly, he gave her the opening she needed. "You never told me," he said, "what you want—a girl or a boy?"

She smiled to herself. Already she had begun to think of the child within her as a full-fledged person, and its gender was definitely male. He would have his father's eyes and curly hair and, perhaps, if such things could be inherited, his sense of humor and even his stubborn streak. She said, "A boy, definitely."

"Girls are much more fun," he objected. "I'd rather have a girl."

It was odd, the way he said that. As though it were his right to have an opinion, which of course it was. She glanced at him quickly, a little uncertainly, and then she volunteered, "I'll...write you, and let you know... what it is."

She tensed herself for the hurt, the impatience, and the insistence she knew to expect from him, and was surprised to receive none of it. His fingers were laced casually with hers, the wind blew the folds of his open shirt across the strong planes of his chest and lifted his hair, and on his face was no disturbance, merely an expression of calm certainty as though the matter had already been resolved and no longer concerned him. "That's not necessary," he replied, "unless you'd care to scribble me a note on the back of a paper mask from the delivery room, because I'll be waiting right outside the door. Unless," he added, looking at her with every sign of sincerity in his face, "you would like me to be with you during the delivery. They allow that at most hospitals now, you know."

She did not know how much longer she could bear the pain of parting from him. He would do that for her, even though he did not know the child was his and even though she was not his lover. He would do it for her because she was his friend and he cared for her.

Tears choked her throat and she had to turn her head quickly. "Oh, Seth, please!" It was hardly above a whisper. "Don't! Don't make it any harder."

"I intend," he told her evenly, "to make it impossible. Kelly, look at me." He took her chin between thumb and forefinger and she quickly jerked it away, blinking back tears. "You don't want to go through this thing by yourself, and you don't have to. I'm offering you—"

"Seth for God's sake," she cried, pulling her hand away. "This is not a game! This isn't a disease," she explained in a slightly more controlled tone, "that will go away in a few months and leave no one the worse off for it. It's a baby, another person, an entire new life! It's *forever*."

"Which is exactly," he told her, still completely unruffled, "why you should be giving more thought to your future. There is no reason for you to be thinking about going anywhere. There will be plenty of room for you and the baby right where you are now, with Trish leaving and Susan probably gone by then too. You'll have someone with you when you come home from the hospital and someone to take care of you both until you get back on your feet again, and you won't even have to go back to work right away if you don't want to. It's the only sensible thing, Kelly, and if you won't think about yourself, think about the baby. Do you really want to bring her home to a one-room hovel of a flat with cockroaches as big as she is and broken windows and lead paint peeling off the walls?" He was smiling gently now, trying to tease her with exaggeration. "Be practical."

She shook her head in dreary helplessness. Practical. If that was the only way to get through to him . . . . "You be practical," she told him. "Babies cry. Babies make a mess. They keep you up all night and demand every minute of your time during the day. That house isn't built for babies. And," she reminded him ruthlessly, "you don't even like children, you told me so. It would drive you crazy, and what about your other house-mates? You'll be looking for others after Trish and Susan leave, won't you? Don't you see, it would never work. It's a ridiculous idea."

He responded to her questions in reverse order. "I won't be looking for other housemates," he informed her. "Trish and Susan were part of a family, not replaceable commodities. And as for not liking children—what else is a bachelor like myself supposed to say? I've never had any experience with them, but I'm a quick study, I'll learn. If there is something structurally wrong with the house," he added mockingly, "that makes it unfit for habitation by babies, I'm sure it can be repaired. And as for the crying and the mess—I suppose I've lived through worse. Are you trying to tell me there's something innately superior about womanhood that enables you to cope with such problems and not me? I doubt it. I'll manage."

It would be so easy, so very easy, to succumb to the temptation of the fairy-tale picture he painted, to relent to his persuasion and let him lead her into disaster—because that was what it would be. He would find out, somehow he would find out, and what had begun as a friendly offer of support and shelter on his part would twist and turn on him and trap him into a lifetime obligation. Nor could she live with him, loving him, yet still separate from him, watching him with other women and trying to be no more than a sister in his life. It would destroy her, and the only chance of happiness she had left now was to be alone with his child. She dropped her eyes, twisting her hands together tightly, and she felt a tear sting her cheek. "Oh, Seth," she whispered, "you're making it hurt so much!"

His hands were on her waist, holding her, drawing her to him so that their thighs brushed, and he bent his head so that she must look at him. In his eyes was an emotion so dark with intensity that it made her breath catch and her heart lurch in her chest, and he said lowly, "For God's sake, Kelly, don't you know that I—"

"Seth!" It was Susan's voice, and they both instinctively turned toward the sound of it. A few dozen yards down the beach Susan was making a positive mess of the barbecue amidst much laughter and playful fanning of the flames threatening to engulf the hamburgers on the grill. "I give up!" she called. "Help!"

His smile was rueful and his eyes tender as he glanced back at Kelly. "We'll finish this conversation later," he promised her. "And"—lightly he brushed his hand over the flatness of her abdomen—"you're going to have a girl."

But the afternoon sped by in laughter and high spirits, slightly overdone hamburgers and champagne in paper cups flavored with bits of sand and sea spray. They shared hilarious anecdotes of their time together and poignant memories, and more than once Kelly's eyes misted over. But it seemed always Seth was beside her, touching her hand or her knee or squeezing her shoulders, and despite the sadness associated with the occasion, she felt content. How would she ever bear to part from him?

Just before sunset Trish suggested they leave, as she was eager to complete the move before dark. Susan and Carl, who were just as eager to be alone, raised no objection, and they began to pack up.

Trish would be riding home with Seth and Kelly, and Peter, who had arranged to borrow a friend's pickup truck, would meet them there. Trish walked Peter to his car and Seth and Kelly carried the last of the leftovers to the Jeep. Now, while they were momentarily alone, Kelly screwed up the courage to ask him something that had been nagging at the back of her mind all day. She inquired, as casually as she could manage, "Why aren't you seeing Melissa anymore?"

He was silent for a moment, appearing to give his explanation the careful thought she deserved. "Do you remember," he began in a moment, "how I told you once that I was afraid all that separation we went through in the beginning with the strike would only make this affair seem more important than it was?" Kelly nodded, and he admitted, "I guess that's what really happened. I thought she was the one for a while, I'll confess that, but it was only because I didn't know her well enough to know differently. It was just one of those tricks you stumble over in relationships—seeing things that aren't there just because you want to see them." *Just like I used to do,* thought Kelly. And then he looked at her. "Sometimes," he told her soberly, "you look so hard for things that aren't there you can't see what's under your own nose."

They had reached the Jeep, and he opened the door to place the hampers they carried in the back. But before helping her inside, he rested his arm casually on the open door and concluded, "I got to know Melissa and I found I really didn't know her at all. There was nothing to relate to. I could never," he added quietly, "talk to her about Vietnam, or about my childhood, or anything that was really important. I couldn't just sit with her and feel comfortable not saying anything like I can with you." Lightly his hand came forward to catch a strand of her hair, and a tingling of awareness began within her, a breathless hope and a sudden clenching of anxiety. His eyes were a very deep brown. He said softly, "There was just nothing there after the passion died."

"Are we ready?" Trish said brightly behind them.

Seth smiled gently, stroked her cheek, and stepped aside to help the women inside.

Trish chattered all the way home, but Kelly heard

none of it. She felt tense, excited, bemused, and afraid to explore the reasons behind it. Beside her, Seth seemed no different than ever, conversing casually with Trish and driving with relaxed confidence along the familiar road to home. But something seemed different, something he had been trying to say to her, both with words and glances, all day. Unspoken promises, unfinished conversations...something she did not understand, something that both frightened and excited her and she did not know why.

Trish's voice pulled her out of her reverie as they drove into the driveway. "Well, will you look at that!" she said curiously. "Who in the world can that be?"

Kelly could see there was a figure standing on the front steps, but she could not guess from this position who it might be. Seth saw too, and though he made no comment, Kelly noticed a flicker of recognition in his eyes, a slight tightening of the muscle in his jaw. She inquired, "Are you expecting someone?"

"Not exactly," he replied, but his tone was grim, and there was an unmistakable tension in his movements as he put the Jeep in gear and turned off the ignition. Kelly gave him one more curious look as they all got out of the Jeep, but discovered nothing in his face.

Kelly went up the short walk first, with Trish and Seth close behind. Seth's hand was resting lightly and protectively on her back, although whether it was to urge her forward or keep her back she was not certain. It was all very peculiar.

And then the man on the steps turned, and she understood. A slow dread tightened in her stomach and dried up her throat. They stared at one another for a long time; he glowering, and she helpless, and then she had to speak. Her voice sounded very small and weak.

"Daddy," she said.

## Chapter Twelve

Her mind was whirling in muted panic, and anxiety was dampening the palms of her hands. Her father—here! Something was wrong, terribly wrong... "Wh-what are you doing here?" she choked, and then on a sudden shaft of fear, "Mother! Is Mother okay? Is she sick or—"

"I am here," her father replied in icy tones of clarity, "because I was invited." His eyes were like daggers and they were focused over her head—at Seth, she thought. "Your mother is fine," he added shortly as an afterthought.

She felt a slight increase of pressure from Seth's hand on her back, as though in reassurance, before he moved around her to open the door. There was an odd, restrained look on his face and she could see the tenseness of his muscles even in the uncertain light. Electric distaste vibrated between the two men so violently it was like a tangible thing, but Seth's voice was carefully polite as he said, "Won't you come in, sir?"

Kelly stepped forward quickly, her mind still swimming with confusion. "I—I'm sorry, Daddy, these are my housemates. This is Trish." She pulled Trish forward. "And that's Seth."

But her father hardly seemed to hear her. He directed himself exclusively to Seth. "There's no need for that," he said, and the harsh, clipped tone of his voice made Kelly flinch even though she did not understand the reason for it. "What I have to say can be said just as well from out here."

"I still don't understand why you're here," Kelly began, but Seth's voice cut through hers.

"Come inside," he insisted, and there was the same sort of deadly violence in his tone that she had noticed in her father's.

Something was going on between the two men and Kelly felt as confused and excluded as a theatergoer who has walked in on the middle of the second act. It was something primitive and savage that transcended the boundaries of female understanding; two male animals sizing one another up and preparing to fight for their territorial rights. It was totally irrational. Of course Kelly had been prepared for the fact that if her father ever met Seth—a possibility that, until this point, had been so remote it was almost unthinkable—there would be instant hostility, but there was no reason for Seth to dislike her father on sight, and it was very unlike him to react this way. She had never seen Seth like this before, so coiled with power and ready for defense, like an animal who had gotten the scent of danger and was ready to spring.

Trish sensed it as well as Kelly did, and was fascinated, but it was she who, with a curt nod from Seth, tugged at Kelly's hand and urged her inside. After a moment in which it seemed for some irrational reason the fate of each of them hung in the balance, Kelly's father followed, and then Seth. The door closed behind them.

Kelly turned, her eyes darting in confusion and subdued alarm from her father to Seth, who maintained their respective positions a few feet away from one another on either side of the small tiled entranceway. They stared at each other in varying degrees of aggression and hostility, and it suddenly occurred to Kelly that each of them knew exactly what this was about, but she was still in the dark. She said quickly, for the moment was becoming awkward and much too highly charged for her liking, "Daddy, won't you sit down? Can I get you something to drink? Will you please tell me—"

And suddenly her father's eyes flitted to Trish. "You're Trish," he said, and Trish jumped. He had a way of barking at people instead of talking, as though he were still in the army giving orders. "The one who wrote me the letter," he added.

Kelly's confused gaze riveted on Trish, but Trish looked as surprised as Kelly was. "Letter?" she protested. "What letter? I never—"

And suddenly the ex-colonel turned his sharp, military eyes back on Seth. Kelly saw the muscles of Seth's arms bunch instinctively but nothing else about him moved. He did not even blink. And suddenly she knew, in that split second before her father spoke, that something dreadful was about to happen. She felt it sinking in her stomach and weakening her legs, and her hand even made a small fluttering motion outward as though to stop it, but she did not know what she was defending herself against.

"And you," her father said slowly to Seth, his voice dripping with contempt, "are the man who's responsible for this. You are the father of my daughter's child."

Kelly gasped and a sharp pain of understanding burst in her solar plexus. For a moment the entire vignette was frozen in sickening clarity before her eyes: Seth, grim-faced and unflinching, shoulders square, fists tight at his sides; and her father, meeting him inch for inch with hatred and barely controlled violence in his eyes.

And then Seth answered, quite clearly, "Yes, sir. I am."

Dizziness spun. Kelly lost her breath completely and the strength in her legs. One hand went automatically to her abdomen in an instinctual protective gesture, and she sank to the nearest chair, struggling for breath and for reason. She saw Trish's eyes, wide and incredulous, and heard her sound of protest, and then everything happened so fast that it was like a high-speed film of a nightmare; it was so unexpected and so rapid that it had all been over several seconds before Kelly could react, and even then she could not believe it.

Seth must have seen it coming; he must have been prepared for it since the moment her father had entered the house, but he did nothing to defend himself, he did not even try to block the blow. The colonel's fist struck Seth's jaw with a force that snapped his head back and cracked throughout the room. Seth steadied himself, brought his hand slowly to his jaw, and never once did his eyes leave his opponent's.

Trish screamed. She rushed toward them, and then Kelly was on her feet and the voice that cried "No! Stop it!" was her own, even though she could hardly hear it over the roaring of her heart in her ears and the gasping of her breath. Her father whirled on her and then Seth's arm shot out, grasping the other man's wrist firmly. "You can do whatever you like to me," he said, and his tone was deadly quiet even through the sound of his harsh breathing, "but if you lay a hand on Kelly I swear you'll regret it."

Her father's face was flushed a choleric tint, his eyes two dark malicious pebbles. He jerked his arm furiously away. "You'll pay for this, you damn hippie," he growled. "You can't get away with this with *my* daughter, not in California or anywhere else. You're going to marry her, do you understand that, boy? You're going to get yourself a job and you're going to—"

"Seth has a job." Trish was babbling incoherently. "What are you—"

And Kelly, her face white and tear-streaked, cried, "Daddy, please! Seth—"

"Will somebody tell me what's going on?" Trish cried, and she was not afraid to put herself between the two combatants. "Oh, my God, Seth, you're bleeding! Will you look what you've done?" She turned on Kelly's father. "He's bleeding!"

"He'll do a lot more than that before I'm through with him."

"Stop it!" Kelly cried, and she reached Seth. A tiny rivulet of blood was staining the knuckles of the hand he pressed to his face, but his other arm went around her shoulders firmly, his hand gently caressing, but his eyes never left her father. She leaned against him, trembling, and he shielded her with his quiet strength.

"Yes, stop it!" Trish declared with one deep, steadying breath. She extended her hands between them, palms downward, in a signal of truce. "It's obvious there's been some sort of misunderstanding, but this is neither the time or the place. Will you look what you're doing to Kelly?" And then, swiftly, she took the colonel's hand in one of her own. "Your hand is bruised; you need ice for that. Kelly." She gave Kelly one quick, desperately meaningful look. "Will you tend to Seth's cut? And maybe later we can all sit down and discuss this reasonably. Mr. Mitchell, will you please come with me?"

"You haven't heard the last of this, boy..." her father began to bluster, but Trish exercised a gentle pressure on his arm to lead him toward the kitchen. And Kelly had read the look in her friend's eyes—it was a command to get the two of them away from each other quickly. She turned Seth toward the bathroom.

"Will you please tell me what is going on?" Her voice was tight and shaking as she fumbled for a towel.

Seth released a painful sigh and perched on the edge of the vanity. But when she turned, his face was rueful, as though it had all been a game, a joke with a surprise ending. "I don't know where to begin," he said.

She turned on the faucet, saturated the towel with cold water, then squeezed it until it was damp. "How did he know?" she demanded. "What was he doing here?" She was afraid she already knew the answers to those questions as she turned to him and commanded harshly, "Move your hand."

She wiped the blood off his fingers and then began to dab not so gently at the cut near his chin, and he winced. "You were expecting him," she accused, trembling with fury and the aftermath of shock. "You *knew*."

"Kelly..." He caught her wrist, removing her hand and its ineffective ministrations with the towel. "Leave that for a minute." Now for the first time she saw uncertainty in his eyes, reluctance, and behind that a deeper emotion she was afraid to try to define. "Look," he began hesitantly, and his eyes dropped briefly to study her hand, which he still held steady with a light grasp upon her wrist. "I know I blew my first marriage proposal, and this"—he cast his eyes with a dry quirk of the brow around the room—"is not exactly how I planned to stage another one, but Kelly—" Now he looked at her, a faint desperation and a deep sincerity darkening his eyes. "I'm not offering to marry you to save your honor or my reputation, like you thought; it's not even that I want to marry you because it's the decent thing to do. Kelly, I *need* to marry you. I can't live without you."

For the second time in less than an hour dizziness swept her, and she reached her free arm out to steady herself against the vanity. What was he trying to say? What could he mean? Her lips parted on a breath, but he stopped her words with a slight increase of the pressure on her wrist. His face was grim, and she was too confused to read the emotions within it. "No," he said quickly, "just listen. Kelly, this is not the way I planned it." Again, with a frustrated sigh, his eyes glanced about the room. "I don't expect you to believe me, but I've been trying to tell you all day, for longer than that. You're the only woman I've ever *loved*, Kelly. And I've loved you for so long that it became almost second nature to me, so that I didn't even see it when I was looking for it. You're the one person in the world who's more important to me than anything else, than anyone else, than even myself. You're the person who makes me feel complete, and alive, and makes me happy to be living, and it seems as though I've known it forever, I was just too stupid to admit it to myself...too stupid and too scared. When we made love," he said on a breath, and there was desperation in his eyes as he pleaded for her acceptance of what he was saying, as well as dread that, despite his best efforts, he would only find rejection again, "it was like—like suddenly a whole new world had opened up before my eyes, one that had been there all along but I had been too blind to see it before. I knew then that you were the one, the only one, the one I had waited for all my life, but I was scared. I tried to tell myself it was just sex, just an accident. I was afraid you would hate me, and it was more important to me than anything in the world that I not lose you. I was desperate. I was so afraid you would run from me, and I thought just having you near, even if I could never have you again the way I had that one night, would be worth it. I even tried to convince myself that what I felt for you wasn't real, and I tried to lose it in Melissa. But, oh, God, Kelly, these past few months have been pure hell, having you so close and not having you at all. That thing with Melissa was just a smoke screen. I may have fooled you, but I couldn't fool myself. Kelly, I love you," he said quietly. "It's as simple as that. I love you as a man loves a woman, as a father loves a child, as a brother loves a sister. I love you with every kind of love there is, it's part of my soul and I can't get it out. It's forever, and it's only for you."

Kelly did not know whether to cry or burst into laughter of pure joy, soaring, sweeping unmitigated joy. There was trepidation in his eyes as he looked at her, but also the beginnings of a small leap of hope, and then pure relief and a happiness so intense it transfigured his face as she simply came to him, stepping into his embrace and returning with trembling in her arms the crushing strength of his. Silently they clung to each other, their breaths unsteady and their hearts thundering a desperate, ecstatic rhythm, needing no words to express what had been there between them all along but savoring the wonder of its revelation. Tears wet her face and she did not know whether the choking in her chest was due to sobs or laughter, for she should have known...she should have known all along how alike they were, that he would be thinking and feeling the same things she was. Yet all these months of heartbreak had been caused because they were working at cross-purposes with each other, trying to protect one another. "Oh, Seth!" Her voice was high and shaking with unleashed emotion. She pressed her face into his shoulder to blot the tears and felt his hands moving in restless urgency along her back, as though trying to convince himself that she was really there, and that it was really happening. "Don't you know—didn't you guess how much I loved you? All this time...all this time...."

She felt his choked, startled breath, his lips against her neck. She tightened her arms around him so hard that she thought she must surely be hurting him, and his returned embrace was crushing, so intense that neither could maintain it for long. "I thought—I hoped..."

he said huskily against her ear. "Sometimes I thought I saw it in your eyes, but I was so afraid, afraid I was wrong, that I'd lose you if I pushed you."

The sound she made as she gradually pushed away from him was half laughter, half despair. "Why didn't you tell me?" she insisted. "All this time— Oh, God, why didn't you tell me?"

He held her arms, his fingers making urgent, caressing movements on her elbows. His eyes were dark with remembered pain. "All I've wanted to do since that night in the desert was tell you," he said slowly. "If I hadn't left when I did I think I would have gone completely mad with trying not to tell you. Why else do you think I stayed away so long, why I made sure you wouldn't answer the phone whenever I called? Still…" There was longing in his face as he looked back. "When I finally did come back, thinking I had the big-brother act down pat again, and I saw you that first night, I almost crumbled. If you hadn't looked so scared, so miserable and embarrassed—"

"But that was only because I was trying to hide what I felt for you!" she cried.

He shook his head slowly, a deep light of wonder mingled with regret in his eyes, and his hands, which were resting lightly on her waist, tightened slightly. "I never would have guessed that," he admitted slowly. "I was too busy trying to protect you from myself… and maybe, to protect myself from being hurt. When I suggested," he reminded her soberly, "that morning that you were still on the rebound from Hampton you didn't deny it. How could I keep from thinking that you were just transferring what you felt for him to me because I was convenient?"

She gasped in sudden horror, pressing one hand to her cheek as she shook her head violently. "I thought that was what you wanted to believe! I never—"

A small smile tightened the corners of his lips as he

looked at her. "We were so busy trying to outguess each other that we overlooked some pretty important facts, didn't we?" And then suddenly his hands left her waist and slid down her arms to clasp her wrists intensely. "I want you to know something, Kelly," he said, his voice low with sincerity. "There hasn't been anyone else since you. I tried to get you out of my head with Melissa, but it didn't work. That fight we had—it was because she thought it was long past time we carried our relationship to its, er, natural conclusion." He twisted his eyebrows as he dropped his eyes briefly. "But I just couldn't make love to her after you." He looked at her. "That's when I finally realized I couldn't go on this way, that I had to have you—as a wife and a lover, not just as a friend. I thought there was time, plenty of time, to let you know how I felt and, maybe, time for you to come to feel the same way. Then I found out about the baby and there was no more time. But how could I tell you then?

"I thought, despite what you said, that you still wanted Hampton and it was just pride preventing you from going to him. I loved you so much that if Hampton was what you wanted then I was determined you would have him. I was crazy with jealousy and torn up inside about the whole thing and I know I acted like an idiot, but what else could I do? And then when the news came that he was already married, it was like a last-minute reprieve from death row, it was like a heaven-sent opportunity. But I knew you would never believe how I really felt after I had made such a fool of myself about your pregnancy. I thought if I could convince you of the sensibility of marrying me that you would at least see I really did care about you, and that maybe, eventually, after we were legally married and the baby was born and you came to trust me again, that you might learn to love me in the same way I love you. And of course I jumped in there with both feet and screwed it up," he admitted wryly. "So," he concluded on a sigh, "I wrote your father, using Trish's name." A slight grimace touched his features. "God, she'll kill me if she ever gets her hands on that letter. I made her sound like a Bible-toting temperance militant with a sermon for a brain and a cliché for every occasion. I knew he'd come here and without knowing what he was doing, act as my reinforcements." He touched his jaw gingerly. "Some ally, huh?" And then he dropped his eyes. "Okay, so maybe it was a stupid thing to do, but time was important. I was afraid you were going to kill yourself working like you've been doing, or worse, that you'd just suddenly pack up and leave and I wouldn't be able to stop you. I panicked."

She looked at him, and she could hardly force herself to speak. The joy of the truth he had told her still flooded and buoyed her, but there was one more truth to be faced. She said unsteadily, "You told him...the baby was yours."

His eyes were very somber as he looked at her. "Not one day has passed since I found out that you were pregnant," he answered her quietly, "that I haven't wished that baby was mine. Kelly." She tried to avoid his eyes, to gain courage, but he took her chin between his thumb and forefinger and forced her to look at him. His eyes held hers so steadily that there was no chance of avoiding the truth any longer, there was no desire to avoid it any longer. He demanded quietly, "You never slept with David Hampton, did you?"

She whispered, "No." And then her head was on his shoulder, his hand hard against the back of her neck, pressing her close, holding her there.

"Oh, God, Kelly," he whispered. "Why didn't you tell me? You could have saved us so much agony."

"Yes, both of us," she murmured against his shoulder, her arms tightening around him. Peace throbbed within her and a bright, shimmering, unquenchable joy pulsed through her, and she wanted to stay like this forever, just holding him, knowing it never had to end. But she forced herself to move away, searching his face for some sign of reluctance or regret. She found only relief there, a burden lifted, a quiet, yearning welcome...and love. She tried to drink it in all at once, wondering over it, savoring it, and then she had to ask, "But how did you know?"

He sighed. "Oh, Kelly, if I hadn't been such a damn fool, so wrapped up in jealousy and fear of losing you, I would have guessed it long ago. And then, the other night you were trying to tell me something, and I looked at you, and I just knew," he said simply.

She smiled. "You always could read my mind," she murmured, and tears hung on her lashes.

"That's going to come in handy," he assured her, "in all the years ahead."

Happiness swelled in her and threatened to burst; it shone with an unquenchable light in her eyes and she wanted to laugh out loud. But she could only stand there, holding the damp towel, and she said, her eyes sparkling, "It may have been just an accident, but it was the luckiest one of my life."

"It wasn't an accident," he corrected her soberly. "It was just nature's way of telling two people who were too blind to see it for themselves that they belonged together."

The moment between them was intense and poignant, it throbbed with pent-up yearning and unfulfilled promise. But the bathroom was no place to make love, and there was no time even for all the things they had to say to each other. They still had an irate father to deal with, and as incredible as it seemed, Peter was due any moment to move Trish's furnishings. Before this night was over they would have to settle more than simply their future. She dropped her eyes, breaking the spell, and began to pat the cut on his face with the towel, more gently this time. The flesh around it was already swollen and beginning to bruise, and the cut, though not long, was deep. "Oh, Seth," she whispered in real distress. "It's going to leave a scar."

But he only smiled at her. "It's one well-earned," he said.

His hands were on her waist, drawing her closer. She let the hand holding the towel drop, and her face moved effortlessly to his. "Careful," he warned with a slight smile, "it hurts."

Their lips met sweetly, gently, and only briefly, for there was a sudden loud pounding on the door and an angry male voice. "Kelly, are you in there? What the hell are you doing in there? I'm not finished with you yet."

Kelly sighed and turned her head against Seth's shoulder, wishing she could just close her eyes and make the world go away. Seth smiled down at her a little ruefully. "Do you think if we don't answer he might forget about us?"

She shook her head slowly and firmly. "No chance. We could climb out the window," she suggested hopefully.

He laughed softly, holding her hands. "One thing I learned in the military is that you don't disobey an order. And that"—he cocked his head toward the pounding that was shaking the door in its frame—"sounds very much like an order to me. We may as well get it over with." He tugged at her hand.

But she held back. She did not want another traumatic scene to threaten the happiness she had only so recently found in Seth's arms, and she foresaw a long and unpleasant night ahead, only a continuation of the scene that had ended in violence only moments ago. She refused to allow even her father, whom she loved but who did not understand her love for Seth, to spoil what had been discovered between them with his accusations and dirty sneers. She said firmly, "I'll tell him to go home. It's none of his business. He's only going to yell at me and call you names and—"

"But it is his business," Seth pointed out seriously. "It's his grandchild."

Sadness crept around the edges of her happiness and she dropped her eyes. This was not the way she had wanted it to be, her father hating her because of a child she loved whose only crime was to be conceived a few months too early, the two most important men in her life fighting with each other and mistrusting each other. "There's nothing we can do about it," she said softly. "Daddy will never understand. There's no point in trying."

"Honey." He touched her cheek affectionately, smoothing back a strand of her hair. In his eyes was complete empathy, an understanding of her deepest thoughts and feelings, and a sturdy confidence she was far from feeling. "This is no way to start out our life together, not for any of us. If I have to spend the next twenty years trying, I'm going to make sure your father likes me. We're going to be a family. We may have started out on the wrong foot, but there's no time like the present to correct that."

She said dubiously, "Seth, if we go out there, we'd better have an awfully good story to tell him."

He winked at her and reached for the door handle. "Don't worry," he assured her. "I do."

She touched his arm. Love brimmed within her for the effort, which, however noble, was doomed to fail. And she had to tell him, "Seth, you don't have to do this. Not for me. It doesn't matter. As long as I have you—" Her voice almost broke on the happiness and the wonder swelling within her. "Nothing does."

He looked at her, long and tenderly. And then he assured her with a smile, "I'm doing this for *us*. You and me, and"—his hand rested and tightened over her stomach—"our baby. Are you with me?"

Always, she thought, and placed her hand in his as they went out to face the future.

## Chapter Thirteen

Trish was obviously at her wit's end in trying to control an outraged parent on her own. Peter had arrived, and Trish was apparently in the middle of trying to explain the entire bizarre situation to him, for he looked thoroughly confused. When the two accused culprits came out of the bathroom, she dragged Peter forward for moral support and, casting Kelly a harried, apologetic look, entreated, "Please, Mr. Mitchell, Seth, surely we can sit down now like civilized people and get this misunderstanding cleared up."

"I don't need to sit down!" bellowed Kelly's father. "And there's no misunderstanding. All I want to know is—"

"As a matter of fact, there has been a misunderstanding." Seth's quiet confidence cut through her father's bluster and made it sound like a tinny echo. His hands rested protectively on Kelly's shoulders as he guided her around him and into a chair.

"There's nothing you have to say that I want to hear, boy," glowered Colonel Mitchell.

"Maybe not," agreed Seth pleasantly, perching on the arm of Kelly's chair. She glanced at him as she took his hand, and there was a secret twinkle in his eyes she did not quite understand. All of a sudden he seemed to be enjoying himself thoroughly. "But for the sake of your daughter and your grandchild, I hope you'll listen."

Peter looked startled, and Kelly's father seemed to notice him for the first time. He shot the intruder a dark glance beneath shaggy brows. "Is this public business?" he challenged.

"I don't know why not," Seth responded easily. "We don't have anything to be ashamed of. Congratulate me." He grinned at Peter, squeezing Kelly's hand. "I'm going to be a father."

Kelly thought her father would burst a blood vessel, and Trish—well, Trish looked as though she had just crash-landed on an alien planet. She gaped at Kelly. Kelly felt a little sorry for both of them, but that emotion was far behind the one that surged through her when Seth spoke with such pride and unmistakable joy of his impending fatherhood. She knew how he felt, she wanted to shout it to the whole world too. They had nothing to be ashamed of.

Peter looked for explanation to Kelly, then Trish, and back to Seth. "Well, that's great," he said at last, still very confused. "Is that what all this fuss is about? Why is everyone so upset? Good Lord, honey," he reprimanded Trish, "I thought for sure someone was on the verge of murder or suicide at the very least."

"You didn't give us a chance to explain," Seth said mildly, his eyes fixed steadily on the ominously glowering ones of Colonel Mitchell, "that Kelly and I *are* married. We have been for several months now. So, like Peter says, why is everyone so upset?"

Now it was Kelly's turn to gape. Trish's legs folded beneath her and she sank heavily to the sofa opposite, staring at them. Kelly paled, and then went scarlet. She was so horrified at the shameless lie that a sputtering protest began to form in her throat, and then she felt Seth's fingers tighten on hers.

Suddenly she understood. No matter what they said

to her father now, no matter how much they loved one another or how quickly they got married, it would not change the damage already done in Colonel Mitchell's eyes. If they lived to be a hundred and gave him dozens of grandchildren and great-grandchildren, he would never look at Seth as anything other than the man who had "gotten his daughter into trouble" and "had" to marry her, and he would never forgive Kelly his disappointment. Seth wanted them to be a family, and it was above all things what Kelly wanted too, and the only way to prevent that stigma that had formed in the conservative mind of a censorious father from passing on to their child was to erase its beginnings. It was not perhaps a strictly honorable thing to do—in fact, it was so crazy and old-fashioned it was almost childish—but then, Seth's method of bringing Kelly's father here in the first place had not been exactly honorable. How well he knew the workings of her father's mind! And how she loved him for it, marveled over it, wanted to jump up and fling her arms around him in laughter and relief, for was there any problem Seth could not solve?

Colonel Mitchell glowered at his daughter suspiciously, a considerable amount of wind taken out of his sails. "Is this true?" he demanded.

"Oh, yes," responded Kelly weakly, although now the choking in her voice was from repressed laughter, not horror. Her eyes glittered with provocative mirth. "Several months."

Trish stared at her.

The door sprang open and Susan burst in, a laughing Carl in tow. "Guess what?" she cried from the threshold, and the radiance in her face left no room for guessing whatsoever. "You'll never guess! You are looking at the future Mrs. Senator Carl Apling!"

Even in their shock over the events of the past hour, a friend's need took precedence over all else. They went to the newly arrived couple with cries of congratulations and welcome, leaving Kelly's father to stand in utter bafflement in the midst of the chaos. At length Susan noticed him, and cried in delight, "Why, Colonel Mitchell! What are you doing here?"

Trish said breathlessly, taking her hand, "Now, you'll never guess!" Apparently she had recovered herself, adjusted to the whirlwind momentum of the events of the past hour, and was now taking great pleasure in plunging her friend into the same reaction. "Seth and Kelly are married!"

For a moment there was a stunned silence, and Kelly avoided Susan's eyes. The deception perpetrated upon her father was necessary and it was for his sake more than theirs, but Kelly did not like to lie to her friends. Something in Seth's stance beside her told her he felt the same way, and that was reassuring.

Then Carl Apling exclaimed, "I knew it! Didn't I tell you, sweetheart? I knew it all along!"

There was a babble of "Well, you're the only one!" and "I don't believe it!" and "When did this happen?" and Kelly's father cut through the uproar with a resounding "You still haven't answered my question. Why did you keep it such a state secret?"

There was a silence, and Kelly began to panic. Not even Seth seemed to have a ready answer for that one. Then Susan looked at them, quickly to Trish, and back to Kelly and Seth with understanding and something strangely like apology in her eyes. "It was because of us, wasn't it?" she said softly. "You were afraid of how Trish and I would feel about it."

And Trish broke in, "Oh, you crazy kids! We've known for a long time how the two of you felt about each other."

"But we didn't want to say anything, knowing you would make the move when you were ready."

"But to keep it a secret from us...."

Kelly felt like a child on Christmas morning being

showered with gifts. Not until this moment had she admitted to herself how really worried she had been about Trish and Susan's reaction, and this was more than she could ask for, more than she could dare expect. She was in their arms, laughing and crying and hugging and all talking at once, then Seth was there too, and she was in the middle of a four-way embrace, wanting for nothing, never happier than at that moment.

Once again her father was the reality that cut through her ecstasy. "Well, this is all very fine," he announced gruffly, "but there are a few things I would still like to know."

Seth turned to him. His hand brushed Kelly's arm in a trailing caress, but this was man's business, and he was well up to it. He told her father seriously, "I'm well able to support a family, if that's what you're worried about. I've been employed at the same job for eight years and in two more I'll be eligible for a sizable promotion."

Kelly put her hand out. "Seth, you don't have to—"

He barely glanced at her. "No, it's all right. He has a right to know. I own this house," he continued, "and I have quite a lot in equity if we should ever need it. I also own some more property upstate that will have doubled its value in another five years, as well as a few investments that aren't doing too badly. I have a college education and I've done my military service—"

For the first time the other man's face registered acknowledgment with an upshooting eyebrow. "Military, eh?" Obviously Seth had saved his best for last.

"Yes, sir."

"What branch?"

"Army. Sergeant."

Colonel Mitchell looked at him long and hard, grunted, and then turned to his daughter. He asked gruffly, "Is this man going to make you happy?"

Kelly knew the battle was won. She slipped her arm around Seth's waist and smiled at him, unable to keep her happiness from showing in her face. "Yes, Daddy."

He looked at her for another moment, then started toward the door. "Looks like I made this fool trip for nothing," he grumbled. "I just hope I can get a flight home tonight. Your mother will be coming out," he told Kelly with an air of resignation, "when it's time for the baby, if I can keep her away that long."

"She's welcome here any time," Seth said. "Both of you are."

The two men's eyes met, and Kelly thought her father almost smiled. But all he said was a very disgruntled "You just take good care of her, you hear?" And for the first time his voice softened as he glanced at Kelly. "She's all I've got."

"I know," Seth said quietly, looking down at Kelly. "She's all I've got too."

Kelly stepped into her father's embrace, her eyes brimming with tears, and he kissed her cheek awkwardly.

Carl volunteered, "Can we drop you at the airport? Susan and I are going that way."

In the hurried good-byes Kelly felt a pang of remorse that the turmoil of the past few moments might have spoiled her friend's announcement. But Susan winked at her on her way out the door and assured her, "We'll talk in the morning." Kelly counted herself blessed to have such good friends.

And still the confusion and the activity was not over. Seth and Kelly pitched in to help Trish pack and move her belongings to the truck parked outside, and all the while Trish kept alternating between "I just can't believe it!" and "I'm so happy for you!" And she giggled. "It's just like an old-time movie, isn't it? The kind you're always watching? Corny, but beautiful." She hugged Kelly. "Isn't it crazy how everything worked out so perfectly? We're all going to be so happy!"

Kelly was in her bedroom, putting her closet to rights again after the two girls had gone through it in search of borrowed sweaters and missing scarves, when Seth came in from seeing them off. "God," he said wearily, sitting on her bed, "this house is so quiet." He stretched back on the bed, his hands propped behind his head and his feet still on the floor, and grinned at her. "Do you believe this night?"

A smile tightened the corners of her mouth, though she tried to look stern as she came over to him. "You're pretty quick with the improvisation, aren't you?"

"Like any good head of household," he returned, "I make quick decisions in a crisis." He sat up, taking her hands and pulling her down beside him, sobering. "It was the only thing I could think of to do, Kelly. I couldn't have him holding anything against the baby, and I could see how it was hurting you."

She nodded. "Do you think he'll ever find out?"

"I have a feeling," Seth answered thoughtfully, "that if he does, it won't make a difference by then." And then he added, "We'll tell Trish and Susan the truth tomorrow. I don't like lying to them."

She giggled. "They'll be teasing us about it for the rest of our lives!"

"They won't get too much teasing out of it," he informed her, "because by tomorrow it will all be legal anyway."

She stared at him. "So soon!"

He grinned. "Not getting cold feet, are you?"

She shook her head adamantly. "But how—"

"I've had the license for a week, all you have to do is sign it. Your blood test is on file from the physical you had, and I had mine done last week. All we have to do tomorrow morning is find a justice of the peace."

She fell back, amazed. "You were pretty sure of yourself, weren't you?"

"I had to be," he assured her soberly, brushing his hand across her cheek. "It was the only thing that kept me from going crazy."

She realized, with a sudden tightening in her chest and a dryness of her throat, that they were alone. The house echoed its unreal silence around them, enfolding them, for it was all theirs; they were alone together and for the first time in complete mastery of the night.

His eyes reflected the dawning realization and the cautious anticipation in hers, and his hand trembled a little as it moved to her throat, his fingers brushing the ridges of the column there and gently caressing the flesh. He smiled faintly, and his voice was soft and a little hoarse. "It's been too long," he said.

Her arms moved around his neck and her lips met his, and she thought, *too long. Entirely too long.* She lost herself in the sensation of his mouth upon hers and his quick breath mingling with hers. His hand rested upon her bare thigh and his fingers tightened there as she drew him closer, opening herself to him in a swift hot flush that could wait no longer. He moved his hand to her waist and pulled his lips away reluctantly, holding her to the hard, rapid beating of his heart while his fingers pressed against her spine and his chest moved with the deep swell of his breath. "Lady," he murmured somewhat unsteadily against her hair, "are you making a pass at me?"

Her fingers worked the buttons of his shirt, moving aside the material to expose his flesh to her exploring fingers. "I'm trying," she responded huskily, her eyes glittering. "Am I doing it right?"

He drew in his breath sharply as her nails brushed across the bare muscles of his chest. "You're doing it right," he said, and his lips came down on hers again.

There was no containing the passion that had been

restrained too long, hidden and denied, nor was there any controlling the joy that opened herself to him, knowing it was forever as she sought only to draw him closer, to melt into him and belong to him as it should have been from the beginning. She gasped and went weak as his hand slipped beneath the thin muslin, moving over her stomach and the outline of her ribs and leaving a prickling trail until at last it found her breast, heavy and waiting for his touch. Wonderful dizziness soared in the gentle massaging motions of his fingers and the breathless exploration of his lips upon hers, and then he drew slowly away. "Kelly," he whispered, his eyes searching her face. "Is it all right? I won't hurt you?"

She smiled and for an answer pushed aside the remaining fabric of his shirt, with her lips and her tongue beginning the discovery of his body she had yearned for so long. "Perfect," she murmured against his chest. "Perfectly all right."

He lowered her gently to the bed, and his eyes never left her as he undressed her slowly, growing in wonder and reverence as he kissed each part of her body his hands uncovered. She realized they had never seen one another in the light before, she had never watched his eyes as he discovered her, never seen the tenderness and the desire there as he made love to her. And when he removed his own clothes and lay beside her, her eyes grew dark with the newness of the discovery, wanting to drink in all of him, marveling over him, knowing that time was hers to possess and be possessed by him in all the days and nights to come.

His fingers began a leisurely exploration of her body, stroking her thighs and brushing across her ribs, teasing her breasts until the flesh quivered and she moaned, her own hands finding again the places about him she most loved, the hollow of his throat and the curve of shoulder, the taut muscles of his buttocks and the furry softness of his thighs. Then he bent and placed one long, infinitely tender kiss upon her abdomen, where even now the child they had created together grew and thrived. She tangled her fingers in his curls and closed her eyes against the brimming tears of happiness and yearning, and when he moved his face to hers she was ready to receive him, drawing him into her, drowning in the swelling tide of love that broke within her again and again and left them both at last dazed, exhausted, and dreamily content.

He lay upon his side, his leg crooked around her knees, stroking her hip, and there was a lazy light deep within his eyes as he murmured, "I sure am glad you said yes. I don't think I could have held out much longer."

"I'm sure," she replied demurely, her finger tracing a small circle on the end of his chin, "that you're referring to your marriage proposal."

He feigned innocence with lifted eyebrows. "What else?" Still he gazed at her with that steady, worshipful light in his eyes, as though he could not get enough of looking at her, discovering her. The faraway smile that seemed to be a permanent part of his face was reflected on hers. "How many months," he inquired, "will we be able to carry on in this magnificently wicked way?"

She snuggled down deeper into the hollow of his shoulder, tightening her arm around his waist. "How about seven?"

"Not long enough," he murmured, kissing her throat. "But it will have to do. After that we get to start all over making a new one."

She laughed sleepily and replied, "Easy for you to say."

"Kelly," he said after a long moment, in which she almost dozed off.

"Hmm?"

"We're going to have one terrific kid."

She tightened her arms and pressed closer to him, her smile deepening as she closed her eyes in ultimate contentment. "I know."

"Kelly." When next he spoke he sounded dreamy, far away, and a little drowsy himself. "How does four sound? Is that too many?"

"All girls?"

"Of course."

She laughed, weakly and sleepily, loving him with all her soul. "Go to sleep," she murmured. "We'll talk about it tomorrow." Yes, tomorrow, she thought just before she drifted off to sleep. Tomorrow and all the tomorrows ahead filled with promises and dreams come true. But tonight.... She moved more comfortably against him, her head pillowed on his chest and her hand entwined with his. Tonight there was just the two of them, and she was exactly where she wanted to be above all places in the world—wrapped in the arms of the man with whom she belonged for the rest of her life—her very best friend, and her one and only love.

# Enter a uniquely exciting new world with

# *Harlequin American Romance* ™

**Harlequin American Romances** are the first romances to explore today's love relationships. These compelling novels reach into the hearts and minds of women across America... probing the most intimate moments of romance, love and desire.

You'll follow romantic heroines and irresistible men as they boldly face confusing choices. Career first, love later? Love without marriage? Long-distance relationships? All the experiences that make love real are captured in the tender, loving pages of **Harlequin American Romances**.

What makes American women so different when it comes to love? Find out with **Harlequin American Romance!**

Send for your introductory FREE book now!

# Get this book FREE!

**Mail to:**

**Harlequin Reader Service**

In the U.S.
2504 West Southern Avenue
Tempe, AZ 85282

In Canada
649 Ontario Street
Stratford, Ontario N5A 6W2

## YES! I want to be one of the first to discover

**Harlequin American Romance.** Send me FREE and without obligation *Twice in a Lifetime.* If you do not hear from me after I have examined my FREE book, please send me the 4 new **Harlequin American Romances** each month as soon as they come off the presses. I understand that I will be billed only $2.25 for each book (total $9.00). There are no shipping or handling charges. There is no minimum number of books that I have to purchase. In fact, I may cancel this arrangement at any time. *Twice in a Lifetime* is mine to keep as a FREE gift, even if I do not buy any additional books.

Name _____ (please print)

Address _____ Apt. no. _____

City _____ State/Prov. _____ Zip/Postal Code _____

Signature (If under 18, parent or guardian must sign.)